da bug

by
Rich Kisielewski

Wolfsinger Publications Security, Colorado

ISBN: 978-1-936099-41-2

Printed and bound in the United States of America

Dedication

In memory of Robert B. Parker without whom
Harry Mickey Shorts would not be

and

Ira Sarde who first taught me the game
making this book possible; he
continues to watch them run from above

Acknowledgments:

The journey Harry Mickey Shorts has taken has not been alone.

First and foremost, many thanks go to Carol Hightshoe and the entire crew at WolfSinger Publications for her continued support and friendship.

All my friends at WritersAnonymous who have been along since the beginning—through the good and the bad.

My bud Tom Hopke has been there always with support, a firm hand and invaluable advice that has carried me through many a day— thanks Tom.

Likewise for Pablo my West Coast voice of reason.

Friends too many to name kept me going and cheer me on today—I couldn't have done it without your support.

And last, but not least, my favorite daughter Tara and favorite son Brian along with Liz, my wife and partner, it don't get no better than you.

And, oh yeah, thanks Harry.

To everyone else, see you at the tables...

Chapter 1

Eighteen years old. Eighteen frisky years old. Million dollar yearling at the Keeneland Sales grows up to be a Triple Crown winner and two-time Horse of the Year before being retired to stud at the age of five. Syndicated for seventy-five million dollars, he goes on to produce over thirty stakes winners including two Kentucky Derby champions. Top stud stallion commanding top dollar in the world six years running. All of it don't mean shit when he's found dead in his stall the morning he's due to service the top mare from Ireland.

~ * ~

"Harry, Ms. Timmons here. Mister Trundle needs your help."

"Ms. Timmons, you can tell him I'll be standing at his door before he knows it."

Maybe I should jump back a few steps and let you in on what's going on here. My name is Harry, because I'm told an aunt promised to lay some bread on me if my mom named me Harold. I don't believe it one little bit because I didn't see a single dime and, to my knowledge, neither did my moms.

Oh yeah, it's Harry, or should I say Harold Mickey Shorts, which wasn't my given name when I was ushered into this wonderful world of ours. My original name didn't cut it in my eyes and the Mick, Mr. Mantle, is my all-time favorite ballplayer courtesy of my dad. Plus, my original last name was way too long. Wearing tee shirts and shorts is how God intended us to dress, so that's how I came up with my new and improved name, "Shorts", which just happens to be a great conversation topic for the ladies.

By trade, I guess you would call me a private investigator, but not your ordinary, run-of-the-mill, every day private dick. Kizmet Incorporated is what my card would say if I had one. Mr. M. Randal Trundle, CEO of a major New York conglomerate, entrusted me with a very personal problem a short while ago and I am now indebted to him forever. When he asks for help, you best jump back because I'm coming through to do anything in my power to mend what needs mending.

And so the story begins...

Chapter 2

I hang my hat in Manhasset, New York, which is a little burg on the North Shore of Long Island. I've been there a few years—second time around. I returned specifically to be close to my kids and, by necessity, my ex-wife. Things couldn't be better with the kids, Max and Briande, who are rediscovering their previously wandering father. Sherry, my ex, isn't constantly telling me to self-perform an act that normally requires two individuals to consummate, so I guess things are looking on the bright side there, too. Not to worry, I'm sure very soon she'll find some reason to remember what I did to her and the kids and revert to hating me again. Happens all the time.

My most recent professional engagement ended about a month ago and I've been taking it easy since then. You could say I was worn down a bit and needed the rest after having experienced the following: helping an old friend and his son get right with the world, corralling some scumbuckets who thought they could play with the big boys—to no avail, and a mother/daughter combo that wore out one particular piece of my anatomy much more than the rest of me.

Ms. Timmons, or Wendy to some, but not currently to me, is the personal assistant to Mr. M. Randal Trundle. She's a foxy package I might add, who continues to elude this private investigator in spite of his best efforts. She is as good as they come in all ways imaginable; just a matter of time…just a matter of time. I know, cuz I'm Harry Mickey Shorts, and almost hardly never wrong.

~ * ~

"Ms. Timmons, it's Harry. I'm downstairs and on my way up right now."

"Mister Trundle is most anxious to see you, Harry," she replied.

"And you, Ms. Timmons?" I inquired.

Dead air provided my answer.

Chapter 3

The executive offices of Trundle's midtown New York corporate headquarters never cease to amaze me. The expenditure of heavy duty greenbacks to outfit the place was evident, but in subtle and understated tones. You couldn't point to anything in particular; it was just all around you. Well, maybe the original Renoir behind the receptionist's work station did make a small statement. A Renoirish kind of statement you get used to after a while. Yeah, right. My ass.

"Harry, come this way. Mister Trundle is waiting for you," Ms. Timmons said as I sat admiring the beauty of a receptionist sitting below the Renoir.

"Always a pleasure to see all of you, Ms. Timmons," I tried.

A shake of her pretty head and an, "As I you, Harry," in reply.

She walked, I followed, thoroughly enjoying the following.

~ * ~

Randle was on the phone with his back to me when I entered his office. He gestured me to a chair with a wave of his hand. Trundle's office appeared slightly different from the last time I was there. I couldn't put my finger on it immediately, but something was different. It would come to me.

He hung up the phone and sighed.

"Harry, it's good to see you again. Sorry to have to bring you down here and drag you away from the kids."

"Not a problem at all, Randle. I am at your service at all times and nothing could make me happier than to see you and to help you in some way," I said.

"Sit, Harry, sit. A cool one perhaps?"

"Why don't you tell me what's wrong and how I can help? Then we can think about a few cool ones to wash away the taste if we need to," I replied.

"Well enough, Harry. I'm not sure where to begin, or if there really is something to talk about. I hope it is just a terrible tragedy and only a case of my imagination running wild. Such a waste of life, and joy, and a pleasure to so many. And I can see from your eyes you are telling me to spill it, aren't you, Harry? Okay, I will."

"In your own time, in your own way, Mister Trundle."

"Sure, Harry. Let's go out on the balcony and enjoy the view while we talk."

We did just that.

Chapter 4

Best damn view in the whole city. Central Park is one hell of a beauty from up on high.

"So," I said.

"So," he replied. "Brian Boru. You may recognize the name, Harry," he started.

"The race horse that just died?" Harry asked.

"Not just a race horse, Harry. He was a champion among champions and perhaps the greatest sire of all time. If he wasn't there yet, he was approaching that status quite quickly."

He stopped for a second and sighed a long sigh. M. Randle Trundle didn't sigh!

"I didn't know you were into horse racing, Mister Trundle," Harry said.

"Have been for a long time, Harry. My brother Danny is the real horse person in the family. He's the one who introduced me to the sport. He's a substantial stockholder in the corporation—I mean stable. I have a minor stake, but large enough to keep my attention from a financial perspective.

"That horse was a sheer joy to watch run. And win. And win he did. He won on all tracks, at all distances, with weights that should have buried him. Nothing, or no other horse mattered; he was just too good for the rest of the animals he ran against. 'Poetry in motion' is what I used to say when I watched him run. We, my partners and I, we bought him as a yearling. We enjoyed tremendous success and garnered great joy from being part of his career and his life."

Randle was quiet for a good minute.

"And now?" I prompted.

"Now, Harry? Now he isn't," he said.

Not knowing what else to say, I said, "Isn't what, Mister Trundle?"

"Isn't there to admire and enjoy. Isn't there to run in the fields and take apples from my hand. Isn't there to lick sugar cubes from my palm and make me smile just watching him fly through the grass as if his hooves weren't touching the ground. Isn't there to smile—yes, smile,

Harry. Crazy, but I swear he smiled just to show you how happy he was, and to say thanks."

Another long sigh.

"All that being said, Harry, he also isn't there to stand at stud and make Board Room Farms boatloads of money as the number one stud stallion in the world. My brother Danny and the rest of the partners are distraught at the loss of Brian Boru and resigned to the loss of future equity. To me, that's money out of my pocket, Harry. Someone took money out of my pocket and I want it. I want it now and I want what BB would have brought in the future."

"Insurance?" I asked. "You and your partners must have had insurance on his life and his, ah, what you call, ah…"

"Standing at stud, Harry. It's called standing at stud. Mares come from around the world to his palatial barn and he would, as you would say, Harry, he would bang away all day. Then he would eat, shit, and run around the farm like he owned it. And Harry, he did. He made Board Room Farms the number one horse farm in the industry," he said.

"And the insurance, Mister Trundle?" I repeated.

"Yes, there was insurance, Harry. An animal mortality policy to cover his life and a policy to cover his stud fee potential. But, Harry, we bought a unique policy from Equine something or other, an outfit in Kentucky that's part of a Bermuda company. Diminishing return policy based on a complicated formula using age as the critical factor. At this point the policy will pay only a fraction of what his potential earnings could have been over the rest of his stud career."

"Excuse me, Mister Trundle, Randle. But horses die all the time. What is it that has you so upset?" I asked.

Trundle thought for a long minute.

"He didn't die, Harry. Brian Boru was killed."

"Killed?" Harry uttered. "You shitting me?"

"I shit you not, Harry," Trundle replied. "I shit you not."

Chapter 5

Cold bottle of Sierra Nevada Pale Ale firmly in hand, I, Harry Mickey Shorts, private investigator extraordinaire, asked the inevitable question.

"Killed?"

"That's right, Harry," Trundle replied.

"As far as I can remember from what I read, the horse died in his sleep. There was no mention of any suspicion of foul play in what I read. Surprise maybe, but natural causes was what was reported in the papers," I stated.

"Correct, Harry," he replied. "And I have no proof that something other than natural causes ended Brian Boru's life. I just have a feeling, Harry. No, it's more than a feeling. It's like the Schooners, Harry. I was right about them and I know something happened to end that horse's life; I want to know what it was. Who it was. Why it was. How it was. Once again, my life has been fucked with and I don't like it when my life is fucked with, Harry."

Two simultaneous sips of cool refreshment stopped the conversation momentarily.

"What can I do?" Harry asked.

"Find out what happened, Harry. Find out if there was anything other than natural causes involved in BB's death. I know you're not an expert in the game of thoroughbred racing, Harry, but I know you've been around the track once or twice in your life. Do what you do, Harry. I don't care what it takes or how long it takes. Just find out so I can rest assured the horse lived as long as God intended and something…or someone else wasn't involved. And, Harry, if something or someone else was involved, then prepare yourself for the shit storm of your life."

"You know you can count on me, Mister Trundle. If it's there, I'll find it. And if I do, let the shit storm begin."

Chapter 6

Kizmet Incorporated lists as its business mailing address a local real estate office on Plandome Road in Manhasset. It sits right at the end of the street my garage apartment happens to be on. And, lo and behold, it just happens to be owned by my ex-brother-in-law or EBIL for short. Big Mel is what I call him when I'm being nice, or need something. Every name in the book and more is what I call him when he is being a major dick, which happens more often than not.

Monday morning and time to find out if I had scumbuckets to chase.

"Big Mel, how might you be on this glorious Monday morning? You're looking exceptionally grand this morning," I started.

Yeah, I needed something.

"Shit on your glorious morning. And shit on your grand bullshit, too. Why are you here and what do you want?" he spat in my direction. "Can't a man have any peace in his own place of business?"

"Venom, Big Mel. Spewing venom like that will cause us to drift apart and lose the treasured relationship we now share. A warm and close relationship..."

"Fuck venom, and fuck our relationship," he cut me off.

I couldn't help but crack up and he soon followed suit.

"Not hanging so good, my man?" I asked.

"The monthly nut's got my balls in a vice and I can't get this big closing to come off before next week. I'm gonna have to max out my credit line at the bank again this month and I'm catching more shit at home than three men should have to endure in a lifetime."

I frowned in sympathy as he shook his head in disgust.

"Long as we're having this pleasant little chat," I started, "can I pick your brain a bit?"

"What could you possibly want now?" he answered.

"Hear about the horse that just died out in Missouri somewhere? Big stud horse they said in the papers."

"Yeah, I saw it," he replied.

"I know you don't partake in the Sport of Kings, but don't you have a bud in town that's known to frequent the racing circles on a regular basis?"

"Why?" is all he said.

"Why? I answered.

"Yeah, why?" he repeated.

"Ah, cuz I could be working on something for a friend that might involve the horses some," I said.

He just looked at me.

"What?" I said.

"Could be…a friend…might involve…" he mimicked.

Saved by the bell again. The door opened and Ms. Bunny Malone, faithful assistant to Big Mel, real estate tycoon in the making, pranced in. And I do mean pranced. She could stop traffic on the Long Island Expressway, in rush hour, on a Friday night, with just a smile and a little twirl. Not related to Einstein in any manner, but a face of sheer beauty, a body to die for, and legs that just don't quit.

"Harry, I missed you so the past week," she purred as she wisped a kiss across my cheek.

Johnson jumped to attention immediately waiting for his cheek to be wisped.

"Missed you too, Bunny," I managed to get out. "How are your Mom and Dad?"

Down, Johnson, down.

"They're good, Harry. It's so nice of you to ask," she said as she headed back to her desk.

Four heads turned and followed her progress back to her desk. Short skirt on long legs that moved in perfect unison to her swaying ass.

Four heads you ask? Me, Mel and a pair of straining Johnsons of course.

"Muller," Mel said.

"Muller?" I repeated.

"Yeah, Muller. He's the horse guy you're looking for. He's usually across the street at the diner having breakfast about this time."

"How will I know him?" I asked.

"Eggs, bacon, coffee and the Racing Form. Can't miss him," he told me.

"You the man, Mel," I answered.

"Yeah, he agreed. The man you owe the rent to."

The EBIL never changes.

"See you later, Bunny," I threw in her direction.

"I'm counting on it, Harry," she replied with a smile that indicated I might be seeing a whole lot of her later on.

Down, Johnson; get down, boy.

Chapter 7

As I crossed the street to see if Muller was still having breakfast at the Manhasset Diner, Big Mel stayed in my mind. Royal pain in the balls as he can be, he still watches over his little sister Sherry, my ex, and our two kids, Max and Briande. Gotta love him for it and thank God he's around to do it.

Eggs, bacon, coffee and the Racing form were all in the back booth with Muller. Or else, there were two guys who fit the description and this one ain't Muller. I'll take my chances.

"Muller?" I inquired as I slid into the both.

"And you might be?" he asked over the rim of his coffee cup.

"A guy looking for a guy named Muller. Mel told me you might be here," I answered.

No response as he looked down at his eggs and Racing Form at the same time. He took his time gathering a generous portion of the eggs on his fork using a piece of toast as a backstop. He then ate the eggs and a piece of bacon with a wash of coffee to go along with the food.

"Mel?" he finally replied.

"Yeah, Mel. I'm his brother-in-law, or ex-brother-in-law actually. You Muller?"

"I know Mel. You, I don't know. Mel I almost like. You, I don't know if I like. I'll talk to Mel. You, I'll decide after I talk to Mel."

With that he got up, dropped a fiver on the table, and walked out of the diner. Not another word.

Talkative kinda guy.

Me, I finished the toast he hadn't touched and the last piece of bacon. Washed it down with some water and split from the diner myself.

I just love it when a plan starts to come together, piece by piece, part by part. Pieces/parts is what I call it. These pieces parts are just getting started. May not look like it to you, but to a trained private detective like me, they're starting to come together. Slowly, but coming together. Alright, very slowly, now leave me alone for cripes sake.

Cripes? Kids taught me that one to replace my normal un-god like remark. Helpful little bastards aren't they?

Chapter 8

Let's recap…

Monday morning, late in the morning in fact, and pieces parts of my newly forming plan to help Trundle are starting to come together. Slowly, but it's forming. I rounded the corner off Plandome Road onto George Street to head up to my place. Not really paying much attention to where I was going, I was actually looking across the street over at EBIL's office trying to get another glimpse of Bunny.

WHAM! I walked right into a living, breathing brick wall and landed flat on my back—stunned.

"You should watch where you're going, laddie," the wall said.

Too stunned to speak and seeing three of everything, I heard a car door slam and the car drive off lickety-split. When I finally got to my elbows, I fell right back to the ground with another thump of my head against the concrete. It was my second cranial brush with concrete in a short period of time. Just in case you haven't had the pleasure—concrete hurts.

From somewhere behind me came a, "You alright, buddy?"

If I was alright I wouldn't be lying on my back seeing stars in broad daylight.

Then the voice of reason rang out loud and clear.

"What the hell are you doing?" Mel boomed.

Voice number one was trying to help me get somewhat upright. Mel watched while continuing to ask, "What the hell are you doing, Harry?"

With much effort, I made it to my feet, thanked voice number one, and started for my apartment. Half way there I could still hear Mel asking, "Where the hell are you going, Harry?"

~ * ~

When you wake up in the dark and don't know where you are, how you got there, or what time or day it is—it definitely isn't a good thing. That's the shape I was in the next time I saw the dark of day.

The wetness and slight pressure on my forehead was an odd feeling. The pounding in my head coupled with an overall body soreness was a bad feeling.

"What the fuck?" came quickly to mind.

"Welcome back, Harry. You almost scared the piss right out of me."

"Who the…what the…where the…?" was all I could get out.

"Harry, its Sandy, Sandy Taylor, your neighbor," was what I heard next and the last thought before I faded to dark chartreuse again. P.I.'s don't fade to black—too ordinary.

Chapter 9

It was light again the next time my eyes decided to take a peak. How long I had been out was anyone's guess, and, since I didn't remember I was actually out, it wasn't one I could come up with. Luckily I had exquisite assistance.

"Good to see you awake again, Harry," Sandy said.

"It's always good to see you, period," I replied.

"You gave me a pretty good scare, Harry. You've been out for fifteen hours and I still haven't been able to figure out what happened to you in the first place. You just staggered up the driveway like you were three sheets to the wind mumbling something about an Irish wall. Made no sense; then you practically passed out in my arms. I got you up to your apartment as fast as I could."

"Couldn't wait to jump my bones?" I asked with total practiced sincerity.

"Harry, you never cease to amaze me. Now, what the hell happened?" Sandy asked.

I started to raise myself on my elbows and said, "Let me get up and…"

The effort didn't last long. I fell back flat on the bed and my head started this swirling activity I'd experienced previously only after getting smacked real hard upside the head. Getting upright wasn't in the cards.

"Take it slow, Harry. Let me freshen up that washcloth and get some liquids in you. Don't move, I'll be right back," Sandy told me.

"Seems like I don't have a lot of choice in the matter," I replied.

I lay still and waited for my angel of mercy to return.

Sandy was a neighbor who happened to enjoy the finer experiences in life that Harry Mickey Shorts was so adept at providing. Being rather adept herself, it was a mutual friendship that suited both parties quite well.

"Here, Harry, lay still and put this washcloth back on your forehead. Mel was here and he wants you to call him as soon as you are able. I think he's worried about you. We were all worried for a bit."

"Thanks, Sandy," I said. "You're a doll."

"Drink some of this water so you won't get dehydrated, Harry," Sandy said. "I'll get you something to eat when you can sit up for more than five seconds at a time."

"I'd much rather be laying down when I'm in bed with you," I replied.

"Oh, you," Sandy said as she got up to leave the room. "I'll be back later, Harry. Get some rest and we can discuss the combination of laying and bed when you are feeling better."

"Maybe I will," I told her. "And I'll be dreaming about more than discussing that combination," I smirked.

A smile and Sandy was gone.

Chapter 10

Harry woke the following morning with the sun shining directly in his eyes. Eyes that produced a mediocre pain in his head when they opened. The distant memory of his neighbor tending to his wounds brought a smile to his face, but only briefly. What happened to him crept into his consciousness, wiping away his smile. It was obviously a matter for deep concern.

Who the hell was that guy that nailed my ass to the concrete? And what the hell for? Was it an accident? Was he waiting for me, or was it just a chance meeting of brick wall and falling P.I.?

So many questions—so few answers.

Since raising himself to his elbows didn't cause an immediate retreat to horizontal land, Harry's attempt to sit up was met with moderate success. After giving himself several minutes to get used to that level of upness, he swung his feet over the side of the bed and headed to the bathroom for a quick piss and a very, very long hot shower.

~ * ~

It was two o'clock that afternoon when Harry entered the premises of one Big Mel, real estate tycoon wannabe.

"Phone broken, asshole?" Mel inquired.

"A bit better, but not tiptop as of yet," Harry answered. "But thanks for asking," he threw at Mel.

"You look like a walking dog turd," he said. "You see Muller? And by the way, you better call your ex-wife immediately. She heard and for some reason is worried about you. The kids are still away so you're cool there."

"I'll call her, just not yet. I saw Muller yesterday morning I think it was, then the world caved in and I seem to have missed a day. Kinda strange dude, Muller. Need to get together with him again sometime in the near future if I can.

"You have any clue what happened to me?" Harry asked.

"Why are you asking me?" Mel replied. "I come out of my office and find your ass laid out on the corner. Some guy was trying to help you and I saw a car screaming around the corner as I headed on over to see what was up."

"Sorry, just thought you might have seen something from the window."

"Nada. I only saw the commotion and felt like being nosy," he finished.

The phone rang and Mel answered it, listened for a minute, then said, "Yeah, he's right here."

Harry took the phone, pressed it to his ear gingerly, and then said, "Yeah."

A minute later Harry was headed out the door with a "Later" left for Mel to deal with. A firm scolding from Sandy for leaving without telling her where he was going prompted his hasty retreat to his apartment. That and the promise of a bacon and cheese sandwich waiting for him there. Harry hoped that would be followed by the proper sequencing of bed and laying with the tender loving care of a concerned neighbor.

Turned out to be a rather horny concerned neighbor.

Care comes in many forms, and since Harry had experienced Sandy's particular form many times before, concerned or otherwise, the bacon and cheese sandwich took a back seat for the time being.

Chapter 11

"Yes, Sherry, I'm fine, Sherry. I swear I'm okay, Sherry. I'd tell you if I wasn't, Sherry," Harry was saying into the phone.

Listening, he shook his head as he had been doing for the last ten minutes.

"I was resting all day and couldn't call, Sherry. I'm calling now and you can tell the kids I'm fine. Really, I…Am…Fine."

A small lie, but the truth wasn't worth the ration of shit Sherry would rain down upon him.

"Yes I will, I promise. The second I feel anything at all I'll go directly to the emergency room. Promise," he continued.

Not a chance in hell it would happen, but a required response if I was to get off the phone ever again.

"Yeah, I'll be over later to see the kids. Yeah, I promise. I gotta go," Harry said as he hung up the phone.

Ya bang the ex-wife once and you can't get knocked on your ass without getting all the concern and crying shit. That'll teach ya, ya schmuck.

I didn't know exactly what was happening, or why, but whatever it was, it wasn't good. Mister Trundle lays the dead horse tale on me and before I can muster a plan, boom, some Irish bloke sends me to queersville. Muller could be a good way to get into it, but he looks like a head case, or a tough one to crack at best.

Thank god for Sandy. Nothing like a good roll in the hay to bring you back to reality and set your bearings straight. And trust me on this one, Sandy is good, too—very, very good.

Was there any connection between Trundle's problem and the Irish brick wall? Not a clue. Patrick's Pub.

That my friends was your first Harry Mickey Shorts QAS—Question, Answer, Solution—of this story. Won't be the last, I'm sure. Which means I'm off to Patrick's Pub to try and get some much needed intel.

Chapter 12

Patrick's Pub is a delightful Irish bar/restaurant located on Northern Boulevard in Queens, New York. It specializes in pretty Irish lasses serving good food and plenty of liquid refreshments.

Dolly, my favorite human liquid refreshment dispenser, met me at the entrance and walked me over to my favorite table. Good view of the clientele and great view of the short-skirted waitresses as they glide about.

"Harry, it's been a while," Dolly said as I sat my weary bones down.

"That it has, Dolly. Much too long," I replied.

"The usual, or have you switched brews on me again?" she inquired.

"Actually, I'll have a half-n-half. Stella for the lighter side of the combo," I told her. "Guy from Atlanta turned me onto it. It's called a JFL."

"Stella Artois? Somebody footing the bill here, Harry? A bit on the pricy side for a private dick?"

"Private dick?" I replied.

"Yes, Harry, a private dick. And by the way, it's been quite a while since the last time it became un-private in my presence."

A thought, an ahem, a smile.

"You have me there, Dolly. I've been working out of town quite a bit of late, plus you were doing the cozy thing with that construction guy last time I heard," I tried.

"History, Harry. Ancient variety," she said.

"Ahem," was the best I could come up with.

"I'll get your beer. You here alone?" Dolly inquired.

"Yeah, I am. But I'm looking for some information. Anybody here tonight that has their finger on who's coming and going around the area?" I asked.

"Lemme check; I'll be back," Dolly said as she turned and headed for the bar.

The familiar sway reminded Harry it had indeed been much too long.

~ * ~

"Harry, this is Shawn. Shawn, Harry. Shawn's gonna have a beer on you and sit and chat for a while," Dolly told Harry.

"Good to meet you, Shawn," I said.

"Yeah," was all he said.

"Have you heard of any guys arrived new in town, maybe from Ireland?" I asked Shawn.

Nice stare on Shawn. Very effective.

"If not new, been here a short time to do some heavy work maybe. Big guy, Irish brogue, maybe hooked up with the horsey crowd," I supplied.

"And you'd be asking why?" Shawn contributed.

"Let's just say I had the unpleasure of making his acquaintance recently. I'd like to find him and have a quick chat about it, and maybe find out who he works for."

"Horsey crowd?" he repeated.

"Yeah, thoroughbreds. Race track people. That kind," I said.

Shawn thought a minute, drank his beer in one swallow, and then said, "Don't know nothin', man. Don't ask me again," as he stood to leave.

"I'll take that as a yes and a no?" I asked.

"You can take it any way you want, mister. Just don't involve me in any of that shit."

With that, Shawn walked away and right out the door.

What kind of a shit pile have I gotten myself into this time, I wondered?

Chapter 13

The EBIL was sitting at his desk when I strolled into his place of employment the following morning, a perplexed look on his face.

Nothing perplexing about Bunny Malone, not one wee bit. What a pleasure just to glance in her direction.

"Big Mel, Bunny," I said as I entered.

Big smile from Bunny; ignored by Mel.

"Mel, man, you with us this morning?" I threw in his direction.

He finally looked up.

"Need some of your special intel. Of the Irish variety this time. Seen any new guys in town lately? Big boy, almost certain he's Irish and could be from the old country," I asked him.

"Irish? Big?" he repeated.

"Yeah. Real big and talks like some of your cousins from over there," I continued.

You could tell he was giving this a bit of thought.

"And, you seen Muller?"

"Big Irish guy. Muller. What are you into, Harry? You been betting the ponies and owe somebody some serious scratch?" he asked.

"Nothing like that. Really, I mean it. It's just I'm looking into something for a guy, I have a quick chat with Muller, then I get knocked on my ass. Wondering if any of it ties together."

More thought from Mel.

"Well, you seen anyone around town who fits the description lately?" I asked again.

"Not sure," he replied. "Let me make a few calls and I'll get back to you later today. This serious trouble, Harry?" he asked.

"Not trying to make it," I replied. "Just helping a friend is all."

"Why do I have the feeling you're yanking my chain here, Harry."

Making like Shawn, I was out the door.

~ * ~

Timmons answered the phone herself and I asked, "Ms. Timmons, it's Harry. Would you know if Mister Trundle is available any time soon for a short get together?"

"Harry, you don't even say hello any more. No how are you; how have you been? Just business," she answered.

"Ms. Timmons, my favorite person in all the world, the light that brightens even my darkest moments, how are you?" I dutifully asked.

"Boots, Harry, boots. Mister Trundle is involved in an all day meeting downtown and goes directly to the airport from there. He won't be back in the office until next Monday. Anything I can do for you, Harry?"

"Plenty you could do for me, Ms. Timmons. Plenty indeed," I laughed.

"Harry, what am I going to do with you?"

"If you'd just let me show you, you wouldn't regret it one bit," I continued to tease.

"I'll let Mister Trundle know you called, Harry. Anything else…never mind," and she hung up.

Chapter 14

Afternoon naps are so way cool. They're like stealing minutes from the time god and loving every bit of it. The phone brought me out of my fun place much before I wanted to.

"Yo, pops. You set for Saturday?" Max asked.

"Max, my favorite son. How you be?" I asked him.

"Your only son, too. I'm dandy, and your favorite daughter, Briande, she's good, too. Now, are you set for Saturday or not?" he asked again.

"Set as I can be. Gonna give me a clue this time?" I tried.

"Clue this, buddy boy," was his irreverent reply.

"One of these days, Maxie boy. One of these days."

"Yeah, yeah. Be here at eight thirty am sharp. Don't know why, but mom's making breakfast for all of us before we leave. She said to tell you you better not screw up her breakfast. She's acting kinda weird about it."

Oh boy.

"Tell her I'll be there. See you then."

"Good deal. Bye," and he was gone.

~ * ~

Once a month, if I'm in town, I get together with the kids and they decide what we will do for the whole day. It's a surprise and they plan the entire event. Briande used to lead, but Max has assumed more of the responsibility of late. I pay of course, but they haven't gone too far overboard yet, so I'm never too worried. There's always a first time, though.

~ * ~

The phone rang soon after I hung up with Max. So much for the resumption of my midday slumber time.

"Harry."

Nothing else, just Harry.

"Yeah, Mel."

"Muller seems to have split town. Nobody's seen him since you had your little encounter on the corner. Shack saw him walking toward Northern Boulevard that morning and that's the last anyone's seen of him."

"That odd for him?" I asked.

"Yeah, it's very odd. He was consistently around in the morning eating breakfast at the diner and off to the track in the afternoon, usually with at least one or two guys. Vanished is odd."

"Odd," I agreed. "Anything on the big dude?" I continued.

"Words been out. Nothing at all from anyone. If he had been hanging around town before that morning, someone would have seen him. Guys that big with something unusual like an Irish brough don't go unnoticed in a town this size."

"Again, odd," I said.

"Harry, it could have been an isolated accident and you just happened to be the person that got in the way. It happens, you know. You've had enough unusual shit happen to you that makes one wonder if unusual shit isn't supposed to happen to you."

"You are right there, Mel. But, I go downtown to talk to a guy and agree to help him out, meet with Muller that morning, then go around the corner and get my clock cleaned. Too neat and tidy for me."

"Could still be coincidence," Mel said.

"Coincidence, maybe," I said. "But where's Muller?" I asked.

"Good point, Harry. Good point. I'll keep on digging and have my track friends see if they can catch anything around the track," Mel said.

"Sounds good. Thanks for the help, Mel," I said.

"Not a problem, Harry. Just be careful, okay. You get in deep on this one and can't get yourself out, my sister will kick my ass six ways to Sunday. The track is a dangerous place to find yourself if you're on the wrong end of the stick. Friends from town have experienced the bad side of the racing business; trust me on this one. Be very careful, Harry."

"Got it, Mel. I'll be as careful as I can. But I still gotta do my job and, as hard as I try, careful sometimes gets lost in the translation. Gotsta split. Later."

"Yeah, Harry, later. I'll call you on your cell if I hear anything else."

Mel worried about me; not a good thing. His normal concern consists of where is the overdue rent and go take care of your kids. Real concern—that's a real concern.

Chapter 15

Saturday morning and still no call from either Trundle or Ms. Timmons. Not a total surprise, but one can always hope for the unusual to happen. Not this time. Nothing new from Mel either, so I moved on with life and turned my attention to my kids.

At 8:30 on the dot, I rang the door bell to my ex-wife's house on Linden Street in Manhasset, Long Island. Max said don't be late and I wasn't about to find out what would happen if I was. Almost immediately, the door opened.

"Hello, Harry, you look good," Sherry, the ex, greeted me.

You look good? I'm used to getting the finger or a fuck you, Harry. That's without having done anything wrong, either.

"Hi, Sherry. You're looking rather fetching yourself bright and early on this beautiful Saturday morning," I replied.

Fetching? Idiot talk from a bumbling idiot.

"Why thanks, Harry. Come on in. The kids are in the kitchen waiting for you; breakfast will be ready in a jiff," Sherry said as she turned and headed to the back of the house.

Still a rock solid pleasure watching the ex sashay away from me. She knew it and put an extra little bounce in her sway. Damn she was good when she wanted to be!

"Dad," came from Briande as I entered the kitchen. She was getting older by the minute. She wasn't my "little girl" any more.

"Cop a squat and let's get some food moving," Max added to the mornings festivities. "We got things to do, places to go, people to see," he concluded.

"I'll give you 'get some food moving' right across that thick skull of yours if you aren't careful," Sherry responded to Max's comment, hands on hips, Tweety Bird puffed out on her apron.

Defiant she didn't look and we just laughed. Two seconds later, she joined in.

"Okay, let's get some food moving," I echoed. That caught me a dish rag right in the mouth.

More laughter all around.

~ * ~

Breakfast done, kids' teeth brushed, a kiss on my cheek and a discreet pinch on my other cheek from the ex, and we were on our way. Today's transportation was a rented 1970 mint Mercedes convertible that blew the kids doors off when they saw it.

"Man, that ride is awesome!" Max exclaimed.

"Very nice car, Daddy," Briande added.

"Yeah, and its due back first thing Monday morning, so don't mess it up. It will cost me a fortune if anything happens to it," I informed them. "Let's hit it," I finished.

All settled in, Max took the lead and said, "Head on over to the Northern State Parkway and point toward the end of the Island. I'll tell you when to exit."

"Still no clues? Briande?" I tried.

"Drive, Daddy. You'll see when we get there," she replied.

"Sheesh, you guys are no fun at all," I kidded them. "How's your moms doing by the way?" I continued.

Quiet on all fronts.

"Guys?" I said.

Continued quiet, then Briande tentatively said, "Weird. She is acting all happy and stuff. It's like something happened not all that long ago and she is all smiles and is like…like…happy!"

"Max?" I asked.

"Ah…happy kinda says it all," he replied.

"Well, that's a good thing," I said. "She should be able to be happy."

"Yeah, she should," Briande said. "But why is she *so* happy?"

They should only know.

Chapter 16

Everyone was laughing and having a good time when Max yelled, "Exit. Get off this exit. This one...don't miss it...exit."

"All right, all right. I'll make it. Cool your jets there, bud," I said as I hit the brakes hard and just made the exit turn off. The sign in front of me said "Roosevelt Field Mall" and I had my first inkling of what the day was going to bring. Expensive jumped to the head of the class.

"The mall?" I inquired.

"Yeah, the mall," Max echoed. "If you're gonna play, you gotta look the part, don't you?" he asked.

"Yes, daddy. You don't expect us to go out there without the proper attire, now do you?" Briande chipped in.

"Go where? What attire? To do what?" I went on.

"Oh, you'll see. Come on, park this hunk of junk and let's get rolling," Max urged.

I gave him a "hunk of junk" look.

"Just park it, okay," he teenagered me.

"At your service, Master Max. And yours, Mademoiselle Briande. The parking of the vehicle and subsequent spending of my money is my utmost priority you can be assured," I deadpanned.

"Don't worry, Poppyson. We got some bucks of our own to spend first. Your bucks only kick in when we have maxed out our bankrolls," Max informed me.

"Meager bankrolls I would imagine?" I said in question.

"You'll be surprised. Mom opened up the coffers for this one and we have a pretty good head start on the potential expenditure limits."

"We'll see," I said. "We'll see."

"But," Max continued "the rest of the day is on you big guy."

Roosevelt Field Mall, like most malls, is designed for one thing—spending money. The kids weren't that hung up on "stuff" cuz they were raised that way even though they grew up in Manhasset where money seems to grow on trees. But, give them the opportunity and they can spend with the best of them.

Shocked the shit right out of me, but the numero uno target for both of them was Golf America and their annual "kids day" sale. I came to learn on this beautiful Saturday morning the kids had both taken golf in gym at school and fallen in love with the game. Flat out head over heels in love with the game of golf. God does shine down on the poor fathers of the world every once in a while.

Basic golf shoes for Max with the only requirement being they had to be water resistant. Two pair of shorts and two golf shirts were all he wanted. Briande went for two pair of shoes—your basic white with white tassels in the front for one pair and a snazzy pair of yellow over tan that looked pretty damn good on her. Next came a few pairs of shorts and two skirts to match the shoes with tops to complete each ensemble.

Any thoughts of us being finished in the mall quickly went by the wayside. The Limited and Esprit were next on Briande's list with similar purchases of shorts, skirts and tops, plus a few pair of those short socks with pom-poms on the back. I have to admit it, the kid had pretty good taste and clothes just looked good on her. She has her mother's build and I'll be beating away the boys sooner than I would like.

Max hit Modell's Sporting Goods and made major purchases of golf-like attire coupled with your array of socks and hats. Kid had his father's taste in clothes—basic stuff that did what it was intended to do. The fitted Yankee hat made his daddy proud.

I was bummed cuz I didn't get to go to FAO Schwartz or The Disney Store. Kids never let their parents have any fun!

A quick stop at the Family Pet Center to pick up a few goodies for Sherry's Airedales and the mall was history. Mediocre damage cost wise and it hadn't cost me a penny yet. Why do I believe that's not going to last much longer? At least lunch wasn't going to do it as we hit Fuddruckers for gigundo burgers with all the fixings, fries, and sundaes for dessert. Briande was her usual dainty self, which was good, since Max and I pigged out like we hadn't eaten in three weeks and had to wash twice to get all the remains off our faces.

"So, where to now my lovelies?" I asked when we were back in the car.

"Eisenhower Park," Max replied.

"Eisenhower Park?" I said in question.

"You heard him," Briande said. "Eisenhower Park and let's get a move on."

"Yes mam, Eisenhower Park it is, mam. And I's hustling, mam, I truly be hustling," I answered.

"Very funny," Max laughed. "Now move it."

We pulled into the entrance to Eisenhower Park and I was directed to proceed to the golf course. They have multiple courses in their layout and I'd played there a few times, but the place was jumping much more than usual.

Reason—Demo Day.

Chapter 17

After parking the car in the far reaches of the lot, we proceeded to the course area.

"Demo Day, guys?" I queried as we approached.

"What's wrong with a Demo Day?" Briande beat Max to an answer. "If you are going to learn to play the game, you need the proper tools to do so. Being fitted with a set of clubs that suits your game and physical abilities is the best way to begin your golf experience," she instructed me.

"Golf experience?" I said.

"What can I tell you," Max replied. "She listens to all that shit they spew to get you to spend mucho dineero on equipment. Me, gimme some clubs and let's whack away at it. But, as long as we're here, might as well see what they got. Know what I mean, pops?" he finished.

"Might as well," I answered.

Here comes my expenditure time I thought to myself.

~ * ~

The kids waited their turn and used me as confirmation that they were serious in their pursuit of "proper tools" to play the game. Max gravitated to the Taylor camp after trying the newest Calloway drivers and Cleveland clubs. Briande went directly to the Cobra sales rep and concentrated one hundred percent of her efforts right there. A lady with her mind made up is a lady you need to leave alone.

I watched Max hit a few drives and it looked like his natural athletic ability carried over to the game of golf. His mechanics weren't quite refined yet, but it wouldn't be long before he would be giving his uncle Mel a run for his money—if he put his mind to it. Knowing my son Max, combined with the look of determination on his face, his mind was already to it.

Briande had the grace of a ballerina and the muscle tone of a gymnast that translated into 150 yard drives right down the middle. A long controlled back swing, full turn ending with her body square to the target meant she had already started working on her game.

That's daddy's girl.

No sense in fiddling around, so we had the reps fit both of them and ordered clubs while we were there. Got a fair discount due to the Demo Day sale and we were all happy when we left. All except my wallet which took a twelve hundred dollar whipping and I didn't even get anything. I take that back. The look on their faces as we left was worth its weight in gold.

As it turned out, buying the clothes would have been a steal and a half.

"So, as I believe I have said before, where to now my lovelies?" I asked when we were back in the car.

"da beach," Briande instructed.

"da beach?" I queried.

"Yeah, da beach," Max repeated. "da beach—Jones variety," he said.

"Ah, Jones Beach, on the south shore of Long Island, the island we happen to be on," I translated.

"Right," Briande sighed. "Think you can find it?" she smiled.

I just love that kid's smile.

"I'll find it," I answered. "And we would be doing what when we get there?" I continued.

"Stopping and getting out of the car," Max informed me.

"What a genius you are. I never would have thought of that," I said as I smacked my forehead.

The cooler and blanket we had packed in the trunk before we left their house now made some sense.

"Jones Beach it is. Sit back and relax and we'll be there in a jiff," I told them.

Max looked at Briande, Briande looked at Max, and they said in unison, "A jiff?"

Chapter 18

Late afternoon, sun starting to head toward sleepy-by land in the west, a picnic on a blanket with the ocean as background music. My kids can do it up when they put their minds to it. People have asked if their mother helps them plan our little excursions. Answer—not a single bit. Our days together are planned 100% by the kids and I'll put their ingenuity up against any other pair of dysfunctional misfits on the earth. Proud of them is the least I can say.

"Sierra Nevada Pale Ale would be the beer of choice at the moment," Max said with authority as he handed me a sweating bottle of the glorious nectar of the gods.

"Right you are, little one."

"And I believe Genoa Salami and Swiss with lettuce and mayo on lightly toasted white will suffice," Briande stated with equal authority.

"Right you are oh favorite daughter of mine," I said.

"Good, then let's eat and enjoy the beauty of nature and the fine company we find ourselves with," Max expounded.

Three beats and we all cracked up in unison.

"I know, enjoy this," Max said in my direction.

"You're disgusting, Max" Briande said. "And you condone such language, father?" she continued.

Three beats and we all cracked up again in unison.

We ate and watched the sun go down for what seemed like forever. It was a good forever. Real good forever. We talked and we laughed. We spent time doing what fathers and their kids don't do enough of and what I'd like to do more often—enjoy my kids.

"Okay, so we squandered your money on clothes and my money on sticks of ignorance. Better equipment then I use myself. Now what?" I asked.

"Dessert and we're outa here," Max said.

He reached into the cooler and handed me a plastic Ziploc bag; nothing for them. Seemed odd before I opened my goody bag.

"Son of a bit…" I almost said.

"Surprised?" Briande asked.

"Surprised?" I finally said when I could get my mouth to say the words my brain was thinking. "I'm…I'm…I'm flabbergasted!" I got out.

"Cool," Max said.

"Very way cool," Briande contributed.

"We saved up and bought them with our own money. It's our way of saying thanks for being our dad," Briande spoke for the two of them.

"Wow!' I finally said. "Van Morrison and Sarah McLachlan together tonight at Jones Beach Theater. Van the Man and I'm gonna get to see him. But wait, there's three tickets here. How am I gonna find two other people to go with me on such short notice?" I said with a straight face.

Two kids piling on their dear old dad told me who I was going to the concert with. Kids with great musical taste I might add.

Two great kids, period.

Chapter 19

"How was the concert?" Big Mel asked without looking up as I entered the office early Sunday morning.

"Amazing," I replied. "Van Morrison is simply amazing. And he and McLachlan put out fantastic sound together. The whole show rocked the house down and warmed the audience from the get. They had us in the palm of their hands and switched up with ease. Plus, the band was dynamite."

"Rest of the day?" he continued without nary a peak from his beloved Sunday Times.

"The whole day was too cool. The kids just never cease to surprise and bring sheer joy to my heart when we do our Saturday thing."

Could have been a verbal sound, could have been him farting.

"You knew? I asked.

"Knew what?"

"About the day; what we were gonna do?"

"Some. I'm playing golf with the kids over at Plandome Country Club next Saturday," he stated matter of factly.

"So you knew. Those little bastards were pretty sure of themselves. Me?"

"You? You what?" ebil said.

"Me, next Saturday?" I asked.

"Clean the shit out of your ears, Harry. I said 'I' was playing golf with '*the kids*' over at Plandome next Saturday. You, I didn't say you. You. Fuck you," he finished without ever looking up.

"I believe you forgot to say 'And the horse you rode in on,'" I finished for him.

"That would be correct. Thank you, Harry. Fuck you and the horse you rode in on, Harry. And by the way, my sister said to tell you thanks. She owes you one and I don't want one word from your mouth on what it is she owes you. Not a sound out of your mouth now, or after she gives it to you. Clear?"

"Clear big guy. Can I repeat the grunts and groans…?"

I was already running for the door before the paper flew.

Chapter 20

"Harry, Ms. Timmons."

"That has such a delightful sound to it—Harry and Ms. Timmons," I said into the phone.

"What am I going….never mind. Mister Trundle will see you at one o'clock today if that's convenient for you…Good. Be on time, Harry."

It is very difficult to respond to the sound of dead air followed by a dial tone.

Since there was no offer from Ms. Timmons of Charles coming to pick me up, I assumed I was to find my own way to Randle's office for our one o'clock meeting. I hopped on the Long Island Railroad at the Manhasset station and promptly dozed for the entire ride into Penn Station. A quick cab ride later and I was waiting patiently in Trundle's reception area admiring the Renoir and the red-headed beauty adorning the reception station.

On the third "Harry" I finally surfaced from my reverie and heard Ms. Timmons calling my name. I did mention she was a red-headed beauty, didn't I?

"Mister Trundle will see you now, Harry. If you can manage to tear yourself away from your current attraction, go ahead in."

She was gone before I could respond, but not before I could admire her "well worth a look" departure.

A knock-knock later and I was shaking hands with Mr. M. Randle Trundle in his spacious office.

"Harry, how are you?" he immediately inquired.

"I'm good, Mister Trundle, I mean Randle," I responded. "How have you been?"

"As well as can be expected, Harry. The company is doing quite well, the stock is at an all time high, and revenues are going through the roof. Requiring more of my time than I would like, but I'm remembering to take the time to smell the roses and suck on some suds."

"That's great. But what I really meant was; how are 'You' doing?" Harry asked again.

"The loss of Brian Boru hasn't left me yet, Harry. Danny and the other members of Board Room Farms seem to have gotten beyond it and are off doing their usual array of business and personal functions like nothing happened. I'm not there yet, Harry. Don't know if I'll get there soon, either," he concluded with a sigh.

M. Randle Trundle was not acting M. Randle Trundle like. Not even close. Not much I could say to make it all better, either.

"Finding out what happened won't fix it, Randle. But, finding out what happened will fix them, if there is a them. And Brian Boru deserves at least that much," I tried.

"Maybe, Harry. Maybe," he whispered.

"Did I hear you mention suds before?" I threw at him.

After a moment of non-recognition, Randle said, "Yes, Harry, I did at that. And I do believe a nice bottle of cool refreshment would be just what the doctor ordered right about now," he said.

"I heartily agree," I replied. "And never forget, if one is good, two can't help but be doubly enjoyable."

A smile crept across Randle's face and he seemed to lift just a little bit.

"Harry, you can say just the right thing to remind me life is good and I'll get beyond this soon enough. Let's go out on the balcony and enjoy some of that life while we can. Suds, too."

Chapter 21

"Lee's Summit, Missouri," Randle said as we settled in on his balcony to enjoy the city of New York and some Bass Ale.

"Bass?" I queried. "Lee's Summit?"

"Had some on my last stopover in England and enjoyed it. We stock it now, but I can have some Pale Ale brought up if you would prefer, Harry."

"Bass is wet. Bass is quality suds. Bass is what you want to enjoy right now and Bass is what we will both enjoy right now."

A smile of thanks from a friend.

"Lee's Summit? What's a Lee's Summit?" I asked.

"We had our string of horses down in Kentucky from the beginning of BRF and collectively always figured we'd be there forever. Our trainer comes from Missouri originally and he got homesick. He worked on us for over a year and finally convinced us to move the string out there. It actually saved us some money by doing so. J'Orr is a good horseman and trainer, a good man, and a good friend."

"Where is this Lee's Summit?" I asked figuring I would probably end up visiting Lee's Summit, Missouri soon enough.

"Just outside of Kansas City," Randle told me. "Not a bad town and they play American league baseball there. We've been planning our visits out there when the Yankees are going to be in town. They beat up on the Royals every time and that really frosts J'Orr's butt. He loves his Royals to death."

"I guess I'll be meeting J'Orr soon enough, Randle?" I asked him. "Question though: you have any dealings with anyone that might employ an Irish guy big as a brick shithouse and just as hard?"

"Irish?" Randle said with a cocked eye.

"Yeah, Irish. Let's just say I had a run in with one in town recently and the timing was kinda peculiar. Irish for sure," I finished.

"This brick shithouse have a name, Harry?" he asked.

"I was too busy acquainting myself with the sidewalk to ask for a name," I said. "He jumped in a waiting car and sped off before anyone knew what happened, mostly me."

"Irish," Randle said in contemplation mode.

From past experience, I knew I'd have to wait a bit before he answered. To kill time, I killed a Bass.

"Broderick," Randle said.

I waited.

"Could be the Brodericks," he expounded.

I waited some more while enjoying a second Bass and the fabulous view of New York from on high. Randle was currently ignoring his (Bass and view) which seemed quite a waste to me on both counts. Which one was worse could be debated forever.

"Big international stable run by the Broderick clan has been a major player and very successful on tracks worldwide. The breeding end of the business was never a priority until just recently; we have bumped up against them continually since they got heavily involved in that end of the business."

"Interesting," I said for want of anything better to say.

"The Brodericks battle pretty hard with another huge Irish stable that we have done some steady breeding business with over the last eighteen months to two years. Guy from the Isle of Mann named Davey Boy McGarry heads up that group. Another bullheaded Irishman. Brian Boru was their exclusive stud stallion of choice and their top mare was scheduled to be BB's breeding barn guest the day he was found.

"The interesting thing is, Harry, the Brodericks are headed up by Mikey Broderick who just so happens to reside in Manhasset, Long Island. He's semi-retired now and the day-to-day business is run by Pauly Broderick out of the West Coast; San Diego I think. He's a hardheaded, hard-drinking, woman-chasing bully of a man—doesn't take shit from anyone and doles it out by the truckload. Wades through the ego-infested waters of the racing business like it's his backyard swimming hole. Smart as he is tough. If you come up against him, be careful, Harry."

"Anyone else from the Brodericks I should know about?" I asked.

"Two brothers—Matt and Mikey, Jr.—run the East Coast operations, John Broderick stays over in Ireland most of the time to run that piece, and Tom runs the transportation side in the US. He's muscle, too, so watch him carefully. Patrick is the mouthpiece, and a slick one, who can play both sides of the street if need be."

"Two simple questions: if there are any, they the bad guys here; and if yes, why?" I asked.

"I don't know, Harry," Randle said. "But if there are any, the Brodericks are as good a bet as any. Mikey, Sr. and I go way back, Harry. Some of it good, some not so good."

I finished my Bass in one long swallow. My knowledge of the horse racing game wasn't bad, but it wasn't good either. The end of the business Randle and I just got through discussing was foreign territory to me, just like most of the rest of that world. Not for long though. Breeding and racing horses was going to be second nature to me very soon, and the bad guys had no idea what was about to hit them.

Chapter 22

"Big Mel, my man, my main man, my biggest, bestest, mainest man…"

"Oh shit, Harry. Give it a rest, will you. And what do you want. I'm busy here as you can plainly see," Mel answered.

What was plain to see was Mel had his feet up on the desk in the back of his office, nap time about to engulf his being. Busy he wasn't. Not by any stretch of anyone's imagination.

"Just letting you know I'm going under real soon. Don't know where I'm gonna be at any time and I may be gone for a week or more at a time. Bunny around?"

"She look like she's around? Hey wait—Bunny, you hiding in the closet? Come out, come out, wherever you are," he squealed.

"Funny, asshole. As nice as I try to be to you, that's the thanks I get." We both laughed at that one.

"Seeing as Ms. Malone isn't here, can you ask her to keep an eye on my place for me while I'm gone? If I'm gonna be around, I'll let her know. And, oh yeah, don't tell Sherry I'm going under. Or the kids. She'll worry and badger the kids and they don't need her shit with me gone. I'll keep in touch with them, I promise."

Mel looked at me with a questioning eye.

"At least I'll try," I said.

"Alright," Mel said. "But don't expect me to make excuses for you when she figures out you're gone again. My ass is out of it and not getting into it. No way, no how."

"Bunny?" I asked.

"I'll take care of it," Mel reluctantly agreed.

"Thanks," I replied.

"This dangerous shit, Harry?" he asked.

"Don't know yet," I answered truthfully. "Might be, might be nothing at all. By the way—you know a guy named Broderick, Mikey Broderick I think?"

"Michael Broderick? The racing tycoon Broderick that lives here in town?" he queried.

"That's the one, I think," I said.

"Everyone in town knows of him. Nobody really knows him, though. Keeps to himself behind heavy security and travels quite a bit. Mark's company does the driving for him exclusively, I believe. From what I know, one tough son of a bitch. I think he's retired from the racing game," Mel stopped. "You mixed up with the Brodericks, Harry? You betting the ponies and in deep? Tell me you're not mixed up with that shit, Harry?"

"Relax, Mel. I'm not mixed up in anything, and I'm not betting the ponies. Once is more than enough for one lifetime."

"Then what?" Mel asked. "Why the questions about old man Broderick? And your interest in Muller? What gives, Harry?"

"Time to split, Big Mel. Take care of Bunny for me and keep an eye on the ex and the kids. I'm good, don't worry. If shit is gonna come down, I won't be coming out of it spotted brown. You can count on it, Mel. Later," and I was gone from the office and headed up George Street to my apartment.

Racing World—get ready for one Harry Mickey Shorts.

Chapter 23

The Daily Racing Form is the bible throughout thoroughbred racing. It contains all the information you need to follow horses running on just about every track across the country. Regional versions carry the race tracks within a certain geographical area with feature articles highlighting the national scene. The Bible, or at least it was once my bible—not any more.

The Belmont, last leg of the Triple Crown, is run at surprise—Belmont Race Course on Long Island. Early in the year the track that's open in the New York area is Aqueduct—Jamaica, Queens. Hop on the A Train and eventually you're there. That's where I found myself on a bright sunny morning soaking up the track atmosphere and looking for Muller. Guys knew of him, but nobody had seen him in a while. What's a while at the track: anywhere from yesterday to forever. No help so far.

Handicapping the races is an art form individual to each person. A bit of the Harry Mickey Shorts education lesson is about to come your way. Guy named Andrew Beyer who writes for the Washington Post invented perhaps the most famous handicapping technique—Speed Rating Handicapping. Attached to every horse in every race is the speed figure that horse generated in that race. Appears on the right side of that horse's line in the form. You also get the horses that finished first, second, etc. in the race. Me, I'm a Beyer guy, and thus, speed figures are gospel.

That is unless I get a hunch or think I know better when I do my last minute handicapping. I was up early that morning and already had my choices for the six races I was going to bet on. I never bet on Maiden races—those are races for horses that haven't won a race before. Too unpredictable. I can lose enough money betting on horses who have run before—I don't need to guess.

Education lesson is now over for today.

I gave up on finding anything useful on Muller and concentrated my efforts on acquainting myself with the Broderick and McGarry barns. That's another horse term—barns. Both ran horses in the US and abroad with the Broderick's having more success domestically and Davey Boy McGarry coming out on top in England and Ireland. Two different styles of racing and each stable seemed to point their purchases and efforts toward their specialty. They dabbled across the waters to keep their name out there and each one seemed to be stepping across the water with more frequency over the last two years. Hence, Brian Boru became very important to the McGarry stable's domestic invasion.

I bet twenty bucks on Princess Tara for Mel in the third race—a claiming race for Fillies and Mares. Those are female horses—a little bonus educational tidbit. Claiming races exist so trainers and owners can purchase horses at predetermined prices and add or subtract from their stables. Horse churn is what I call it. Business is how they see it and it keeps the industry going.

Princess Tara ran away from the pack and put a nifty $80 in Mel's pocket. I'll explain how the betting and odds work later. Time to squander some of my money for the time being.

Chapter 24

A day at the track is a trip unto itself and can last forever. You get caught up in the handicapping as horses are scratched—taken out of the race by their trainer or owner for a myriad of reasons—or extra weight is added. Each horse is assigned a particular weight to carry for that race. It is a way of evening out the chances for each horse in the race against the better or lesser horses they run against. The weight is a combination of the jockey's actual body weight and extra weight (lead) added to the saddle to get to the assigned weight.

Harry the educator—what a burden. Let's move on.

More fun is the people watching. Track people and spectators alike. The track people are always there and have a tendency to congregate in the same places every day. I've spent a few days at the New York tracks since my return and naturally do my P.I. thing while I'm there. Being able to understand people is a key in my business and the more you practice, the better you get at it. Sit back in the shadows and just observe.

One particular group of five or six guys, depending on the day I was there, would hang around the area that contained the $100 betting windows. "Shoe Tying Willie" is what I called this one guy who was always with this group. They were there every time I hit the track, so I assumed they used the same routine every day. Or should I say Willie used the same routine every day. Here's what I saw:

Willie was the ring leader of the group, always doing the most talking, never going to the windows to bet. Same manner of dress each time I was at the track which was as nondescript as you can get. Short sleeve drab colored shirt over no-name pants of equally drab color. Not mismatched—just not noticeable. The other guys had some color to their get-ups and you couldn't help but notice them. All part of the gimmick. Notice the crowd, but not every player in the crowd.

Their particular gimmick went something like this: hang out and bullshit by the back railing overlooking the seating area in front of the "big bet" windows. They knew all of the stable hands that did the betting for the owners and/or trainers. Each one of them watched a different direction while they seemed to be engrossed in their tales of whoa and glee. Laughing and carrying on like they were oblivious to what was going on around them. When a stable bettor appeared, their game was on.

Two guys from the group would gravitate to the widows and start horsing around within sight lines of the windows. Just enough action so you had to look to see what was going on, not enough to cause enough commotion to draw the attention of the track security personnel. Willie would slide over to the other side of the windows and pretend to be tying his shoe lace. Just close enough to hear what the stable bettor would say when he placed the bet. Now they had the "inside information" from the stable and would use some of their pooled money to bet on the sure thing.

Sure thing? There's no such thing as a sure thing at the track you say. Of course you're right, but stables prepare some of their horses to run in specific races, at specific distances, under specific conditions. The horse may not win very often, if at all, but given the perfect setup with the right preparation, the horse becomes a champion. Stables do it and Willie and his boys count on that happening when they get the "inside info."

Slick gimmick as long as the stable knows what they are doing and there aren't two stables setting up for the same payday in the same race. Or the horse needs to take a shit before the race and runs like it.

I watched Willie and his boys cash much more often than not.

Me—I cashed once and not nearly enough to make it a winning day at the track. It was another day of P.I. skills honing, though. We can talk about spectator watching at the track at a later date.

Chapter 25

Ticket in hand, affairs in order, Harry Mickey Shorts was headed to Lee's Summit, Missouri to try and get a handle on what happened to Brian Boru—if anything. The Kansas City Royals were on a ten day road trip and wouldn't be in town while I was there. Make it easier to concentrate on the task at hand.

The plane landed right on time and I found Buddy, one of the ranch hands, waiting for me. I didn't need to rent a car since they had plenty of extra wheels at the ranch for me to use. Since small talk didn't seem to be a Buddy specialty, we rode in silence. I arrived at Board Room Farms with the same amount of knowledge I had when I left New York.

J'Orr was standing by the corral as we pulled up and he walked over to greet me. Knew it was J'Orr when he stuck out his hand and said, "I'm J'Orr," and I happened to be the only person standing there at the time. Another stable hand had taken my bag and was headed up to the main house.

"Harry Mickey Shorts," I replied. I like to be formal when I meet a guy for the first time.

"Call me Harry," I continued. We were old friends now.

"Good to meet ya, Harry. Mister Trundle says you're good people and that's good enough for me."

J'Orr paused for a minute like he was putting his thoughts in order.

"Place is still a bit out of sorts with what's happened and all. The boys here loved that horse and we still can't believe he's gone. Boru was a special one, he was; to the stable and to all of us that work here. Going to miss him terribly," he said

"Sorry for the loss," sounded like the thing to say, so I said it.

"Well, Mister Trundle says you're interested in the horse business and we should help you out. Whatever you need you just let us know, all right, Harry? What's here is at your disposal and all the boys know you'll be around asking questions. They're at your disposal as well."

"That's cool, J'Orr. I appreciate you putting up with me, especially at a time like this. You guys just go about your business and I'll try and stay out of your way as best I can. Watching is as good as talking most of the time for me."

"Good enough, Harry. Stu there will show you up to the main house and get you settled. We'll be eating lunch right about noon, so feel free to roam around till then. I gotta get to some things done before hand."

"Thanks, J'Orr. See you at lunch."

J'Orr headed off toward what looked like a huge barn. I followed Stu up to the main house. Stu was about as talkative as Buddy. At this rate I'd gather enough information to figure out if there was anything to be concerned about in a little less than a hundred years. To quote my beautiful ex— "You should live so long, Harry."

Chapter 26

The main house was a "serious" main house. Not what I expected to find at a horse ranch. The entrance had double doors at least ten feet high, each five feet wide, solid oak. Board Room Farms engraved on both doors. You walked into a wide open space with a spiral winding staircase twenty feet straight ahead of you. Oak floors everywhere and flowers brightening up every surface you could see.

"Welcome to Board Room Farms, Mister Shorts. I'm Ham. Anything you need while you are staying with us you just ask me and I'll make it happen. Your bag is up in your room and there's some coffee there for you as well. Let me show you the way and then I'll get out of your hair and let you get settled in."

"Thanks, Ham. I won't be long."

"Lunch is at twelve noon sharp and the boys are usually mighty hungry by then. Wouldn't be late if I was you," Ham said.

"I'll be there bright and early," I told him.

My room was at the end of the hall and next to the floor's community bathroom. I peaked in and was again surprised by what I saw. Big old claw foot tub standing in one corner and an enclosed shower stall filled the other corner. Double sink counter with a huge mirror lining the entire back wall. Like the rest of the house, the room seemed like it was big enough for a half court basketball game. Long as I was in there, I relieved myself of the three cups of coffee I'd had that morning and then headed back to my room to unpack.

"You must be Shorts," caught me while I was leaning over to pick up my bag off the floor, my back to the door.

"Nice ass," followed in a husky, smoky, sexy voice.

Straightening up but still facing away from the door, I turned to see who it was that was admiring my ass. I must be getting slow as the doorway was empty when I got myself turned around. I walked over to the door and looked down the hallway at what had the makings of an intriguing cowgirl mystery. Tight jeans over snakeskin boots with a thumb stuck in the corner of each back pocket that didn't obscure the finely shaped ass and long legs neatly tucked into those jeans. Denim shirt completed the outfit and, if I was a betting man, I'd bet the front view wouldn't disappoint either.

"Yo," I tried.

A half turn and what I thought was the hint of a smile vanished around the corner at the end of the hall.

Picture the old cowboy westerns and a grisly old coot clanging a metal rod inside a metal triangle. Loud metallic sound reverberating throughout the bunk house and surrounding property. That's the sound I heard and knew right away it was chow time.

Chapter 27

The dining room was big—even bigger than I expected. It had to be fifty feet from one end to the other and a good twenty feet wide as well. Long wooden tables filled the center of the room and smaller tables were set up against the walls to pile food and drinks on.

"Shorts. Come on over here and grab a seat before the grub's all gone," J'Orr shouted from the head of the table at the far end of the room. Farm hands were all filling their plates and sitting wherever there was an open seat at the tables.

"Grab a plate and go on over to that table under the picture of Boru. That's some of the best pulled pork you're ever gonna get this side of... of...of wherever you can get yourself some pulled pork. None better anywhere I'm telling you. Slaw's pretty fair, too," J'Orr said as he wiped his mouth with what looked like a linen napkin.

"I'm all over it, J'Orr," I told him as I headed over to the table. It looked about as good as he described and I filled my plate with a good helping of each. Cornbread looked and smelled great as well.

I headed back toward my seat next to J'Orr with the best pulled pork anywhere and, just as I was about to sit, the mystery was solved. Taking the other chair next to J'Orr directly across the table from me was the raven haired beauty I had encountered in the hallway outside my room.

I was right—head on view didn't disappoint one bit. I managed to sit down and place my plate on the table without spilling any of my food. May sound easy to you, but it gets a bit more complicated when your eyes are transfixed on the vision sitting across the table from you.

As she sat, her presence commanded the attention of the entire table. I had no doubt it did every time.

"Harry, this here is Kate Martin. Everyone calls her Doc," J'Orr said. "Best damn vet you're gonna find in the horse business. She's a great gal and a real good horse person all around," completed the introduction.

"Pleased to meet you, Ms. Martin. Name's Harry Mickey Shorts," I offered.

"Doc will be fine, Mister Shorts. Kate if you feel you must be a little formal at any time," she responded.

"It is a pleasure, Doc. You can call me Harry, and if you feel you need to be a little formal at any time, you can call me Harry."

Brought the same half-smile I had seen not that long ago and a few chuckles from the hands sitting within hearing distance.

"Can I get you something else to eat, Doc? That salad can't keep you going all day," I offered.

"Salad is fine, Harry," she said. "You don't have to worry about me. I get what I need when I need it," was accompanied by another of those half-smiles I was getting to like a lot.

"Suit yourself, Doc. I'm sure we will have the opportunity to share another meal before I head back east," I said.

J'Orr, who had been an interested bystander up to this point, said, "We all eat meals together same time every day, Harry. Doc here usually joins us unless there's an emergency somewhere on the ranch. I'm sure you'll get to see a lot more of her in the coming days."

"I'd count on that, Harry," Doc said as she got up and headed out of the dining room.

All eyes went with her and lingered...exit, stage right.

Chapter 28

After popping my eyes back in my head and having finished putting my stuff for the next week away in my room, Stu took me for a tour of Board Room Farms. Turns out Stu is right hand man to J'Orr and took me up to the main house only because he just happened to be there when I arrived.

A twenty thousand acre ranch sounds like a big place, and it is. The corrals behind the main house were used to exercise the horses and cool them down after they finished their workouts. The quarter mile training track was on the other side of the corrals and conveniently led directly to the back side of the largest corral.

Harry Mickey Shorts—corral expert.

The ranch currently had forty-five horses occupying the multiple set of barns on the property. The majority were BRF owned race horses with a few boarders and recreational animals thrown in the mix. They were needed for city slickers like me who happen to be hanging out at a working racing stable ranch.

Stu asked, "Know how to ride, Harry?"

"Um, riding isn't something I picked up along the way, Stu. I've done quite a few things in my life but riding just doesn't happen to be one of them," I replied.

"Not a problem, Harry," he said. "We can fix that right quick."

"I was afraid you might say that, Stu."

~ * ~

We completed the walking tour of the ranch with a look at where the hands lived and slept. Last place on the stop was the spartan living quarters given to the exercise riders and young jockeys tied to the stable.

"Pretty basic accommodations," I stated.

"Danny and the rest of the owners give them a place to stay and feed them three good meals a day—every day. They get medical attention when they need it and most benefits a regular company gives their people. Benefits that are unheard of in the rest of the racing circles, Harry."

"That's very generous of them. Why?" I asked.

"Why? It's simple, Harry. You treat people fair and make them belong and they are gonna treat you fair in return. That's Board Room Farms' mantra as Mister Trundle calls it and we all believe it. People and animals all get treated fairly and we can't ask for much more than that."

"Sounds fair to me," I replied.

"Bugs stay here free and ride the majority of the claiming horses for BRF. They stay until they lose the bug and then head out on their own. Most of them continue to ride for the stable as much as the stable will let them. Loyalty," Stu finished.

"Bugs?" I asked.

"Sorry, Harry. I sometimes forget what we know and take for granted around here when I'm talking to people who aren't in the business."

"No problem, Stu. So, what's a bug?"

"Harry, the term "bug" is used to describe an apprentice or student jockey who is allowed to carry less weight due to his or her inexperience. The term "bug" comes from the weight concession symbol found in the track program (an asterisk "*") which looks like a bug. Another name is 'bug boy' which you'll see some times," Stu told me.

"Interesting," I said. "Sticks until they win enough I would guess," I said.

"Good guess, Harry. And with Board Room Farms' record on the track, it doesn't last long for our bugs," Stu said proudly. "Let's go up to the house and get something cool to drink before I give you the rest of the tour."

"Sounds good to me, Stu. I could use a cool one right about now," I replied.

And we did just that.

Chapter 29

As Stu and I came into the dining room, we met a round little guy that could probably carry one of the horses around the track on his back. Looked like an ox in clothes.

"Hey, Cookie. This here is the fella we been waiting for from out East," Stu said to him.

"Let me guess," I said. "You the cook?"

Cookie looked at me and laughed long and loud.

"Him the cook? That is a hoot," Stu laughed. "Cookie would probably burn the water if he tried to boil a pot of it. Cookie ate so many cookies when he was a kid his mom eventually started calling him Cookie. Name stuck and, as you can see, most of the cookies stuck to him, too."

Cookie and Stu both laughed at that one.

"Good to meet you, Cookie," I said as I stuck my hand in his direction. "Name's Harry, Harry Mickey Shorts."

"Good to have you here, Harry," Cookie said as we shook hands. "You need anything, you just ask. I do a lotta things around the main house here and I'll see to it you get what you need.

"That's cool, Cookie. Stu and I were looking for something cold to drink. I'm sure Stu is working all day, but I could sure go for a nice tall beer if there is one around," I said.

"Stu knows his way around. Come on with me and I'll show you where we keep the beer. Then you can help yourself anytime you want from here on in."

"Don't you be showing him how to open them bottles and how to drink it, too," Stu said to Cookie.

"Have to be neighborly to the new fella, Stu. Like I said, Harry, I do lots a things around here and drinking a beer now and again fits under "lots a things" wouldn't you say?" he asked.

"It does in my book, Cookie. And I'm sure Stu there has had a cold brew or two in his day," I answered him.

"See there, Stu. Man knows what things are and knows you pretty well in the short time he's been here," Cookie said.

"Maybe I'll just come along with you around back, Harry. Just to be neighborly and all," Stu said with a smile.

Cookie led the way through the main house that proved to be as big inside as it looked from the outside. The back porch looked out on the pastures that went on forever. You could see horses running free as far as your eyes would let you. The young ones chased the older horses and it was a sight Harry had never seen before.

"Some view from here," Harry said. "They always out there running free and clear like they don't have a care in the world?"

"Nah. Those horses aren't in training right now and we let 'em run free to gain strength. Also, gets the young ones runnin' and buildin' up stamina. Soon enough the boss will get us to training the two year olds and the young ones will have the run of that there meadow to the right. Some sight to see them frolicking through the high grass like a bunch of little kids playing hide and seek," Stu said.

"I'd love to see that," Harry replied.

They watched the horses running in the field for what seemed like a long time to Harry. The sound of Cookie's voice brought Harry back to the task at hand.

"This here barrel is full all the time, Harry. The boss always says we work hard and we should be able to play hard, too. The boys come around here end of the day and have a few beers, talk about what happened on their part of the ranch that day. J'Orr wants all of us to know what's happening in every part of the business in case we need to fill in for somebody gets himself hurt or sick. Don't happen often around here, but we all can do most things should the need arise."

"That sounds like a pretty sound way to run a ranch in my opinion, for what it's worth," Harry said.

"J'Orr be here end of every day to hear from the hands what's going on. He's the boss, but he can't be everywhere all day and the boys appreciate him listening to and caring about what they have to say. J'Orr will change some things every so often based on what one of the boys will tell him," Stu said.

"No kidding," Harry said.

"Truth be told, Harry. And your opinion is right on, it's a pretty sound way to run a ranch in all of our opinions. Especially J'Orr's, and he has Mister Trundle's backing on just about anything he wants to do around here. Boys trust J'Orr and he trusts what the boys tell him, too," Stu said.

"Now, how about we have us a neighborly break and pop the caps on a few of them long necks?" Stu finished.

"I'm down, kiddo. Hand me one of those and let's get neighborly," Harry replied.

Chapter 30

Cookie took the three dead long necks and headed back into the house. Stu and Harry headed over to a pickup truck out behind the house. Stu got in the driver's side and fired it up. With Harry safely riding shotgun, Stu threw the truck in drive and proceeded into the pastures following a small road that ran between the fields.

"How far do the fields run," Harry asked.

"Don't know for sure, Harry. Something over five thousand acres of fields on the whole spread I believe. That field over there on your right was Brian Boru's field. He'd run out there with some yearlings and we'd watch for as long as the boss would let us," Stu replied.

"I gather you like it here?" Harry asked.

"I do, Harry, I like it here plenty. Been with Board Room Farms going on seven years now and I couldn't ask for a better place to work. Just lately things have been a little off kilter. Boru passed on us and all the boys took it hard, me included. We loved that horse for sure, but the boys also know he was what made this stable and he can't be replaced. I'd be lying if I said that me and the rest of the boys aren't worried some."

"I can appreciate how all of you are feeling, Stu. While I don't know all the details, seems odd Brian Boru just up and died. He just didn't wake up in the morning; that what happened?" Harry asked.

"That's about it, Harry. Looked fine the day before and was scheduled for a session that day. No reason to think anything was wrong with him or he wouldn't be just as fine that day as well. We were all shocked the way it happened. Doc come over and just said he's dead, plain as day," Stu said.

"Who found him?" Harry asked.

"Don't really know who it was found him," Stu said. "Buddy was the one that tended to Boru pretty regular since the accident put Jackson in the hospital."

"Jackson? Who's Jackson? And what accident is that?" Harry asked.

"Yeah, Jackson was the one took care of Boru from sunup to sundown, most every day. He made sure he got fed, had water and hay all the time, and got to the shed when he was supposed to be there. Cooled and washed him down when need be and slept with Boru more than not. Loved that horse Jackson did," Stu said.

"What happened?" Harry followed up.

"Jackson went into town to get some supplies over at the feed store and got himself hit by a truck. Banged up pretty bad and been in the hospital more than a month now. Supposed to get out next week and he'll have to be laid up over here at least another month. Broke his leg, his arm, and some ribs, too. Looked real bad at first, but the doctor up at the hospital says he's gonna be alright in a few months."

"They get the guy?" Harry asked.

"Nope. Whoever done it took off and left Jackson all broke up and laying in the road. Happened out back of the feed store and nobody was around to see how it happened. Jackson never saw it coming and didn't see what hit him," Stu said.

"Bummer," Harry said. "Police have any leads?" Harry asked.

"Nothing so far," Stu replied. "J'Orr does most of the talking to the police, but he told us a few days ago they had nothing to go on so far."

Stu's cell phone rang and he answered it while Harry looked out the window at the young horses running and playing in the field. Boru's field.

"Will do," Stu said into the phone and closed it.

"Problem?" Harry asked.

"Nah, just a broken fence over to the north field. I need to go over there and make sure it gets mended right away. I'll drop you at the main house and head on over if that's alright with you, Harry?" Stu asked.

"Not a problem," Harry answered. "Thanks for the tour and I'm sure we'll have a chance to talk some more over the next couple of days."

"Sure enough, Harry. Whatever you need is yours," Stu replied as he turned the truck back toward the main house.

Chapter 31

Sitting in a rocker on the back porch, long neck in one hand, scratching the neck of a lazy old hound dog with the other, Harry was enjoying Lee's Summit, Missouri. The sounds of a working horse farm were background music to Harry's faraway thoughts. The last Saturday he spent with the kids and the happy state his ex was currently in filled his mind. Sherry deserved to be happy and his kids were becoming something very special to him.

The sound of someone calling his name from somewhere far away jarred him back to reality.

"Harry…hey Harry…you with us, Harry," J'Orr called out to him again.

"Sorry, J'Orr. Yeah, I'm with ya, kiddo. Just caught me day-dreaming there a bit," Harry replied.

"No problem, Harry. Stu told me you were back here at the house and I figured I'd come by and see if there was anything I could do for you."

"Thanks, J'Orr. I'm good right now and happy to sit here, drink some beer and keep this old hound dog company. This is all somewhat new to me and I'm trying to absorb everything I've seen and heard up to now. I do need to catch up with Doc and maybe have her give me a tour of the breeding shed when she has time."

"Doc's helping out at the animal hospital this afternoon. She spends a few afternoons a month volunteering her time to work with the local vets at the hospital. Money's a bit scarce around these parts and she gives them whatever time she can spare. I'm sure she'll be back for supper and you can make arrangements with her then," J'Orr said.

"Sounds good to me. That's great what she does for the hospital," Harry replied.

"Doc cares about the animals and about our community, Harry. She's about as good people as you're gonna find anywhere, bar none," J'Orr continued.

"I believe you, J'Orr. How'd she come to work here at Board Room Farms?" Harry asked.

"She's pretty proud of what she's accomplished and likes to tell the story herself," J'Orr said. "I'll leave it to her to fill you in when you two get together."

"Sure enough," Harry said.

With that J'Orr backed down off the porch and went on his way to do whatever the boss of a thriving horse farm does. Harry had no idea what that was, so he proceeded to drink his long neck and keep his current porch companion happy.

~ * ~

From deep in his subconscious, Harry could swear he could hear a voice calling his name again. This was beginning to form a pattern and getting very confusing; Harry couldn't afford to have his subconscious confused. His mind was out there far enough without somebody playing with it.

As he slowly regained consciousness, Harry thought he could hear a familiar voice through the fog saying, "Nice ass, Harry." When he finally opened his eyes, flipped over and turned toward the door, the room was empty, but the familiar hint of jasmine lingered in the air.

Doc was back.

Chapter 32

All hands on deck!

Well, all hands were out on the back porch at least.

After a quick squirt, a comb of his hair, his head back in order again, Harry proceeded down to the main floor and out to the back porch. Cookie was holding court with stories of his upbringing in Kansas and the boys were loving it.

"The teacher's standing up there in front of the room and keeps asking, 'Who's got those cookies…I said, who in this room has brought cookies to my class which is against the rules…' he's saying," Cookie goes on telling the boys, "I didn't know what to do, so I bent down under my desk and I ate every one of those cookies. Popped up with my cheeks so big I coulda burst both of them," as he puffs out his cheeks twice their normal size. The entire group burst out laughing and Cookie looked like a kid again, cheeks puffed out, hands out, bouncing up and down.

"Come on, Harry," J'Orr said when he saw Harry at the door. "Grab a beer and sit on down with the boys and me. If we can get Cookie to quiet down, we were gonna go over the day's doings like we do at the end of every day."

"Be pleased to, J'Orr, as long as Cookie doesn't spit any of that shit he's got stuffed in his cheeks on me. I'll sit right over here by Doc."

"Good a place as any, Harry. Hand him a beer, will ya Buddy? Let's get to it: anything we need to hear about from today's activities?" J'Orr asked the group.

"The fence up on the north pasture is fixed and shouldn't be a problem anymore," Stu reported.

"Any idea what caused it?" J'Orr asked. "Second time this month that fence needed mending in about the same place if I recon right."

"Sure is," Stu said. "Can't figure out how it could have given out like that. We re-dug them posts another foot deeper when we fixed it the first time. We found it down on the ground like we never been there before to fix it the first time. Some of those yearlings got over there they would have been half way across the county by the time we found the fence down again," Stu said.

"That's troubling," J'Orr said. "Any of you boys see anyone or anything suspicious around the ranch the last few days?"

Nothing.

Silence from the group.

"Well, let's keep our eyes open and especially sharp next week or so. Okay, boys?" J'Orr told them.

From the back of the porch, a skinny string bean of a kid who couldn't have been more than fifteen made a noise like he wanted to say something. A few of the boys half turned toward him, but then turned right back around when they saw who it was. J'Orr saw him as well.

"Harry," J'Orr said to the group as a whole, "the young hand in the back there is Thomas, Danny Trundle's son. He's out here with us for a few months to get some experience with the horse business and get away from a few scrapes he got himself into back east."

J'Orr paused to let that hang over the group awhile.

"He's been working real hard since he got here and tends to the fields and the stalls in the barns most of the time. You want to say something, Thomas?" J'Orr asked him.

"Well I…ah, I…I mean, I…"

"Just spit it out, Thomas. You're one of the hands on this here ranch and got as much say as the rest of us do."

"I, ah…I'm pretty sure I saw those flashes up on the hill again today. I know nobody else has seen them but, they are real, and I've seen them about every third day or so. I'm actually positive I saw them again today," Thomas said with as much conviction as he could muster.

"Flashes?" Stu questioned. "What do you mean flashes?"

"Like flashes of light," Thomas said. "Flashes of light that are there and then gone, then back again. Usually two at a time when I see them, up on the hill toward the old Rogers spread," he explained.

"They swirling in the air like little flashing green and red colors?" one of the hands said to get the rest of the boys laughing at young Thomas.

"That's enough of that," J'Orr said to quiet down the group. "Are you sure about this, Thomas? You have any idea what caused it?" he asked.

While Thomas shook his head indicating he had no idea what was causing the flashes of light he had seen up on the hill, Harry knew exactly what it was and it troubled him. He couldn't think of any reason someone would be up on a hill, far away from the main grounds of the ranch, watching what was going on through high powered binoculars.

Binoculars, that when facing into the sun at just the right angle, would throw what looked like flashes of light back at the ranch. The same flashes of light Thomas had seen on more than one occasion.

Somebody wanted to know what was going on at Board Room Farms and didn't want anyone to know they were doing it.

Chapter 33

"Didn't see you around the ranch today, Doc," Harry said as they walked through the house. They were both headed toward the stairs that lead up to the living quarters in the main house.

"I was out most of the day. Didn't get back until just before the end-of-the-day meeting out on the back porch," she replied.

"Went right on out to the porch when you got back?" Harry asked.

"Might have, Harry, might not have as well," Doc answered him.

"Didn't happen to be up on the second floor at any time, did you?" Harry continued.

"Might have, Harry, might not have as well. Might have gone directly to my house to drop my things off before heading over to the porch," Doc answered him again.

"Might have at that," Harry said. "That jasmine you're wearing?" Harry asked.

"Why yes it is, Harry. Very perceptive of you. Just a bit behind each ear and a dab in one other place if you must know. Some reason you're asking, Harry?" she said with the slyest of smiles forming on her face.

"Thought I caught a whiff outside my door before I came down to the back porch. Maybe I was mistaken," Harry told her. "A dab? Someplace special?" he continued.

"Yes, a dab, Harry. And everyplace is special, Harry," she told him. "Just some places are more special than others. You would agree, wouldn't you, Harry? There are some places that are more special than others," she teased as she took a step closer to him while playing with a button on her shirt.

Harry closed the gap between them with a step of his own and whispered softly in her ear, "Some places are very special and, if handled in just the right way by a knowledgeable and practiced individual, with care and reserved abandon, can produce feelings of amazing delight taking one to places you might never have dreamed existed."

Harry was half way up the stairs before Doc even realized he wasn't standing in front of her any more.

~ * ~

His trusty notebook and pen in hand, Harry made notes on what he had learned so far during his stay at Board Room Farms. Carrying his laptop when he was on the road wasn't always practical, plus it was a pain in the balls. A notebook and pen take up a lot less room and weigh a fraction of what a laptop weighs.

What had he learned so far?—not much was what he had learned so far. J'Orr ran the place, had a good handle on how to run a ranch as far as Harry could see, and he seemed to be well liked by the ranch hands. Stu was his second in command and was given a good bit of responsibility by J'Orr to keep things in order. The ranch hands responded well to both of them and loved Brian Boru, at least according to J'Orr and Stu.

Things to check on: what happened to Jackson, who knew he was going into town on that day, and when did they know? Who's Buddy and where did he come from, what did he do before Boru died, and what is he doing on the horse farm now.

Thomas could be a tricky one. Maybe get Ms. Timmons to give him the lowdown on Thomas and the scrapes he got himself into before being sent out to Board Room Farms. Why send him here and why didn't anyone give Harry the "heads-up" he was out here. Plus, he had to verify the flashes of light Thomas claimed he saw. Why hadn't anyone else seen them? Who was Rogers and what had happened to him?

And of course, there was a very important piece to the puzzle that was going to require some extensive first hand investigating—Doc. If anyone was going to give Harry something solid to move on, it might be Doc. A visit to the breeding shed needed to be scheduled along with a full accounting of what transpired in the days leading up to Brian Boru's death, plus Doc's findings after he was found dead. There was a lot Harry still needed to do with Doc and, as he looked at his notes, the combination of the words "something solid to move on" and "Doc" caused a tingling where it mattered most to Harry.

PLACES Harry wrote on the last line of his notes for today. *SPECIAL PLACES* in capital letters.

Chapter 34

Why it surfaced in his mind at that very moment, lying on top of the bed trying to catch a quick cat nap before dinner, he had no idea. It often surprised Harry when certain things would float in and out of his mind for no apparent reason. But, as we have come to know, the mind of Harry Mickey Shorts is a mysterious place indeed.

This particular mind nugget was a nagging brainteaser from Harry's last visit to the office of M. Randle Trundle. Something had struck him as being different with the office and he couldn't put his finger on what it was at the time. He had thought about it for a day or two, and then it was forgotten, replaced by a thousand other details from his personal and business lives. It was back though, and Harry hated nagging details hanging over his head, or in it, about as much as he hated the nagging of his ex-wife. If she didn't have those long legs and great ass…never mind.

It was there and gone almost as quickly as soon as he heard the beginnings of grub being set up for that night's dinner. A quick three S's (shit, shower and shave for those that have forgotten) and he'd head on down to join the boys and his favorite vet in the whole wide world—Doc. Also happens to be the only vet he knows, but why quibble.

~ * ~

Once a week at Board Room Farms, the hands are treated to something special for dinner. Never the same day, never the same special surprise and, as Harry was to learn, nobody really knew who planned the specials.

Tonight was "special" night for this week.

Beer was the normal beverage of choice for most of the boys at dinner. Lemonade and iced tea were available all the time for those that chose not to down a few long necks with dinner; plus now there was Thomas, too. Tonight's surprise was a fully stocked bar set up at the end of the room. The early arrivers were hungrily filling their glasses with precious liquids topped off with very small amounts of mixers, if any.

"Harry," greeted him as he stood just inside the entrance to the room taking in the sight.

"Evening, Stu," Harry said.

"The boys don't get into town too often and we don't allow hard liquor on the ranch. This is a real treat for them and they deserve the opportunity to blow off some steam now and again," Stu said.

"I'm sure they do," Harry replied. "Make for an interesting morning, though."

"That won't be a problem. Cookie over there will keep an eye on all the boys and shut down anyone that gets a bit rambunctious before it gets to be a problem."

"Good idea," Harry said.

"And the boys all know they have normal chores in the morning. We have a horse business to run here and the horses don't take no days off. They screw up one of these special deals and the boys know they will disappear for good. We trust our hands, Harry," Stu said with confidence.

"I'm sure you do, Stu. Well, when in Rome do as the Roman ranch hands do, I always say," Harry said with a smile. "A little Absolut and Tonic will hit the spot quite nicely, I think."

"Make that two," Harry heard a familiar voice say from behind him.

A hint of jasmine confirmed his suspicions.

"Evening, Doc," Harry said as he turned to face his thirsty companion. "An Absolut and Tonic coming right up, that is if I can get past the boys and up to the table."

"I'm sure you're resourceful enough to satisfy my current needs, Harry," Doc said.

"Needs with an 's'?" Harry inquired.

"One need for now, Harry," Doc replied. "Why don't we work on one need at a time and see where that takes us," she finished.

"If one need at a time is your desire, one need at a time it shall be," Harry replied.

"What I desire and my current want of an Absolut and Tonic are two different needs entirely, Harry. One does not preclude the other from happening and, the sooner one need has been satisfied, the sooner the others may become a reality."

At that very moment a bell sounded from across the room putting an end to Harry and Doc's playful back and forth. J'Orr was standing in the entryway about to address the group that now filled the room.

"Boys, you all figured out tonight is our special dinner night for this week. Have a few drinks and enjoy yourselves compliments of Danny Trundle. He's providing the firewater for tonight's festivities. He called me today and wants all of you to know he appreciates the hard work you boys do around here. He also wanted me to let you know he's got a line on a top stud stallion that should be here in the next week or two. Won't replace Boru, we all know that including Mister Trundle. But he wants you boys to know Board Room Farms ain't going nowhere and will be a top stable for a long time to come."

That brought a whoop and a holler from all the boys.

"So, drink up and let's have some fun tonight. Got some mighty nice steaks to put on your plates and the biggest one's got my name on it," J'Orr finished up.

As everyone filled their glasses and headed to the table to dine on fine steaks and all the fixings, needs and desires beyond an Absolut and Tonic were going to have to wait their turn for now.

Chapter 35

The horse farm alarm went off at 6:35 the following morning. Harry had left the window in his room open an inch or so when he went to bed. The sounds of men making a working horse farm go were echoing throughout his room.

The prior evening hadn't ended quite as Harry had planned. Dinner was over rather abruptly and Doc was nowhere to be found as the tables emptied. She had been sitting at the other end of the table and, at some point earlier on, she must have left without Harry noticing.

So many needs, so many places, so little he could do.

Resigned to starting the day much earlier than originally intended, Harry got out of bed and headed down to the kitchen to find coffee and something to eat. One saving grace of not ending the evening with Doc and heading up early to bed meant at least he wasn't hungover too bad.

"Morning, Harry," greeted him as he hit the bottom of the stairs.

"Morning to you too, Cookie," Harry returned.

"Get you some coffee to start your day?" Cookie offered.

"Love some," Harry answered. "Wouldn't happen to have some donuts or éclairs or a nice crumb coffee cake to go with the coffee, would you now Cookie?" Harry asked expecting the worst.

"No donuts. No coffee cake either, Harry. But I can fix you up with some homemade biscuits and sausage gravy that will stick to your ribs pretty good. Most of the boys start their day with a few and we haven't lost anybody yet," he kidded.

"Biscuits with sausage gravy will have to do I guess, Cookie. Lead the way and I shall follow," Harry said. "Seen Doc yet this morning?" he continued.

"Nope, I sure haven't as of yet. But she's got a little kitchen over at her place and doesn't normally come over to the main house for breakfast most days," Cookie offered.

"Where's her place?" Harry asked.

"It's behind the breeding shed over past the last corral," Cookie told him. "Can't rightly see it unless you go clear around back of the shed and head out about a hundred yards or so," he finished.

"Thanks, Cookie. I'll look her up a little later," Harry said.

"Thought you might be doing that sooner or later," Cookie said with a grin. "Let's get you some of those biscuits and gravy, Harry. Man needs to get a good belly full when he has the potential for some hard man's work ahead of him. Know what I mean, Harry?"

"I know exactly what you mean, Cookie. Let's hope I'm gonna need those biscuits before too long," Harry said with a wide grin.

~ * ~

Properly fed, washed up and dressed, Harry headed out to the main corral to see what goes on at a horse farm on a normal day.

Harry found J'Orr and another guy out by the training track watching the younger horses during morning workouts. The training track looked as good as most race track courses Harry had seen.

"Yo, J'Orr. How they looking this morning?" Harry asked.

"They're looking late, that's how they're looking, Harry," J'Orr said. "This here is Board Room Farms Assistant Trainer, Franklin Harvey. Franklin, this here is Harry Shorts."

Nods and a shake of hands ended the introductions.

"Late?" Harry asked in J'Orr's direction.

"Yeah, late," J'Orr repeated. "We should have been done long before now but the boys had to clear out one of our riders this morning before we could start workouts. Horses are used to getting out to the track at the crack of dawn around here, Harry. Getting started late throws them off a bit and the workouts this morning are showing it. Lately, it seems shit never stops around here."

"Trouble?" Harry asked.

"Trouble with a capital "T" you could say, Harry. Our bug boys ride in the mornings if they aren't off racing. One of the stable's best bugs, kid by the name of McDonough, been causing all kinds of grief for a spell now and Franklin came down this morning to officially can his ass. He barked long and loud about it and I had to have the boys haul him and his stuff off the premises."

"He gone for good?" Harry asked.

"Gone for good and good riddance," J'Orr said sharply. "I firmly believe the kid stiffed one of our horses last week and I woulda run him straight out of here myself after that if I coulda, but we handle things in our own shops, and the racing business decisions are owner and trainer territory.

"Sorry, Harry, but we gotta get these horses' workouts done and Franklin is due back in Florida later today."

"No problem, J'Orr. Nice to meet you Franklin," Harry said, then he started back toward the main house.

Chapter 36

Harry noticed a red Land Rover coming up the entrance road and then veering off toward a small road that went behind the barns. Could only mean one thing—Doc was back on the grounds and it was time for breeding—shed that is. The other would come in due course.

The main house was fairly empty with all the hands out tending to the morning chores. The whole breeding end of the business was virgin territory to Harry. It would require some extensive notes if the job was going to be done right. When you don't know what you're up against, and you don't know much about the territory, you are invading unknown waters. Learn what you can and figure out the rest as you go.

Worked before, no reason it wouldn't work again. Notebook and mini-recorder in hand, it was time to do Doc.

"Hey, Doc. Lemme give you a hand with that stuff," I said as I came up behind the Land Rover parked outside her place.

"Thanks, Harry. I'm trying to get to all the things you never have time for around here when the breeding season is going full blast. Although it seems like it has always been in full gear since I got here," she said.

"Must be weird now without Brian Boru. How many other breeding stallions are in the stable?" I asked.

"Three more, Harry. Nowhere near the status of Boru, but they have sired some fairly good foals of their own. Boru was in a class by himself and business has gotten pretty slow since he's gone."

"Let's get these things inside and then maybe you can show me the shed," Harry said.

"It's a little more than a shed," Doc said a bit more than put off.

Harry thought for a few seconds and then figured out how Doc had interpreted his remark.

"Not your place, Doc. The breeding shed; I was hoping you could show me the breeding shed and explain what goes on in there. I'm sure your place is great," Harry tried.

Thinking first, Doc replied, "Okay, Harry, I'll buy that one. My brain is still fuzzy from the circumstances surrounding Boru's death. I still find myself up at night trying to figure out what could have happened. I just can't make heads or tails of it," she said.

"Well, you tell me what happened and everything you know surrounding his death and I'll try and help you make some sense out of it if I can. If I can't, maybe just talking about it will make you feel a bit better," Harry told her.

"That's mighty nice of you, Harry. Not too many people I can talk to around these parts about stuff that happens here on the ranch or to me for that matter. They accept me for what I am and know I'm good at what I do, but I'm still a girl on a horse ranch full of male hands," she said with a sigh.

"Doc, I'm here for you, anything you need," Harry said.

"Thanks, Harry. A girl has needs you know," she said.

"I know, Doc, I know," Harry replied with high hopes he would be able to satisfy at least one of those needs in the very near future.

Chapter 37

Supplies safely stored in Doc's place, with no offer of a tour of the premises for Harry (much to his dismay), they headed out to the breeding shed. Doc thought a walkthrough would be best before she and Harry got down to talking about the circumstances surrounding Boru's death.

Doc led the way as she gave Harry some background on the new breeding shed at Board Room Farms.

"Mister Trundle's desire was to have a state of the art facility that also had the warmth and charm he wanted people to feel when they came to BRF.

"Warmth and charm?" Harry repeated in question.

"We have tours all the time plus friends and relatives of the people who send their horses to be covered. It's not all 'wham bam thank you mam' in our shed, Harry."

"I'll keep that in mind," Harry replied.

As they rounded the corner from behind one of the barns, the "shed" came into view.

"That's it, Harry," Doc said. "The building straight ahead with the cupola on top."

"A what on top?" Harry asked.

"A cupola," Doc replied. "The definition of a cupola is 'a dome-shaped or quadrilateral-shaped ornamental structure located on top of a larger roof or dome, often used as a lookout or to admit light and provide ventilation.' We use it for both, light and ventilation, plus it looks great. It's one of the things that people talk about after visiting Board Room Farms."

"Live and learn," Harry said.

"I hope so," Doc replied as she walked on.

"How big is it?" Harry asked. "How many square feet?"

"I'm not actually sure," Doc replied. "I saw plans once that put it at around nine or ten thousand square feet, but I think the final structure came in somewhere under that. Bigger than a bread box, though," Doc finished.

"I'll say," Harry answered. "Can we go in?"

"Let's," Doc replied leading the way.

As they entered the building, Harry saw a stairway heading up to the second story directly in front of him and a room to the left. Couches, chairs, antique tables and a floor to ceiling stone fireplace filled the room.

"Go on in, Harry. This is where we entertain the owners, trainers and anyone else that comes to see our breeding facilities. Off to the back there is a small size commercial kitchen we use if we do it up real big."

Harry's gaze fell upon a hugh portrait of Boru that filled a major portion of one of the walls.

"The star gets his due in his place of business, Harry," Doc told him.

"Just like you said—warm and charming," Harry observed.

"Let's go upstairs," Doc suggested.

The stairs led to what amounted to several observation points where you could look through plate glass windows down into the breeding areas. Wide open space with two story ceilings providing plenty of room to get the business at hand done. The building was made completely of fine wood and all the walls were padded for safety. Something called a "stock" was set up in each section. It was a three sided stall just big enough to fit a horse, padded all around. It was used to get the mares ready for their "dates" according to Doc.

"Some place," Harry told Doc as they headed back down the stairs.

"Thank you, Harry. We're very proud of it just as we are of everything here at Board Room Farms. Come on, I'll show what happens at my place," Doc said.

"I can't wait," Harry replied.

Chapter 38

The living room in Doc's place was warm and cozy with more pillows than Harry had ever seen in one room. He removed six pillows from his half of the couch and stacked them on the floor next to the coffee table.

"Here you go, Harry," Doc said as she came into the room and handed Harry a tall vodka and tonic.

"Thanks, Doc. What are you having?" he asked.

"Same as you," she replied. "It's my favorite."

Two people with the same favorite drink Harry thought to himself.

"Mine too," he lied, choosing to lead her on a bit while wishing he had his favorite Vodka Gimlet instead.

Doc was seated on a high backed chair directly across from Harry with her feet curled up under her.

"So, what do you want from me?" Doc asked.

Harry almost spit out the small amount of drink he had in his mouth at the time.

"Um, want from you?" Harry repeated in question.

"Yes, what do you want from me, and how?" she replied.

A small spray did escape from Harry's mouth with that comment. Doc leaned over and handed him another napkin to clean his chin exposing a clear view of her cleavage for Harry to peruse.

"Something wrong, Harry?" she asked. "Am I not asking the right questions?"

"Ah, ah," Harry stammered.

A sly smile on her face, Doc asked, "You do want me to tell you what I know about Brian Boru's death, don't you, Harry?"

Composure returned, Harry replied, "Yes I do, Doc. That is what I want from you right now…" with an appropriate hesitation to leave the statement open ended.

"Then I will, Harry. It could be a long night, so let me freshen up our drinks and we can get started," she said as she rose, crossed over and took Harry's glass.

Her walk into the kitchen was slow and methodical for maximum viewing effect.

"Need my help in there?" Harry offered.

"No, not yet, and not in here," she replied.

The small beginnings of a Boing! surfaced in Harry's pants.

"Here's your refill," Doc said when she returned to the living room. The slight forward lean necessary to hand Harry his drink caused a furthering of his hidden malady.

"Thanks," Harry said trying with all his might to stay focused on the issue at hand.

"Is everything okay?" Doc asked with a hint of that same sly smile evident on her face.

"Everything's fine," Harry replied. "So, tell me what you can about the circumstances surrounding Brian Boru's death."

"Harry, I've thought about nothing else since that morning. He was fine the day before and I checked him that afternoon as I always do the day before he has a session scheduled."

Doc stopped and took a long sip of her drink. It was obvious the stress of Boru's death had not left her as of yet.

"That morning started just like any other morning here. I was up at four-thirty and headed over to the main house about five to see if J'Orr had anything special going on like I always do. As I got to the back porch there was a commotion starting in Boru's barn."

"Commotion?" Harry asked.

"Yes, a few of the hands were yelling. I couldn't make out what they were saying. I started to head over to Boru's barn when Buddy came out yelling for somebody to get some help. I didn't know what was happening, so I took off on a dead run for the barn. Buddy was just ahead of me heading back into Boru's barn."

Doc stopped and took another long sip of her drink. She used the tip of her tongue to remove a drop that had found its way to her upper lip.

Boingo Supremo!

"Harry, I know this is important to you for some reason, but I feel like I'm forcing the words from my mouth right now. Why don't we find something else to amuse ourselves with for a little while. Maybe later on I'll be in a better frame of mind to tell you what you need to know. That okay with you, Harry?"

"Sure, Doc. Any suggestions on how we might amuse ourselves?" he asked.

"Well, unless I'm mistaken, and the bulge in your pants would seem to indicate I'm not, if we adjourn to the bedroom we may be able to find some way of amusing ourselves for a time."

"Doc, your powers of observation serve you well. Let us adjourn and see what we can do to free your mind and body. You concentrate on the mind and I'll do my best with the body."

Chapter 39

Lying in bed with a beautiful woman you just made love to is a wonderful thing. Unfortunately, we had tumbled onto the floor at some point in our gymnastic go-round and found ourselves scrambling up the side of the bed for softer ground.

Still a wonderful thing even if it takes a few minutes to get there.

"Thanks, Harry. It's been a little while and it feels good to know I can still turn a man's fancy now and again," Doc told Harry.

"Doc, you can do anything you want to my fancy and anything else you can get your hands on, any time you want. Seems you didn't forget your way in the little while you have been away," Harry responded.

"As they say, it's like riding a bike. You never really forget and remember pretty quickly once you get back on."

"Speaking of getting back on," Harry said as he proceeded to do just that.

~ * ~

The dinner table was almost full when Harry finally made his way downstairs, having returned to the main house after his extracurricular activities. He had showered and was now looking presentable. He and Doc would need to resume their conversation sometime soon since other "things" got in the way and they never finished their talk. He grabbed a seat in the middle of the table and instantly noticed the glow emanating from the right side near the head of the table.

Doc looked up, smiled at Harry, and turned back to continue her conversation with J'Orr.

"Hey, Harry. Went looking for you this afternoon, but couldn't find hide-nor-tail of you anywhere. Where'd you go off to all that time?" Stu shouted from across the table.

Seemed everyone at the table heard Stu and looked at Harry waiting for his answer.

"Ah, I guess you must have just missed me," Harry responded weakly. "I was in and out, here and there," he finished.

"Hey, Doc," Stu said as he looked down the table so she could see him. "Any chance you can vouch for Harry being 'in and out' a good part of the afternoon?" he asked.

Doc started to blush at the question just as the whole table erupted in a chorus of, "Oh, Harry. Do it, Harry, do it," over and over again.

Since there wasn't a damn thing she could do about it, Doc stood and joined in with the Board Room Farms Memorial Choir, louder than anyone else at the table. Harry stood and took a bow prompting a standing ovation from everyone in the room—including Doc.

Chapter 40

"I've thought about it over and over again, Harry. There are some days I think of little else," Doc was saying as they stood outside the corral watching the young horses go through their morning exercises.

"Nothing at all seemed odd about Boru prior to that morning. No sign at all he was ill or acting strangely even?" Harry asked.

"Harry, he was fine. Perfectly fine I'm telling you. Brian Boru was the number one asset of Board Room Farms and my personal number one priority. I love all the animals on this ranch and I care for each one equally as well. But Boru always came first in my mind and in my actions," she concluded.

"Well, maybe there wasn't anything to see. Maybe he just plain died and there wasn't a single thing any living person could have done about it," Harry told Doc.

"As much as it pains me to say so, I hope you are right and it was just Boru's time," Doc said with a heavy sigh.

"At least you have all of these other beautiful animals to care for and help keep your mind occupied," Harry said trying his best to console her.

"You're right, Harry. My days are full and very rewarding doing something I love more than anything."

"More than anything?" Harry smirked.

"Most times, Harry, most times," she responded with a smile. "Let's go over to my place and we can finish that talk we started yesterday. Who knows what I might love doing best after we finish talking," she said as she spun and headed for her cabin.

~ * ~

"Now maybe I can tell you what you need to know," Doc said as she got back into bed with the two cold beers she had gotten from the fridge.

"Pretty nice picture you paddling off to the kitchen bare-assed and all," Harry said. "Entrance wasn't all that bad either."

"Paddling," she started. "Bare-assed is the best you can do to describe how I gracefully glided into the kitchen?" she continued with a hurt look on her face.

"Well I…" Harry stammered.

"Entrance? Entrance you called it," Doc said as she took a long slug of her beer.

For want of anything better to do, or say, Harry did the same.

Putting her beer bottle down on the night stand, Doc said, "For those comments, you better give me an entrance the boys will be singing about for a week."

Talk would have to come later.

Chapter 41

"There wasn't anything there," Doc said to start the conversation off. "The initial physical inspection and subsequent autopsy showed nothing. Not a damn thing," she concluded.

Harry had a pillow propped up against the headboard, beer in hand, as he listened to Doc.

"I looked at every inch of that horse twice. There was no evidence of any foul play. None. Absolutely none I'm telling you," she said. "The autopsy was the most thorough autopsy ever performed on an animal by two of the best in the business. Nothing. They found not one single thing, Harry."

"I believe you, Doc. I know you did everything you could and more. When you examined Brian Boru, did you observe anything at all out of the ordinary? Maybe not evidence of foul play, but just something odd. Not what you expected to see, or smell, or hear, or feel. Did you get the inkling there could have been something wrong, but you couldn't put your finger on what it was? Anything?" Harry asked.

Doc had been sitting upright in bed and sat back when Harry asked the questions he had just posed to her. The sheet that had been covering her as she sat up straight didn't follow her when she sat back exposing her breasts in all their glory. At least that was what popped into Harry's head—all their glory and the glory that would be his.

"Behave yourself, Harry," Doc said. "You may be on to something here and it's not going to be me," she half-smiled in his direction.

"On to something?" Harry asked.

"Yeah, on to something, Harry. When I examined Boru I was so intent on finding what caused his death it was like I was in a trance. I focused in on him and blanked out everything else that was going on around me. And everything that existed in the space around me in his stall."

She stopped and thought for a few seconds.

She must have been cold sitting there, so Harry pulled the sheet up to cover her a bit more. Keen-eyed private eye spying erect nipples gave Harry the notion to help a damsel in semi-distress.

"A buzzing," Doc said. "Now that I run the picture of everything that was going on at the time through my mind, there was a buzzing somewhere in the immediate area. I don't know what was buzzing; it was a faint sound somewhere behind me, I think. It came and went and then was gone altogether. Maybe ten or fifteen minutes after I first got to Boru. Yeah, faint, and then gone," Doc finished.

"Any idea what kind of buzzing it was?" Harry asked.

Doc thought.

"A buzz like a saw somewhere in the distance or something in the sky overhead?" Harry tried.

"No, not that kind of buzzing. The mosquito in your ear buzzing that annoys the hell out of you but you can't swat it away kind of buzzing. Like that, Harry," Doc said thoughtfully. "J'Orr has the place sprayed faithfully to keep the insects down to a minimum around here, so it was kind of odd to hear a noise like that. Yeah, like an insect buzzing around is what I remember."

"That's good, Doc," Harry told her.

"Does it mean anything, Harry?" she asked.

"Doc, nothing means anything and everything means something. When you put things together, you find out which one applies."

"I don't have any idea what you just said, Harry, but right now I have a mind to put certain things together. So, start applying yourself and you better mean it."

A good P.I. always does as he is told. Application began…in earnest.

Chapter 42

Harry was dreaming his cell phone was ringing somewhere off in the distance and he wasn't answering it. Problem was, it actually was ringing and he wasn't answering it because he was still asleep in Doc's bed.

"Harry, answer the fucking phone, will you," Doc murmured still half asleep herself.

No need, it stopped ringing.

"You going to see who's looking for you, Harry?" Doc asked.

"At this very moment, I know who's looking for me, and I know exactly what she wants," Harry answered.

"Do you?" Doc asked. "Oh, you sure do," she purred as Harry gently cupped her breast and pressed his intention against her warm behind.

As Harry disappeared under the covers, he knew just what he was looking for. He found it without much trouble at all.

~ * ~

Sitting at the kitchen table in the main house, Harry read the morning paper while he sipped his second cup of coffee. With the ranch's day well under way, Harry was left to his own thoughts, thoughts dominated by the shadow of a big horse gone forever and the possibility of a new beginning for Harry Mickey Shorts.

"Morning, Harry."

Harry looked up to see J'Orr coming toward him, coffee cup in hand.

"Morning, J'Orr," Harry replied.

"Mind if I sit?" J'Orr asked.

"Please, sit," Harry said as he put the morning paper aside.

"You gonna be heading back east soon, Harry?" J'Orr asked.

"I think so," Harry responded. "I don't think I can do much more here and maybe there are some answers out there to find. Then again, maybe not. Maybe there are no answers to be found anywhere and a beautiful animal's time just came due."

"Maybe you're right, Harry. And Doc?" J'Orr asked.

"We talked. We're good she and I," Harry replied.

"I like that lady, Harry. We all like her. She's family. I wouldn't want to see her hurt in any way if you know what I mean, Harry."

"J'Orr, I think you can sense I'm kind of a wanderer who hasn't found himself in a place, or time, that suits him yet. Got a family back east and I care deeply for them, but my future isn't there as far as I can see. Doc's a lady I could care for, and I do. But I'm not ready yet or I wouldn't be heading out again. She knows that and we're cool for now. I know where to find her and she can get me any time she wants or needs. I'll be back again, you can count on it."

"Good enough for me, Harry. You need anything from me or my boys, you just have to ask and it's done. We appreciate you coming out here to try and help," J'Orr said as he reached out to shake Harry's hand.

"As I said, you haven't seen the last of me, J'Orr. And if there is something to be found out there, you can count on me finding it," Harry replied as he shook J'Orr's hand.

Chapter 43

Eyes closed, drink in hand, Harry reran his visit to Lee's Summit, Missouri through his mind as the plane carried him back to New York. Doc had been off at the animal hospital when he left. He wished he had had the opportunity to say goodbye to her one more time.

Doc. Doc, Doc, Doc he thought. A smile came to his face. Thoughts like the ones he was now thinking hadn't come to him since, well, since never. Not even when he was married for whatever that was worth, if you could call what he and Sherry had a marriage.

No, this was definitely different. Cool, but definitely different for sure.

"Whatcha drinking there, partner?" Harry heard as he woke from his personal thoughts of joy. It brought him back to the present.

"Huh?" he replied to the person sitting in the seat next to him.

"I said..."

"I heard you," Harry cut him off before he could repeat his question. "It's a vodka and tonic."

You sit in first class, which is not Harry's normal mode of air travel, and you can hope for some peace and quiet. Doesn't always happen that way

"Bourbon and branch here for me," came in response. "Fact is, I need another of these babies. Hey sweetie, can you rustle me up another of these," he said to the flight attendant as she passed his seat. "And get my partner here another of whatever it is he's tossing down there."

A semi-sneer at Cowboy Bob, a look at Harry, and the attendant went on her merry way perhaps to return with their refreshments before the plane landed.

"You sleeping the flight away there, boy. Name's Dickson. Cattle feed's my game. Make a fortune and my wives piss it away. What's yours?" he finished.

Harry looked at him and wished he was still thinking wonderful thoughts of Doc, and...

"Your name I mean," Cowboy Bob continued.

"Harry," he replied realizing he probably had no choice. "Harry Shorts."

"Pleasure to make your acquaintance, Harry Shorts. I'll call you Shorts you don't mind."

"That's fine," Harry said trying to be as polite as possible. He had the feeling Cowboy Bob and he weren't going to hit it off before long. Just a feeling, but Harry trusted his feelings and they had done him good in the past more often than not.

Much to his surprise, the flight attendant brought two refills and only spilled a small drop in Cowboy Bob's lap putting down his drink. She actually landed Harry's drink on his tray.

"Lookit here, sweet thing. You got some of my drink on my pants. Maybe you wanna reach down there and pat it dry for me; maybe take a little longer than need be to make sure it's real dry," he said to her with a wink.

The flight attendant leaned over so her mouth was right next to Cowboy Bob's ear. In a calm and collected voice, just loud enough for Harry to hear, she said, "You annoyed me greatly on the flight out to Kansas City, Cowpoke Bob. You're annoying me even more now. If I reach down into your lap, I'm gonna rip your gonads right out of your shriveled up scrotum and stuff them down your throat. Would you like me to do that, Cowpoke?"

To stunned to speak, Cowpoke Bob mumbled out a, "Don't think so, ma'am." He proceeded to toss down his drink and put his head back, eyes closed, pretending to go to sleep to hide from my new favorite flight attendant.

Harry winked at her, she winked back, and all was right in the air. Plus, when Harry looked down at his napkin, a feisty flight attendant by the name of Paulette had provided her home telephone number in New York City.

Chapter 44

"It's another beautiful day in paradise," Harry spat in Big Mel's direction as he strode past him and into the back of the office.

"A what?" Mel responded to Harry's back.

"Another beautiful day in paradise," Harry practically sang out. "The sun is shining, I'm here communing with my favorite ex-brother-in-law, and best of all, Bunny should be here soon to brighten up our day even further."

"Yeah. Whatever you say, Harry. At least you got the Bunny part right."

"Seen Muller since I've been gone?" Harry asked.

"Oh, were you gone somewhere. It was so peaceful around here the past week or so I hadn't noticed anything was missing," Mel said.

"I'll ignore that rather hurtful insult and repeat myself if I must," Harry said to Mel. "Seen Muller since I've been gone?"

"No. Morning Bunny," Mel said as Ms. Bunny Malone pranced through the front door.

"Morning, boss man," Bunny started and then squealed with delight as she said, "Harry, you're back. We missed you."

"We?" Harry asked with a slightly raided eyebrow.

"Oh, don't mind him," she said gesturing toward Mel with a turn of a rather delightfully bare shoulder. "He growls like a bear but he worries about you when you are off on one of your cases."

Harry regained his senses after witnessing the shoulder turn. "Mel, baby, if I had only known how much you cared all this time."

"Harry, don't make me tell you to go fuck yourself in front on this young lady," Mel retorted.

"Mel, shame on you," Bunny said. "But as long as you brought it up, I'm not doing anything for lunch, Harry," Bunny concluded with a smile that could launch a thousand ships and ruin a thousand pair of shorts.

"I'll order something in," Harry told her. "Anything in particular you want?"

"Something that goes good with whipped cream, lasts a long time, and it has to go in smooth," she cooed.

"Oh, for Christ sake," Mel huffed as he got up out of his chair and left the office slamming the door behind him.

"I don't know what could have gotten into him," Bunny said. "I have to go get ready for an open house, Harry. You'll be able to handle my lunch order I presume," she said.

"I have no doubt at all I'll be able to provide exactly what you are looking for, Bunny. Do you have any doubts?" Harry asked.

"None what so ever," she replied.

"Noon?" Harry asked.

"Noon it is, Harry. Be ready," she said as she sashayed to the front door.

"Oh, I'll be ready," Harry replied already three quarters of the way there.

With the office now empty, Harry hit the speaker button and dialed a number he had dialed many times before.

"Ms. Timmons office, may I help you?" came over the speaker.

Timmons either had gotten a new assistant or a temp was manning the desk. Sexy voice, though.

"Is she available," Harry asked.

"Let me check. May I ask who's calling, please?"

"Yes you may," Harry replied.

Silence.

After a few seconds, Harry said, "You may ask now if you would like."

"Oh, that's a clever one. May I ask who is calling, please?" the sexy voice said.

"Yes you may," Harry replied again and laughed. Before he gave sexy voice a chance to reply, he said, "It's Harry Mickey Shorts. You are?" he continued.

Silence again.

"Um…" was all that came across the phone line.

"Ms. Um what?" Harry asked.

This was kind of fun he thought to himself.

"I'll…I'll, ah…I'll check and see if Ms. Timmons is available," she finally got out.

Harry waited and decided he had had enough fun for the time being.

"I'm sorry, Mister Shorts. Ms. Timmons isn't in her office at the moment. Can I take a message?"

"Why yes, Ms. Um. Please have her call me on my cell when she returns," he replied.

"I'll be sure and do that, Mister Shorts. And for your information, it's Timmons, Tammy Timmons," she said as the phone line went dead.

I'll be damned Harry said both to himself and the dead phone line.

Chapter 45

With Harry's visit to Board Room Farms safely chronicled in his files, it was time to move on to the next piece of the horse racing puzzle—the Brodericks.

His computer already powered up from his file updating, Harry utilized several internet search engines to see what was out in net-space on the Broderick clan. Not surprising at all, Harry ended up printing out a full ream of paper worth of information on them including racing results, family personal history and social items—the good, the bad and the ugly. The Broderick clan was a busy and well publicized group and not always for good reasons.

Their success on the racing circuit was a well known and very well documented fact. The best of the stable's horses seemed to run on the west coast giving Pauly Broderick bragging rights within the family's training ranks. He compounded his dominance by shipping the cream of his crop to all the big races country-wide even when it meant competing against the rest of the Broderick's east coast horses. A well publicized shouting match between he and Mikey Jr. at Belmont last year made all the trade rags.

Mikey Jr. dominated the New England racing circuit and more than held his own on the New York/New Jersey tracks. An interesting quote in the New York Post had Mikey speculating on just how successful he would be in New York if his fellow Broderick family trainer would share the stable's quality horses equally instead of "hogging up the family success all for himself."

A wee bit of family squabbling perhaps. The need to go elsewhere to establish his own dominance in the making perhaps. Perhaps, perhaps.

Matt Broderick was down in Florida with an inferior string of horses when you compared them to the other two Brodericks. He found his success shipping what he had to the Midwest and smaller tracks on the east coast that Mikey Jr. couldn't be bothered with. Some insiders in the business quietly speculated that the real training talent in the Broderick family had yet to hit the spotlight that the two older Brodericks currently dominated. Some insiders in the business also quietly wondered when

Mikey Broderick Sr. would let the younger and less heralded Broderick have his day in the race track sun.

And then, and it was a big then, there was the social side to the entire Broderick brood. As quiet and hidden as Mikey Broderick Sr.'s life was, the younger "Brods," as they were sometimes collectively called, love the party scene. Any party scene, on any given day, in any city whether they were racing horses or not.

Borrowing a well known phrase for his own use, Pauly had been quoted more times than you could count: "We race hard, and we play hard; and not necessarily in that order." None of the three were ever married, but the publicly detailed romances and flings Harry found everywhere he looked gave much credence to Pauly Broderick's credo.

Harry had the feeling he could get to like the Brodericks if he tried or had the chance. That possibility hadn't presented itself yet, but he had the sneaky suspicion their paths would cross before long.

Next assignment—it was time to make the acquaintance of the younger brother of Mr. M. Randle Trundle.

Lunch beckoned. Harry was positive his ever present can of Ready Whip whipped cream needed replenishment. A little dab may do ya, but slathering it on in huge and strategically placed locations will do ya way better.

Harry could hear the head waiter's voice beckoning them now:

Welcome back Mr. Shorts and Ms. Bunny to Chez Harry. On the menu for this afternoon, for the gentleman and the lady, we present two divine selections that have served to please both of you immensely in the past. Dessert should prove most delightful with the whipped cream of course on the house and anything else that moves I have no doubt.

Bon Fucking Appetite!

Chapter 46

"Ms. Timmons," Harry said in greeting as he entered the Trundle headquarters building.

"Mister Shorts," she said in reply as she turned and headed for the elevators.

"How's Tammy?" Harry inquired to her back and a rather delightful looking back it was.

She stopped dead in her tracks, hesitated, and then turned ever so slowly to face Harry who had continued walking in her direction.

"Tammy Timmons, for your information, since you have asked, is fine. Tammy Timmons, also for your information, is not a subject you and I will discuss at this time or at any time in the future. Tammy Timmons, Mister Harry Mickey Shorts, will never be mentioned by either myself, or yourself, ever again. Are we clear on that, Mister Harry Mickey Shorts?" Ms. Timmons concluded.

"Loud and clear, Ms. Timmons. Just so I am totally clear on it, she your sister? She look like you? A man has a right to know what it is he will never have the opportunity to discuss again, doesn't he?" Harry asked.

"Jesus H. Christ on a pair of broken crutches," Ms. Timmons said as she turned again and headed for the elevators.

"Must be a real hottie," Harry whispered to himself low enough to ensure continued protection of the family jewels.

The elevator doors opened and Ms. Timmons walked into the reception area. She never looked back at Harry.

"He's all yours, Clare," Timmons said to the receptionist and proceeded to walk through a door that said Do No Enter.

"Mister Trundle will be right with you, Mister Shorts. Please be seated. Can I do anything for you?" she asked.

Harry hesitated, thought better of it, and said no.

With much to admire, Harry was content to wait out the fifteen minutes it took for Clare to announce Mr. Trundle would see him now. He now knew her last name was Morrison, she lived on the Upper East Side with her baby sister, and they both were newly detached from short term "things" as she called them.

"Harry, it's good to finally meet you. Heard a ton about you from R and thrilled you've agreed to help us out with this unfortunate fuck of a mess."

Harry figured he could pretend they had met and he knew who this guy was. Or, he could make sure and ask.

Fuck of a mess stuck in his head.

"You must be Danny?" he tried.

"Yeah, sure, I shoulda said right off. I'm Danny, R's little brother. Come in, come in. Babe, hold my calls, will ya," he threw at Clare as he headed for Randle's office.

"Babe?" Harry mouthed in her direction as he followed.

"Stupid Asshole," she mouthed back and smiled at Harry, her new found friend.

Harry smiled in return and nodded the nod of what could eventually be.

"Sit yourself down, Harry. Scotch, beer? What's your poison?" Danny asked.

"A beer would be great. What's yours?" Harry continued.

"Mine?" Danny said as he got Harry a beer.

"Poison, your poison," Harry explained.

He can't be that fucking dense, can he, Harry thought to himself.

Danny handed Harry a glass and a beer, as in the can said "Beer" on it. Nothing else.

"Scotch. I'm a scotch man, Harry. A man's drink," he finished.

In his mind, Harry told himself Danny didn't just tell him he was a fairy-assed girlie-man for drinking beer, but...

Harry decided to let it slide. Danny was not exactly ingratiating himself in Harry's eyes from the jump.

"Interesting can," Harry said holding up the can that said "Beer" and nothing else. "What exactly is it I'm drinking here?"

"Beer," Danny responded.

Maybe I was wrong Harry thought to himself. Maybe he actually is that dense.

"Yes, I can see that, Danny. But normally a beer can says what kind it is, who made it, where it is from, and like that," Harry told him. "This can has just one word on it—Beer."

Before Danny could answer, the door opened and Randle swept in. He took one look at Harry, looked directly at what he was holding in his hand, and proceeded to shake his head in disgust.

"Danny, I've told you before, and I'm telling you for the last time, peddle that piss-water wherever you want, but not within fifty miles of me or anyone I know. Now take that away from Harry and pour it down the drain. Now!"

Turning toward Harry, Randle said, "Harry, let me make a call and I will personally get you a proper beverage to wash away the taste of that shit Danny has unfortunately subjected your palate to."

Danny grabbed the "Beer" and scurried away. Randle made his call as Harry waited patiently wondering what in the name of holy fuck was going to happen next.

Chapter 47

A pair of St. Paulie Girls in hand, Randle led Harry out onto the balcony. Danny followed behind like a cowering puppy dog that had just gotten his ass kicked for crapping on the rug, can of Beer in hand.

"Sorry I was late, Harry," Randle started. "Since you've already met my brother, let's sit and talk. Danny, pull up another chair and listen for now. When spoken to, speak. Until then, just listen and try and learn something. Okay?"

"Yes, Randle," Danny replied.

Harry didn't think Danny was very pleased at the way he was being treated by his big brother at the moment. Inwardly seething might express it best.

A pull on his Paulie Girl accomplished and enjoyed, Randle spoke again.

"What have you found out so far, Harry? I was under the impression Danny had been in touch with you while I was away, but I have learned I was mistaken."

Randle turned his attention to Danny and said, "Is that an accurate assessment, Danny?"

"Um, I guess so," was all Danny said in response.

"You guess so," Randle repeated disgustedly. "Let's move on."

Harry had the distinct feeling there was little brotherly love between the Trundle siblings at the moment.

Randle shook his head, blew out a breath, and said, "Bring your chair over here, Danny. Jesus, I could just brain you some times. Come on over here and together let's see what is going on with Board Room Farms. And please, put that can down and get yourself a real beer out of the cooler in the corner."

Cooler in the corner, Harry thought. M. Randle Trundle, CEO extraordinaire with a cooler on his balcony overlooking Central Park. Harry had really turned him into a normal human being; well, Harry's version of a normal human being at least.

"Tell us, Harry. What have your travels unveiled?" Randle asked.

"Yeah, whataya got?" Danny said.

Randle looked at him, Danny shut up.

"Well, not much so far," Harry started. "As you know, my investigation got off to a very rocky start and what I thought was going to be a key contact dried up before I could cement the connection. The trip to Lee's Summit was informative and the background information I got gives me an excellent base to work from; but, again, nothing materialized that points me in any particular direction."

Fortification, St. Paulie Girl style.

"I'm on to more fact gathering now and the only thing I've gotten is more facts. Nothing points in any direction at all; facts are facts and what happened exists. If there is any connection in what I have so far, I haven't seen it yet. But you know how it works, Randle. Turn over enough rocks, something slithers out."

Harry stopped at that point and got that Harry look when the light bulb goes on over his head.

"Music," Harry blurted out.

"Music?" Randle repeated.

"Whataya mean music?" Danny said.

Randle looked, Danny shut up.

"Music," Harry said again. "It just hit me. I was sure there was something different about your office the last time I was here, but I couldn't put my finger on it. It just came to me. When I was sitting in your office just now, I heard music. So soft you could barely make it out, but there was definitely music coming from somewhere in your office."

Randle smiled while Danny had a confused look on his face.

"Music, schmusic. Who gives a rat's ass if R has music playing in his office," Danny blurted out.

Brushing off Danny's insightful analysis of Harry's find, Randle said, "Very observant, Harry. You're the first person that has noticed the addition. I had it installed not all that long ago and, when I hear a song that catches my ear, it has allowed me to point my thoughts in a different direction other than one hundred percent work related activities.

"I believe you would call it your 'mind's ear', wouldn't you, Harry?" Randle asked.

"Absolutely correct, Randle," Harry answered. "And a fine addition I might add. I can only hope I had some influence in your decision," Harry subtly inquired.

"Influence you did, Harry, as only you can do best. I have found it very pleasant to put my mind to work while my 'mind's ear' concentrates on something totally different. Never before could I have done such a thing. Never before you, Harry. Influence you surely did."

"Influence what?" Danny asked. "Mind's ear? What the hell's a mind's ear? What the fuck are you two guys talking about?" Danny asked showing how confused he really was.

"Don't worry about it, Danny, it's not important," Randle told him. "Go inside and get yourself another can of Beer and let's enjoy New York. Okay?"

"New York? What the…"

In a huff, Danny got up and left, leaving Harry and Randle to clink bottles and enjoy a friend's smile.

Harry wondered how two brothers could be light years apart such as Randle and Danny were. He could only wonder how Danny had built such a successful racing stable in a business as cut-throat as thorough-bred racing purported to be.

Maybe Randle wasn't as junior a partner as he had led on. Maybe Randle knew much more about the racing business than he had said, and maybe Harry would find out soon enough.

Chapter 48

Harry always enjoyed the peace and solitude of working late at night in Big Mel's office, the only light provided by the computer's monitor. The object of his late night excursion was one Davey Boy McGarry.

The visit to Randle's office had refreshed Harry as every visit to see him did. Refreshed, maybe, but he was even more frustrated by his lack of progress on the case.

Case. Was it a case? Was there anything to find, or had it just been time for a magnificent animal to go to the big corral in the sky. Was Trundle's intuition wrong this time? Was his meeting with a big brick shithouse and the disappearance of Mueller just several coincidences that happen to have occurred at that time and place? Was it always so dark in here Harry wondered?

"Shit on a lightly toasted shingle," Harry said to nobody that was listening.

Davey Boy McGarry was born poor and lived poor for the majority of his early life. Crime on the back streets of Dublin got him sentenced to six months on a horse farm as part of a rehabilitation program the government was trying out. Mucking stalls eventually led to owning stalls, which naturally led to owning the horses that went into the stalls. And own he did. Horses every which way you can imagine that blossomed into commanding the world of the backstretch.

At the age of twenty-nine, Davey Boy McGarry owned one of the largest stables of thoroughbred horses in Ireland. How he did it nobody was totally sure, but he did it. How much of it was procured legally, nobody knew for sure. All that was known was it happened and that now, at the age of thirty-five, he owned the most prosperous stable in all of Ireland. Davey Boy McGarry had conquered Ireland and he now had his sights set on the United States of America.

According to the Irish rags Harry was able to view via the internet, McGarry had left a trail of trainers in his wake on his way to the top. Lack of results meant lack of job in McGarry's eyes. For a short time he actually trained his horses himself after telling the press, "These bums I entrust my horses to can't win enough to pay their own wages never mind make me successful against the stiff competition out there. I'll have to do it myself and show the lot of them what bums they are."

Months later McGarry was a bum himself. At least he must have been; he fired himself and hired another trainer away from the then second best stable in Ireland. Feeney was his name. He had been with the Cloverland Squires stable for ten years. Why he left them and picked up with McGarry nobody knew, or at least nobody was saying if they did know. Perhaps it was money, which Davey Boy had plenty to throw around; but, more than one trainer in his service had turned up physically worse for the wear soon after his sacking. Or so the reports Harry was able to read speculated.

Feeney had controlled the horses in McGarry's stable for the past two years. He had rung up such an impressive string of horse meetings and winning percentages he was voted Trainer of the Year both years running. As one scribe wrote, "Feeney's success can't be argued with, but with McGarry, he's just a bum in the making waiting to be sacked like the string of successful trainers before him. Better him them me," the writer concluded.

Funny, nowhere in any of the articles Harry accessed did it mention Feeney's first name.

Another void in everything Harry read on McGarry, contrary to the well publicized shenanigans of the Broderick bunch, was even an inkling of McGarry in the public social circles. No mention of a wife or girl-friend. No mention of him going to any of the big social events tied to the racing community. No mention of him being seen out and about on the town squiring around the requisite bombshell of the month. Nada, period. Strange, Harry thought, but stranger things had perplexed him before.

Harry gathered up the half-a-ream of printouts he had accumulated on McGarry and his operations and called it a night. Now he was well versed on both the Brodericks and McGarry. Now it was time to see if either had a hand in Brian Boru's demise.

Chapter 49

Sunday morning in the Shorts world meant nothing happened until several cups of coffee and the entire Sunday paper had been consumed. In his earlier days, it was sometimes Sunday afternoon by the time the previous night's activities had cleared and his vision wasn't still impaired.

On good weather days, the activities occurred on the front deck of his garage apartment which was above the driveway overlooking the main house. Hopefully his neighbor Sandy and her bombshell of a daughter would be sunbathing to increase his morning's enjoyment. It was still a tad chilly this time of year but one could always hope, couldn't one. Present weather not permitting any out-of-door lounging, the dining room table was the scene of the crime.

A fine mist meant staying indoors this morning.

Somewhere between the travel section and the arts section, well after the favored sports section had been devoured front cover to back page, Harry's Sunday morning ritual was disturbed by a ringing doorbell.

"Can't a guy read a newspaper and enjoy his coffee in peace?" Harry said out loud as he went to see who was bothering his ass. A pleasant surprise greeted Harry as he opened the door at the bottom of the stairs that led up to his apartment.

"Morning, Harry," Sandy said. "I had plans to go into the city this morning. Unfortunately, they just got cancelled. Feeling a little lonely, I thought you might be able to cheer me up."

"You know you are always welcome here, kiddo," Harry said. "What have you got there? It smells damn good as do you by the way. Oh hell, what am I thinking, come on in here," he finished as he took the platter from her and ushered her up the stairs.

"When I got the call this morning canceling my New York plans, I whipped up a batch of waffles and some sausage," she said. "I know you agree Sunday morning is a great time for a big breakfast."

"Having shared a few with you already, you know I agree, Sandy. And unless I'm mistaken, you do enjoy a hefty helping of whipped cream on your waffles. Am I right?" he asked.

"Right you are, Harry. Just as long as there is enough whipped cream left for dessert activities," she said with that mischievous smile Harry had learned to love so.

"I happen to be in possession of a new can of said dessert enhancing material," Harry started. "And might I add, should the lady so desire, breakfast could be warming in the oven while two consenting adults indulge themselves in a most delicious dessert currently being served in the rear of the apartment."

"I'm consenting if you're serving, Harry. Fire up the Ready Whip and let's indulge ourselves in a most delicious manner."

Breakfast was well warmed by the time Harry and Sandy had enjoyed a most delicious dessert.

Chapter 50

After Sandy's departure, the remainder of Sunday was spent going through the mountain of paper Harry had printed out on the Brodericks and Davey Boy McGarry. Thorough private investigator protocol meant it was necessary to read every word of every paragraph of every page to make sure the smallest detail wasn't overlooked. More often than not, it is a waste of private investigator protocol time.

Scanning the Broderick information while he had it on the computer had generated the same understanding of what was contained in the printouts after he had finished reading them. Just more of the same nada producing nothing more to go on. Harry did confirm Pauly Broderick had a better winning percentage than the other two Broderick trainers. He also confirmed McGarry had crept up ever so slightly on the Brodericks on the US track circuits while maintaining his European dominance over them.

So what you say? You happen to be in very good company. Harry thought the same thing—so what. Knowing how many races or how much prize money either stable had won did not get him any closer to knowing what, if anything, was going on when it came to Brian Boru and Board Room Farms. Not a damn bit closer.

One thing did come of the endless hours Harry had spent accumulating and pouring over the Broderick/McGarry information—more and more races over the past year saw both stables entering horses in the same races. Head-to-head competition had become a common denominator and it was heating up as the year's big races drew closer. But it also seemed to be confined to Pauly and Mikey Jr.'s horses and the McGarry horses. Matt Broderick's string of horses didn't go up against a McGarry horse once in the last six months. Matt's winning percentage was improving while the other Brodericks' had dipped a bit.

Coincidence you say—maybe.

Matt having had the inferior string of Broderick horses you might think—maybe.

The McGarry stable's penchant to run only on the bigger race tracks in higher purse races—could be.

In the P.I. business, too many maybe's and could be's when added together have the potential to mean there's more than meets the eye behind the combination. Or, as Harry had seen many times before when investigating said combinations, eventually they don't mean shit.

There was one important piece of knowledge Harry found most interesting when he was done with his reading. No maybe or could be about it. A certain rider was well on his way to losing his bug after winning a bunch of races for the trainers named Matt Broderick and Feeney. And you guessed it—the bugs name was none other than McDonough. Yes, the same McDonough who not so long ago rode almost exclusively for Board Room Farms.

That, my kiddos, is one coincidence that bears serious further investigation.

Chapter 51

Harry had always found that when his head and his eyes hurt from too much investigating, liquid refreshment was the best cure. From past experience, Harry also knew more cure was sometimes necessary and infinitely better than less. He had practiced this procedure often enough in the past.

This was one of those times.

Not having hoisted a few with his favorite ex-brother-in-law in far too long a time, Harry started up the block to Mel's office to convince him brews were in order. As he entered the real estate office Mel called his work domain, Harry was stopped dead in his tracks, and the thought of drinks with Mel went out the window.

Why, you ask?

Standing there with her back to Harry, in all her glory, was none other than his ex—Sherry.

"Mel," was all Harry got out of his mouth.

Sherry turned to face Harry. That smile that used to make his knees melt and his Johnson do the jig spread across her face.

"Harry, what a surprise to meet you here," she said.

Mel smirked behind her back just to irritate Harry.

Johnson-jigger time.

"And you, Sherry," Harry contributed. "How are the little ones doing?" he continued for no reason at all.

"In the couple of days since you last saw them, they're just fine, Harry," Sherry said to embarrass Harry as she knew it would. "They are off on a school trip for the whole day."

"Sherry was just about to walk back home, Harry. As long as you're here, and seeing as how swamped I am right now, why don't you give my little sister a lift home?"

Not a single piece of paper on his desk. Swamped my ass, Harry thought.

"Better than that, Harry, why don't we just walk back to my place together? It's not a bad day for a walk and I'll let you buy me an ice cream cone on the way if you're nice to me," Sherry said.

Mel, the smirking asshole, had noticed Harry's increasing JJ dilemma.

"Sure, Sherry. But how about we stop off and have that drink we've been meaning to have?" Harry countered.

"A drink would be nice, Harry. We can sit and talk for a while and then you can walk me on home."

Harry could have sworn Sherry's body did the tiniest shimmy possible as she said that.

"A drink it is then," Harry said not sure exactly what he was getting himself into.

"You two kids enjoy yourselves while the kiddies are away for the day," Mel said to bust Harry's balls no doubt.

"Oh, we will," Sherry said as she turned to get her jacket to go. "I can always count on Harry to enjoy himself after a couple of drinks."

Thoughts swam randomly through Harry's mind. Couple of drinks? We were going for one drink. She's counting on me to enjoy myself. Is there enjoyment in the cards for her as well? All I wanted was a couple of innocent beers with Mel and now I'm heading off to I don't know what with my ex for a couple of drinks and who knows what else.

Oh, well. When in doubt, go with the flow, and the flow pointed toward a few drinks and a good time had by all.

God Save the Queen and Harry Mickey Shorts.

Chapter 52

"Two Absolut Gimlets; splash one and Fly-By the other," I told the waitress who came to our table. Cute little package who had a habit of waiting on me when I frequented this local establishment, which was often when I was in town.

Sherry had a look of "what the fuck" on her face after I ordered the drinks.

"What?" I said.

"Splash one and Fly-By the other?" she repeated what I had said in the form of a question.

"Yeah," I said in return. "Put just a splash of Roses Lime Juice in one of the Gimlets and barely any in the other. Like when the jets do a Fly-By over head at parades, or shows, and they are gone before you know it. As the bottle of Roses flies over top of the Gimlet, maybe a drop or two might end up in the glass."

"And she knows what that means?" Sherry asked.

"Been here before and I may have ordered a Gimlet or two," I replied.

"You never cease to amaze me, Harry," she said.

"I'll have to keep on trying, won't I?" I answered.

The drinks arrived and Sherry was spared a response to that question.

"To good times gone by and better times ahead," Sherry toasted.

"For both of us," I said as we clinked glasses.

We each sipped our drinks and exchanged glasses after Sherry's expression told me she had the Fly-By.

"So, Harry, what have you been working on that has kept you out of town?" Sherry asked.

Debating what to tell her, I decided to do something totally out of the ordinary. I'd try the truth.

"A guy I know asked me to look into the death of a horse that occurred recently," I started.

"That stud horse I read about in the papers—Brian Boru?" she asked. "Somewhere out in the Midwest, wasn't it?"

"You follow the horses?" I said in shock.

"No, of course not, Harry. It was on the front of the sports page Max was reading. I just happened to see it. It caught my eye so I read the article. Strange," she finished.

"Strange?" I mimed.

"Yeah, strange. The article said he was like nineteen or something and died of natural causes if I remember correctly. That right, Harry?"

"Eighteen, actually. And what's so strange about a horse dying of natural causes?" I asked her.

The conversation was flowing and the drinks were going down much too easy. Sherry's was almost gone as well.

"Two more, Harry?" cutie-pie asked as if on cue.

"Sure. Two more of the same," I answered. "And can we get some nuts if you have any?"

"I could use some nuts," Sherry said and smiled that god-awful my ass is gonna be in trouble smile.

I downed the rest of my drink.

I asked, "Cold, Sherry?" which had been prompted by my noticing nipples the size of silver dollars causing extreme protrusion in the front of Sherry's tee-shirt.

"Actually no, Harry. To tell you the truth I'm feeling really hot right now. Totally hot in fact. Almost to the point of uncontrollably hot," she continued.

I can't stand it when she licks her upper lip with the tip of her tongue "o" so slowly.

It's been a long time since Wee-Willie Johnson partook in a one day two-bagger.

"We out of here?" I asked.

She downed the rest of her drink.

"We're out of here," she replied.

The next round of drinks weren't touched. Two horny-assed adults skipped the two blocks to her house and you can figure out the rest.

Chapter 53

There's nothing like lying in bed in the late afternoon after a most enjoyable romp in the hay, even if it's with your ex-wife. It's like stealing from the cookie jar and not getting caught. Plus, I might add, we're talking some mighty scrumptious cookies.

Sherry's head was resting on my shoulder and her hand was resting elsewhere. To break the ice, I started.

"To repeat myself from some time earlier today, what's so strange about a horse dying of natural causes?" I said to drift the conversation back to a comment Sherry had made earlier while we were at the bar.

"Oh, it wasn't that the horse died of natural causes," she said. "What was strange was that I was just talking about that particular horse a week or so before it died."

"You were?" I asked.

"Yeah, I was."

Quiet.

"Okay, I'll ask. Who were you talking to about Brian Boru? Where and why?" I asked.

"Well," she started. "I, um, I kinda was, I a…I saw a guy a few times," she finally spit out.

That's why the kids said she was acting kinda happy. Get a little—be happy. And here I thought it was cuz I boinked the ex one time.

"A guy?" I quizzed. "How many times? When? Who may I ask? Is it serious?"

"He's got family local," she finally started. "He was in town and Cara introduced me to him when we were out one Friday. She met him the night before at some bar and I think they knew each other from before."

"Do I know them?" I asked.

"I don't know. His name's Matt. His father is from Manhasset and still lives in town some of the time from what I could gather. He's got something to do with horses and travels a lot. We started talking about horses, where he gets to travel to, and that horse's name came up in the conversation."

"Matt what?" I asked.

Could not possibly be.

"Matt Broderick," Sherry said.

Could possibly be—is in fact.

"Matt Broderick," I repeated.

"Yeah, you know him, Harry?" she asked.

"No, just heard his name somewhere. Or the Brodericks at least," I lied.

"Anyway, he was here for about two weeks, maybe a bit less, and I saw him a few times. Nice guy but he talked about horses all the time and how big he was gonna get. It was late and he got semi-drunk the last time I saw him. That's when he talked about that horse. The Brian horse."

"What did he say?" I asked.

"Something about breeding and a partnership with something, or somebody is what he said, I think. I looked up breeding later but you know I don't understand the horses, Harry. Don't want to, either."

"He say anything else, Sherry?"

"He said lots of stuff, Harry. You want all the details? Didn't you get enough before? I need to spell it out for you, Harry?"

"About the horse, Sherry," I said.

"Oh."

She laughed.

"Just that it was all fixed and life was gonna get much better for him real soon," she said. "He said he'd show the rest of them, I think is what he said."

"Interesting," Harry said out loud.

"What is?" Sherry asked.

"Oh, I was just thinking. Forget about it, kiddo. He still around?"

"Nope. Turned out he split the next day and I haven't heard from him again. He's down south somewhere and said he probably wouldn't be back up here until the Belmont, whenever or whatever that is. He was fun, but not what I need in my life, or the kids life either. You know what I'm saying, Harry?"

"Yeah, Sherry, I know. They don't need another wanderer in their life, or in yours. Good you had some fun, though," I finished.

"Yeah, it was, Harry. It's good to have a guy pay attention to you and make you feel special once in a while. You forget the mother part for a short while and become a woman..." she trailed off.

"You deserve a lot more than that, Sherry. And if it's attention and feeling good you desire, than hold on to your hat, because a Harry Mickey Shorts storm is about to rain all over you like you've never seen before."

Sherry got as much as she deserved and more…Harry Mickey Shorts made damn sure of that.

Chapter 54

"Oh shit" were the first words that popped into Harry's head. They were the third and fourth words that came to mind as well.

It was dark when Harry opened his eyes and finally realized where he was. Still was that is. It wasn't supposed to be dark. It couldn't be dark yet. Sherry was sound asleep lying on her stomach, the covers jumbled all around her. She was facing away from Harry and the natural instinct of seeing a gorgeous naked ass staring him in the face got his juices flowing again.

Maybe there was enough time.

His juices flowed freely.

"Don't be a total asshole, Harry," he said to himself.

A quickie might make me only half-an-asshole he tried to rationalize.

Give it up, Harry.

He tried.

"Sherry," he whispered softly into her ear as he gave his ex a gentle pat on that gorgeous ass of hers.

"Harry," she murmured.

"Hey, kiddo," he whispered.

She turned toward the sound of his voice and had her tongue in his mouth and his dick in her hand before Harry knew what hit him. His small attempt to indicate their present circumstances to her went for naught. His hand found her breast which was quickly followed by a rock hard nipple finding his mouth. Sherry moved to straddle him. Seconds later they were rocking in unison, faster and faster, until Sherry let out a low moan letting Harry know she had found her "spot" as she called it. A minute later she collapsed on Harry's chest, her breathing slowly returning to normal.

It was then that she opened her eyes and said, "Oh shit!"

She sat up and looked out the window by the side of the bed.

"Harry, it's dark out," she said.

"I know that, Sherry. I was trying to tell you that before..."

"Harry, it's dark out," she repeated as if she hadn't heard a word he said.

She sat there looking out the window wondering what time it was and what time the kids were due home. Unconsciously she must have realized Harry was still inside her as she slowly began to rock in place. Tiny movements, but movements Harry couldn't help but feel.

"Sherry," Harry said.

"One minute, Harry," Sherry answered from somewhere else.

She gently moved back and forth matching the slow rhythm of her breathing, arching her back and raising her clasped hands as if to touch the ceiling. The long low moan she released as she let go brought a smile to Harry's face. It was good to know he could still do something good for his ex-wife after all the heartache he had caused her throughout the years.

All would have been right with the world if the front door hadn't opened at that very minute.

The kids, Max and Briande, Harry and Sherry's kids, were home.

Sherry had thought to use the signal when she and Harry had first gotten back to her house. She remembered it before they had another Gimlet and laughingly made their way to her bedroom in the back of the house. That was what she was trying to remember when she had said, "One minute," to Harry before. Before she got caught up finding her "spot" for the third time—three memories she would hold onto for as long as she could. Hold on to them until she needed to refresh her memory and she would have to deal with that when the time came.

Memories with Harry no less.

"Sherry," I whispered.

"I heard them, Harry," she replied.

"If you wouldn't mind, dear, if you don't climb down off there I think my dick is going to fall off," I said.

Sherry had all she could do to stop herself from cracking up. Harry could be the funniest guy in the world at the worst possible moment.

"Sorry," she said as she dismounted her valiant steed.

"Thank you," I said. "Is it still attached?"

"Stop it you idiot, they'll hear you."

"That's if they didn't already hear you howling at the moon before," I cracked.

"Fuck you, Harry."

"I believe you did that three times so far, Sher. Care to try for a fourth?"

She muffled a laugh at that one, too.

"What are we going to do?" I asked.

"We have a signal. When I'm sleeping, I leave my 'My Kids Suck' coffee mug on the table and they know to keep quiet and not to come in here and bother me. I left it out before we came in here."

"Came being the operative word there, Sherry?"

That got me a swift shot to the side of the head.

"Get your clothes on and climb out the window," Sherry said.

"What?" was all I could think to say.

"Put your clothes on, go over to the window, climb out, and go home. I don't think we want them to know we are in here together doing whatever, do you?"

"Whatever felt pretty good by the way, Sherry."

"Yeah, Harry, it felt real good. Each time better than the one before. And thank you, Harry. But now, get your ass out of here before I call the cops and have you arrested for impersonating an Iron Mike fucking machine. I can play ravished victim better than most as you very well know, Harry," she said.

"And as you can attest to, I can ravish with the best of them."

I ducked.

"I'm going, I'm going. Tell the kids I said hi from before and I'll see them soon."

"Sure, Harry. See you soon?" she asked.

"Yeah, Sherry. I'll see you soon, too."

Feeling like a cat burglar overdosed on catnip, I climbed out the rear bedroom window and crept quietly up the driveway on the side of the house. As I got to the sidewalk, I started to cross the street and heard, "See ya pops," from the front door letting me know Sherry and I were a bit noisier than we thought.

Chapter 55

The boys were gathered on the back porch like they did every day at the end of the main work day. J'Orr was holding things up for a few minutes while he waited for Stu to get back from the other side of the ranch.

Stu finally showed.

"Okay, boys. Pretty good day's worth of work out there today. The new shed is up and we shouldn't have any storage problems any more. Good work all around."

A few murmurs as the boys took credit for what they had done. The new shed was twice the size of the old one and all the supplies had been moved over without a hitch.

"Be a little extra for dinner tonight to thank you all for your hard work. So, anything we should know about?" J'Orr asked the group.

Since most of the hands were either tied up with the new shed and relocating the supplies or off with Stu tending to the outer corral, it didn't seem like there was much to report.

"You wanna say something, Thomas?" J'Orr asked.

"Well, Mister J'Orr..." he hesitated. "Well, I think I seen it again today."

Thomas had started to use words like "seen" that he never would have used normally. He desperately wanted to be accepted by the rest of the hands and tried to be like them any way he could. Vocabulary like "seen" instead of "saw" was one small way of trying to fit in.

"What did you see, Thomas?" J'Orr said over the chorus of bullshit the hands were laying down on the kid.

"Up on the hill. Just like the other times. I was loading the hay like you told me to and I looked up and saw them. Two flashes and then they were gone. I only saw them once," Thomas finished excitedly.

Seen becomes saw when Thomas got excited and didn't have time to think it through.

"Okay, Thomas. Any of you other boys see these flashes or whatever they are?" J'Orr asked.

No response.

"Then," J'Orr says, "let's keep our eyes open and see if anyone else can spot these flashes Thomas keeps seeing. Up to the Rogers place, that right, Thomas?"

"Yes, sir. That's where I seen them," Thomas confirmed.

"Okay, boys, let's get cleaned up and have us some supper. Save room for dessert if you hear what I'm saying," J'Orr told them.

"Stu, hang back a second will ya," J'Orr said to Stu as the rest of the boys filed out.

"Sure, J'Orr," Stu told him.

J'Orr waited a minute for the last of the boys to leave, then said, "What do you make of what Thomas says he keeps seeing, Stu? I thought he was just making shit up when Shorts was out here, but now?"

"Don't know what to make of it, J'Orr. Boy don't lie about nothing else and can't see why he'd lie about this. He works his ass off and wants nothing more than to be one of the boys, prove his worth to Mister Trundle I reckon," Stu said.

"I hear ya, Stu. Let's do this then for the next few days. Send one of the men up to the ridge overlooking the Rogers place and tell him to lay low. Let's see what he finds up there and tell him to keep his mouth shut 'bout it. You got a guy you can trust to do that, Stu?" J'Orr asked.

"Yeah, I got just the guy. I'll have him do it for two or three days and see what he comes up with. If he don't see anything in that time, I'll get back to you and we can decide to keep going or pull the plug on it. Sound okay to you?" Stu asked.

"Sounds fine, Stu. I sure hope that kid ain't jerkin' our chain about this. But then, what if he is seeing those flashes. Why's somebody looking down on our spread and who's telling him to do it?"

"J'Orr, I hope the kid's straight on this. I like the kid. Whatever he done to get Mister Trundle to send him here is none of my concern. He busts his butt and been toeing the line since the day he got here. I sure hope he's straight on this…" he trailed off.

"Me too, Stu. Me too," J'Orr said.

Chapter 56

Harry was sitting in the back booth of the Manhasset Diner having breakfast and reading the USA Today sports pages. Two eggs over easy, bacon, white toast and coffee lay half-eaten in front of him.

"What the..." Harry got out as the waitress dropped an identical order on the table across from Harry. The waitress left as quickly as she had appeared, and before Harry could finish his sentence, Mueller sat down.

"Morning," Mueller said as he started in on his eggs.

"Um, morning," Harry replied.

"Best breakfast anywhere," Mueller said matter of factly. "No bullshit, just food. Missed it."

Man of few words Harry noticed.

"Been away?" Harry tried.

No response; Mueller just began shoveling in his food and picked up his Racing Form.

They ate in silence and read.

Eggs finished, Mueller said while he worked on his bacon, "California—needed some sun."

Harry looked up and nodded. "Sun's good," he replied in Mueller's direction as he continued on his toast.

"Yeah, San Diego is nice this time of year," Mueller said into his racing form.

Harry thought on that a few seconds. "Anything special about San Diego?" he asked.

"Navy town. I'm not Navy. Town across the border into Mexico—a tourist attraction I don't care about. Beaches—no use for them. Del Mar I've been," Mueller expounded.

"Del Mar race track I presume."

"Yeah. Watched some races and some people that move out of there."

"Any people in specific?" Harry continued the game of twenty questions.

"Just people," Mueller said.

"Rogers mean anything to you?" Harry asked.

Mueller never even looked up.

Harry didn't know what else to ask at that point, so he picked up his USA Today and read the sports pages some more.

Mueller read his form.

Without warning Mueller folded his Racing Form, stood and started walking away from the table. "Same time tomorrow; track later," he said over his shoulder loud enough for Harry to hear.

"Guess I'm going to the track tomorrow," Harry said to himself. At least Mueller left a piece of bacon for Harry to enjoy.

~ * ~

"Mueller's back," Harry said as he entered Mel's place of business. He had crossed the street and walked over to Mel's office after he had left the diner.

"When?" Mel asked. "You see him?"

"Just had half a breakfast with him at the diner. Walked in, sat, ate, talked, left," Harry told Mel.

"Sounds like Mueller," Mel said. "He say where he was? Why he left so sudden?"

"California, I think," Harry replied. "And no; the why portion was a little fuzzy," Harry said to remain vague on that part of the conversation.

"Piece of work," is all Mel said in response while shaking his head.

"Yeah, some piece of work. We're going to the track tomorrow I think," Harry continued.

"You think?" Mel questioned.

"Yeah, I think. As you know, he's not too easy to pin down and, what you do get, you have to decipher."

"I'm with you on that," Mel said. "If you are going to the track with him, that's big. I don't know anyone else that has actually 'gone' to the track with Mueller. Been there when he was there, yes; but went there with him, no."

"Well, we'll see tomorrow," Harry said. "We're suppose to have breakfast at the diner and I guess go to the track from there."

"Mueller is a man of his word. If he said you're going to the track, you're going to the track," Mel said. "Just be careful with him, Harry. Nobody really knows Mueller and people have tried. He don't let people know him. Period—don't happen."

"Got ya, Mel. I'll catch you in the morning before I head over to the diner."

"And, oh yeah," Mel said. "Sherry called me this morning to say thanks. Didn't say what for, just thanks. Something I should know?"

Harry smiled.

"You didn't do it again, Harry, did you? Tell me you didn't?" Mel said.

Harry's smile widened.

"Ah, you putz. That dick of yours is gonna get you fried one of these days. Mark my words," Mel said as his voice got louder, "gonna fry your ass…" Harry heard as the door closed behind him.

Mel was probably right but there are worse ways to go Harry thought to himself as he crossed the street and headed up to his apartment.

Chapter 57

When he had finished listening to the messages on his machine, Harry downloaded the past performances for the following day off the internet. He took the sheets and a cup of coffee out onto his deck to handicap the races he would be seeing with Mueller at the track the next day.

The Beatle's White Album was on the stereo and Harry was pretty sure some Emerson Lake and Palmer was to follow. Maybe their first Works album which just happens to be a Harry ELP fave.

So, what the fuck happened today, Harry thought to himself as he sat at the small plastic table he kept out on the deck. Why was Mueller back and why was he playing to Harry for no reason at all. And excuse me, but who the fuck was Mueller anyway. Mel's guy, but so what. Who was he really? I better find out. How—the track!

Maybe a long drawn out one, that that was a QAS none the less.

It was after eleven where Harry was and after twelve noon somewhere else in the world. Harry dumped his coffee over the side of the deck railing and went in and got himself a beer. Not a "Beer" like one of Danny Trundle's "Beers," but a real beer in the form of an icy cold bottle of Harp. He kept different beers around for different occasions and different guests—this seemed like a Harp occasion to Harry.

Back at his table, Harry began handicapping the races. When he was done he realized it was a mediocre card that probably wouldn't cost him much money. There wasn't anything close to an outstanding betting opportunity jumping off the pages to get excited about. Anyway, what Mueller was up to would dominate his attention and he didn't want to get distracted by winning or losing.

~ * ~

Ringing. More ringing. Where the hell was the ringing coming from and why wouldn't it stop. Stop the fucking ringing!

Harry woke and realized the ringing wouldn't stop unless he answered his cell phone. The cell phone that was in his jacket that he had hung on the back of one of the dining room chairs when he got home. He hustled in and grabbed the phone just as it stopped ringing.

"Shit," he said out loud.

Whoever called must have heard him because the apartment phone starting ringing right away.

He hit the speaker button he recently had installed and said, "Harry."

"No, it's not Harry," was the response he heard next.

"Not a question, I'm Harry."

Wiseass he thought.

"Then you must be the one I called. Harry Shorts is it?" was the next question.

"Yeah, that's me. Who's this?" Harry asked.

"I represent Mister Michael Broderick. He has requested a meeting with you and asked me to facilitate this meeting."

"That's what. I asked who?"

"Excuse me?"

"Who. I like to know who I'm speaking with when I'm speaking to them," Harry said.

"Oh, I see. My name is Harlon Weatherbay and I…"

"I know, you represent Mister Michael Broderick, Weatherby," Harry repeated before Weatherbay could finish his statement.

"It's Weatherbay, Mister Shorts. Not Weatherby. Weather-bay, like the body of water," he repeated again.

"Fine. You're a bay not a bee. I stand corrected. Now that we have that behind us, Weatherby, what is it Mister Broderick wants and why with me?" Harry asked.

"As you have been making inquiries about Mister Broderick and his family, Mister Broderick wishes to meet with you and personally provide whatever information you require," Weatherbay said.

How the fuck does Mikey Broderick know what I'm doing, Harry thought.

"Fine. When?" Harry asked.

"Mister Broderick will be in town Thursday and is free for lunch at noon if it suits your schedule," Weatherbay stated.

Weatherbay pronounced it as if it was spelled "chedual".

"Thursday's good by me," Harry told him.

"Jones shall be around to pick you up at your apartment promptly at 11:45 am," Weatherbay responded.

"Then 11:45 am it is," Harry agreed. "I'll put it on my "che-dual" immediately," Harry said as he signed off.

So, Mikey Broderick wants a meet with Harry Mickey Shorts. Just so happens Harry Mickey Shorts would like a meet with Mikey Broderick, among other Brodericks. If Harry Mickey Shorts was to be so lucky, maybe additional Brodericks will be in attendance come Thursday at noon. If not, then Harry Mickey Shorts will just have to make his own luck.

Harry walked back out to his deck whistling a fair version of "Sitting on the Dock of the (Weather)bay."

Chapter 59

"A vision in pink that would make sore eyes feel like a million bucks," is how Harry greeted Bunny Malone as he entered Mel's real estate office the following morning.

"Oh, Harry," she blushed.

"Ebil: you, my man, you look like withering shit," Harry threw in Mel's direction.

"Fuck-off, Harry. Leave me be and I'll ignore you and the rest of the world the best I can," Mel groaned.

Harry hunched his shoulders and looked at Bunny.

"Boss man went into the city last night to hang with some college fraternity brothers who flew in from Boston. Seems they were out a bit late and, from what I can gather, they were slightly less than coherent shall we say when the evening concluded," Bunny said.

"Blitzkrieg city there, Big Mel?" Harry asked.

"Let me repeat: fuck-off, Harry, and leave me alone."

"You got it big guy. I'm off Bunny but I'd love to see you if you're gonna be around toward the end of the day," Harry tried.

Mel looked up, grabbed his head and looked down again.

"Sorry, Harry. I'm going to see my mom tonight. Rain check?" she asked.

"For a vision in pink, all the rain checks in the world," Harry charmed.

"I'm gonna puke," Mel gagged and Harry ran for the door.

~ * ~

Harry was sitting in the back booth of the Manhasset Diner having breakfast and reading the USA Today sports pages. Two eggs over easy, bacon, white toast and coffee lay half-eaten in front of him.

The waitress dropped an identical order on the table across from Harry. Before he knew it Mueller was sliding in behind it.

"This is a case of deja-vu all over again, I believe," Harry said.

"Yeah, whatever makes you happy," Mueller said as he started in on his eggs. The Racing Form came up and Harry didn't see Mueller's face for the next ten minutes.

Harry ate and read the USA Today.

"Track," Mueller said without coming out from behind his paper.

"If you mean am I going to the race track with you as we had planned, the answer to that question is yes," Harry replied.

"Good," Mueller said, nothing more.

Mueller dropped a fiver on the table, got up and walked out the front door of the Manhasset Diner on Plandome Road. He stepped directly into a black town car that was waiting for him at the curb.

Harry Mickey Shorts, being a top-notch private investigator and thus sensing it was time to go, dropped a fiver on the table, got up, and followed Mueller out the front door of the Manhasset Diner on Plandome Road. He also stepped directly into the black town car that was waiting at the curb. Or so he assumed it was also waiting for him since he saw Mueller get into it.

"Track?" Harry asked when he was seated in the car.

"It's where the car is headed," Mueller answered.

"Then I guess the track it is," Harry followed up.

With that Mueller put his head back, closed his eyes, and promptly went to sleep. Harry assumed Mueller was sleeping since he didn't say another word until they arrived at the entrance to the track.

Harry's firm belief that Mueller was a weird fucking dude was being strengthened the more time he spent with him.

Without a word to Harry or the driver, Mueller opened the car door and was about to get out.

"You forgot your Racing Form," Harry said to his back.

"Done with it," he heard Mueller respond.

"Aren't you going to need it?" Harry asked.

Mueller turned and looked Harry right in the eyes, then said, "I know who's running," and turned toward the front gate.

"Thanks for the ride," Harry said to the driver. He grabbed his copy of the Form and jumped out to catch up with Mueller who was almost at the entrance to the park.

"And the fun just keeps on coming to the privileged few," he said to Mueller's back.

Chapter 60

Mueller was standing off to the right side of the entrance talking to a man in a jogging suit. A very big man in a jogging suit who seemed to be guarding a private entrance to the park.

Mueller flashed him a pass of some sort and had it put away faster than it came out.

"Him too," Mueller said to the very big man as Harry came up beside him.

"Right this way gentlemen," the very big man said as he stepped aside and opened the door for them. "Enjoy your day," he concluded

They went into an eight by ten room that had no windows and only one door. It opened automatically and Mueller stepped into what looked like an elevator.

Harry followed.

The elevator door eventually opened into a segregated portion of the clubhouse section on the upper floor of the track. Harry had been in the clubhouse before but this was different. The carpet was plush and the person that came over to greet Mueller was wearing a tux.

"Good to see you again, Mister Mueller," tux man said.

"Sidney," Mueller greeted him as well.

"It is a pleasure to have you here with us today, Mister Shorts," Sidney said to Harry with a slight bow.

"Thank you, Sidney," Harry responded.

"Come on," is all Mueller said as he headed for an open space that led to an outside seating area off the main room. Yeah, it was right on the finish line.

As instructed, Harry followed.

Mueller was leaning against the railing looking down on the early arriving crowd when Harry caught up with him.

Before Harry could get out one of the seventy-five or so questions he wanted to ask Mueller, Mueller turned to him and said, "Don't ask me shit. You got that, Shorts. Don't ask me how I got through security to get up here; don't ask where we are or who owns it; don't ask me why I have access to it. Don't ask me shit and we can have a nice peaceful day at the track."

With that he turned back toward the track and picked up the glass that had been waiting for him before he even got there.

"Touchy fuck, aren't we, Mueller," Harry said. "Okay, I'll play. We're here and I'll suck it up and attempt to enjoy the meager surroundings. Not what I'm used to when I go to the track, but…this glass mine?"

"I have mine, so that would make that one yours, wouldn't you think? You're supposed to be the private dick, aren't you?" Mueller asked.

Harry ignored the sarcasm Mueller was flinging in his direction and tasted "his" drink. Not surprised at all, the Absolut Gimlet was perfect. A bit early in the day for one, but it was in fact noon somewhere in the world.

~ * ~

At noon where they were, Sidney brought a platter of sandwiches and two pitchers. He placed them on a table along the terrace wall where Harry and Mueller were sitting. From the color, Harry surmised one was beer and the other probably lemonade.

"Eat," was all Mueller said after Sidney left.

Harry bent at the waist, and while shuffling over to the table, he muttered loud enough for only Mueller to hear, "I's be eating, masta. You's be seeing me eating right quickly now, masta. Be drinkin' da beer too if you's wants me's ta, masta."

"Enough, asshole. Shut the fuck up and get a sandwich. I have to see somebody, but I'll be back before the first post," Mueller said.

He picked up half a sandwich and left before Harry could respond.

"Come back whenever the fuck you please," Harry said to the place where Mueller had been standing. "Not like I have any say anyway," he continued spouting off to nobody.

Nice sandwich. Good beer. Good view. All was right with Harry's world…for the moment.

~ * ~

Harry spent time reviewing the handicapping he had already completed. He coupled it with the scratches (horses originally scheduled to run and withdrawn by their trainers) for the day and any changes to either jockeys or the amount of weight the horses would be carrying. That done, he was set for the day. Now he only had to follow the betting patterns for each race and make enough to retire.

Fat fucking chance.

I promised I would explain how betting works at the track, and with a little time on my hands before the first race, now might be the best chance for it. A fairly simple definition I once saw is paraphrased as follows:

Paramutual wagering is a system of cooperative wagering invented (c.1870) in France by Pierre Oller. According to the system, the holders of winning tickets divide the total amount of money bet on a race (the pool), after deductions for tax and racetrack expenses. The uniqueness of paramutual betting lies in the fact the gambling public itself determines the payoff odds (e.g., if many people have bet on the actual winner of a contest then the payoff will be low, simply because many winners will divide the pool). Paramutual wagering is the accepted betting procedure at major horse-racing tracks throughout the world…the modern paramutual system depends on high-speed electronic calculators, known as totalizators or tote boards, to record and display up-to-the-minute betting patterns.

Summarized, you, the betting public, wager money on the horses in the race and those that pick the winners share the total money bet on the race minus the track's cut. You can bet the horse you fancy to finish first, second or third (win, place or show) or bet "exotics" like daily-doubles, exactas or triples. Why don't we leave the exotics for another lesson and for now you can go bet on a horse to win, watch him lose, say shit-fuck, then tear up your ticket.

Works for me.

Chapter 61

Mueller strolled back into the private box just as the first race was about to go off. Harry had polished off several sandwiches and half the pitcher of beer waiting for the first race, and Mueller, to arrive.

"Bet?" Mueller said as he sat down next to Harry.

"Yeah, I did. Got the six horse to win and coupled him with the two and four in the second race in the daily double," Harry replied.

"The six?" Mueller said sounding very doubtful of Harry's selection.

"Yeah, the six," Harry confirmed. "You don't like the six? He just came off an extra eighth of a mile race and finished strong with dynamite speed numbers. Lost by a nose."

"The four," Mueller said.

"The four. Why the four?" Harry asked.

"Dropping in class and losing six pounds at the same distance he won at two races ago. Slightly lower speed number than the six on a day Secretariat would have run like a donkey."

Harry looked at his form, looked at Mueller, said, "Shit-fuck. You're probably right."

"But, I also bet the six," Mueller said. "Toss up."

As the race went off, Mueller got up and walked over to the table with the sandwiches. The horses were coming down the stretch by the time he sat back down, sandwich and beer in hand.

The six and the four battled neck and neck down the stretch and hit the wire at the same time. The photo-finish sign came up on the board and Harry sat back thinking he had lost to the four, Mueller's fucking four.

Mueller had barely looked up, continuing to munch on his sandwich while Harry jumped up and down screaming, "Get up six, get up you piece of shit six."

After what seemed like forever, the number six was moved up to the top of the board meaning Harry's horse had won. His ten dollar bet would pay off nicely. Calmly, Mueller reached in his pocket and pulled out two tickets, dropped one in the waste can next to his seat and handed the other ticket to Harry.

"Nice pick. Cash this for me when you do yours," Mueller said to Harry.

It was a one hundred dollar ticket to win on the six. Harry's fucking six.

~ * ~

Mueller was on his second sandwich when Harry returned to his seat. Flush with his own winnings, Harry handed Mueller the wad of cash the son-of-a-bitch had won.

Time to find out what was up.

"So, why are we here, Mueller?" Harry started.

"To watch the races," Mueller replied.

"No, why are we really here?" Harry said again.

Mueller finished the last bite of his sandwich, washed it down with a sip of beer, and then turned toward Harry.

"Why?" Mueller repeated. "Why? Because you needed some help. You needed help whether you wanted to admit it or not. I'm here to give it to you. Don't ask why and don't ask how I know what I know. I just do. I put the word out you wanted to meet with the Brodericks. That's done. Meet with Michael Broderick but watch your back at all times. You know the drill—don't trust anyone but yourself, and now me. You can trust me; trust me on that. Be careful because you are stepping into their world and they play for keeps, very serious keeps. Just do what you do and remember at all times to keep focused on what you came to do. Don't stray."

Mueller stood and drained the rest of his beer.

"I have to go. Stay and enjoy the rest of the card and ask Sidney for whatever you want. A car will be in the same place when you are ready to leave and take you back to Manhasset. We'll talk again soon, but don't look for me until I find you. Questions?"

Harry said nothing.

"Good. Bet out on the four in the fourth race and then play small the rest of the card. Nothing else worth losing much money on."

With that, Mueller turned and left.

While he digested what Mueller had just said to him, Harry missed the start of the second race. Good thing since his horses finished dead last in the race. The four horse in the fourth race was the third favorite and went off at odds of five to one. As Mueller suggested, Harry bet out on the four and wagered all his winnings from the first race plus some—a one hundred dollar bet to win on the four. If he won, he would be five hundred dollars richer.

After the sixth race, Harry decided to beat the rush home and headed out. He thanked Sidney for his service, tipped him generously, then went out the same way he came in. The car was waiting for him just as Mueller had said it would. As the car took off, Harry reached into his pocket and began recounting the six hundred and forty dollars he had won, mostly thanks to Mueller.

The big question was—who in the hell was Mueller anyway? Answer—I don't know. Solution—well shit, I don't have one. A Harry Mickey Shorts QAS not worth the time it took to state it.

Chapter 62

Harry was sitting at the table in his apartment reviewing everything he had on the Brodericks when the phone rang. He hit the speaker button so he could continue looking at the information before him while he took the call.

"Shorts," he said.

"Harry, its J'Orr. You got a minute?"

"Hey, J'Orr, how you been, man?" Harry answered.

"Good, Harry. I'm good. I wanted to run something by you if you got time."

"Sure, shoot," Harry said.

Harry was focusing his full attention on the call now.

"Do you remember Thomas, Mister Trundle's son? You met him when you were out here with us," J'Orr started.

"Sure, I remember him," Harry replied. "He okay?"

"Oh, yeah, he's fine. Nothing like that. He's working hard and keeping his nose clean," J'Orr told Harry.

"Good," Harry said.

"Anyway, do you remember the flashes Thomas said he saw up on the hill? He was the only one that saw them and we all kinda pushed it aside."

"Yeah, I remember, J'Orr. What about it?" Harry asked.

"Well, Thomas said he saw them again and I decided to find out if the kid was fuckin' with us or not. I had Stu put one of the hands up on a bluff overlooking the Rogers place where Thomas said he saw the flashes. Just to confirm it one way or the other," J'Orr told Harry.

"Makes sense," Harry said. "Find anything?"

"Stubbs, the hand Stu sent up to the bluff, he came down today and says he saw a guy ride up to the spot where Thomas saw the flashes and spend an hour or so laying on the ground looking down on the ranch. Didn't do nothing but lay there with what he thinks were binoculars and spied on the goings on down at Board Room Farms."

"You shitting me?" Harry said to J'Orr.

"No, Harry, god's honest truth. Thomas really did see something up there. It was a guy watching our spread. We're gonna send Stubbs up there again tomorrow to see if he comes back. Thought you might want to know is why I called," J'Orr said.

"Yeah, thanks, J'Orr. Don't know why the guy would be up there, but I sure'd like to know who sent him up there. Let me know if your guy sees him again, okay?" Harry asked.

"Sure thing, Harry. Want us to grab him and bring him down here if he comes back?" J'Orr asked.

"Nah, just keep an eye on him for now. I need to find out more about Rogers and who bought his spread. You can always get the guy later if we need to," Harry told J'Orr.

"You the man that knows, Harry. And by the way, Harry, Doc says to say hi," J'Orr said.

Harry was quiet for a second while he thought of Doc.

"Tell her I said hi right back. Good lady and I hope to see her again soon, but don't tell her that, J'Orr," Harry told him.

"Will do, Harry. Good talking to you and we'd welcome you back to the ranch any time."

They hung up and Harry thought of Doc some more. Hell of a woman is what he thought. Good times, good memories. Damn good memories. Gonna have to find a reason to head back out to Lee's Summit sometime soon he thought to himself.

Harry went back to the Broderick intel and soaked up everything his brain could hold. Maybe he could throw Rogers name into the conversation with Mikey Broderick and see what happens. Maybe he'd bite if he's involved in any way. Don't know till ya try.

Doc.

Definitely gonna have to find a reason to head back out to Lee's Summit some time very soon.

Chapter 63

There comes a time in every investigation when something that isn't expected or anticipated happens. A clue that breaks the case or at least points it in a new direction. A witness or piece of information materializes out of nowhere and falls in your lap.

That's what normally happens.

Unfortunately, it hadn't happened for Harry yet. He was waiting but nothing appeared to be sneaking over the horizon as far as he could see.

Gotta hope for the best.

~ * ~

On Thursday at 11:45 am, a car appeared in Harry's driveway just as Weatherbay had promised. Harry had been anticipating his meeting with Michael Broderick and was anxious to meet the "man" of the Broderick clan. If Broderick underlings were present, that would be gravy.

"Mister Shorts," the chauffer said as he opened the door for Harry.

"How are you, Jones?" Harry guessed.

"Very good, sir," Jones replied.

Good guess.

When Harry was comfy in the back of the car, Jones headed out onto George Street and took a left toward Plandome Road. Not knowing where the Brodericks lived, Harry sat back and enjoyed the ride.

Michael Broderick's house was smaller than Harry would have expected. It wasn't in one of the "hoity-toidier" sections of Manhasset. It looked like an average house, on an average block, in a section of Long Island that started at about $750,000 for something you'd want your mother-in-law to live in. Basic housing.

Jones opened the door and, as Harry got out, he was met by a tallish bloke with a shock of red hair that couldn't be missed. Harry guessed he was an Irish lad from the old country.

"Mister Shorts," Red brogued. "Mister Broderick is waiting for you in the den. Follow me," he said as he started up the path to the side of the house.

"Thanks, Red," Harry said to his back.

Red never looked back.

"This way, Mister Shorts," Red said as he opened a door in the rear of the house and stepped aside to let Harry go by.

"Thanks, Red," Harry said to his front this time.

Harry walked into a small mudroom and was met by another Irish fellow, this one much larger and older than Red. He took Harry's jacket and showed him the way.

Sans jacket, Harry followed him. The green sweater vest on the gent Harry was following had a Notre Dame insignia over the left breast and did a poor job of hiding the gun he was carrying on his left hip.

"Go Irish," Harry said softly hoping it might prevent him from getting shot later on if things went haywire.

"Mister Broderick is in here," he said as they approached an arched doorway that led to a fairly large family room.

As Harry entered the room, Michael Broderick put down the book he had been reading and rose from a wing backed arm chair to shake Harry's hand. He put out his hand, so Harry assumed it was to shake his own.

They shook hands and Broderick told Harry to take the other chair across from the one he was sitting back down in.

It must have been noon, because at that moment Red came into the room and placed a large glass of Guinness in front of each of them.

"To your health, Mister Shorts," Broderick toasted.

"And to yours," Harry reciprocated.

The Guinness was genuine and Harry assumed there must be a keg somewhere in the house. Guinness that good doesn't come out of a bottle or a can.

"This is delicious," Harry said.

"Thank you, Mister Shorts. My weakness but I restrain myself to only two glasses per day. I enjoy them both immensely."

"Call me Harry," Harry told him.

"Okay, Harry. I prefer Michael, but the tabloids seem to like Mikey for some reason which I haven't yet been able to decipher."

"Michael it is then if that is okay with you?" Harry said.

"Michael will be fine," he replied. "So, word has it you have some interest in the Brodericks, Harry. Is it me personally, my sons, or our business you have interest in?"

"I guess it would be all of the above, Michael. I don't know what I'm looking for, so I'm looking at everything I can find. I found the Brodericks among other people and things," Harry responded.

"And why are you looking if I may ask?" Broderick asked.

"I believe in the honest approach to life," Harry started. "I'm looking into something for a friend that involves a horse he owned, a horse that recently died. You and your stable have been connected with that horse and I'm following connections."

No obvious ticks or look of guilt came over Broderick. He seemed to be considering what Harry had just told him before he spoke again.

"You speak of Brian Boru, I presume?" Broderick queried.

"I do," Harry confirmed.

"And what has the tragic death of a fine animal got to do with me, my sons, or our business?" he asked.

"I don't know. That's why I'm looking. You look at things and you find things. Some good and some bad. The bad is what I'm looking for and I'll know it when I find it, if I find it."

"Come, let's have lunch," Broderick told Harry.

Chapter 64

Seated in the breakfast nook off the kitchen, Red brought Harry and Michael Broderick their lunch. Hot Reuben sandwiches with a side of potato salad filled the plates Red put down in front of them.

"Thank you, Patrick," Broderick said to Red.

"Looks great," Harry commented.

Patrick, not Red, he now knew.

"I like the taste of corned beef," Broderick started, "but I can't stand the rest of the fixings that go with it. I'm probably the only Irishman in the world who wouldn't give his right nut for a baked potato. A nice Reuben and potato salad I like, though. Coleslaw I like, too, but cabbage, no thanks. My father was the same way and it drove my mother crazy. Lucky for me, my wife isn't Irish..." he let drift into the air.

They started in on their lunch and Harry noticed the room emptied.

"They know to leave when I want to discuss business," Broderick said noticing that Harry noticed. "They aren't far, but they won't bother us unless it's necessary. People don't come to my house often and, those that do come to my house, they very rarely make it necessary," he finished with a healthy chunk of his Reuben ready to enter his mouth.

Harry started on his sandwich and found it to be delicious. They ate in silence for a time and Patrick brought them each a glass of beer that tasted like Harp to Harry. Michael Broderick obviously didn't want for much from what Harry could see.

With half his sandwich gone, Broderick said, "Randle Trundle is a good man and he and I have known each other, and butted heads, for what seems like forever. We have done some business together both here in the states and abroad. You couldn't know this, but my interests run far beyond the racing business that you can readily see. He's a tough son-of-a-bitch, but fair. I like him. His brother, that Danny prick, him I don't like."

He stopped there, started eating his sandwich again and then took a long drink of his beer.

"The racing business has been good to the Brodericks, Harry, and we have been good for the racing business. We may not be the top stable out there, but we can compete with any of them domestically. We're getting stronger across the sea every day. To do that you need horses, Harry. Good, quality horses; no, excellent, quality horses that you train well and place in the right spots at the right time."

"You have been very successful," Harry interjected.

Michael laughed and ate some more of his sandwich.

"I'm not part of today's success, Harry. I built our business as my father did before me, but I have very little to do with the day-to-day operations now. My sons are in control and don't always conduct themselves as I would like; but the business thrives and they have become good horsemen. Matt is still learning and he's very impatient, but he's got the sense and you can't teach that," Michael said. "Pauly is, well, Pauly is Pauly."

They finished their lunch and Michael sat back in his chair. Glass in hand, he said, "You have questions, Harry. Ask your questions. I'm going to ask my man to sit in. Weatherbay runs my affairs these days and knows some things even I don't know. I'm sixty-eight years old and I like to hunt and fish up in Maine. I watch the boys and how the business is doing but I don't interfere."

As if on cue, Harlon Weatherbay came into the room and took a seat at the table.

"Thanks for coming, Harlon. Mister Shorts and I have had a very enjoyable lunch and a pleasant talk. Because of my respect for M. Randle Trundle and Board Room Farms, I have offered him the opportunity to ask some questions and I thought you might be of some assistance with it."

A guy that could have been Patrick's twin, Red Junior, brought another round of beers and a cup of tea for Weatherbay.

Michael Broderick stood and said, "Excuse me for a minute before we begin. I have to piss."

He left and since Harry had to go as well, he did.

Chapter 65

Everyone properly relieved, they sat back down at the table.

"What can we answer for you, Mister Shorts," Harlon asked taking the lead.

"Let's try this. How about if I throw out some names, or subjects, and you answer with the first thing that comes to mind? That okay with you?"

Weatherbay was about to protest when Broderick said, "Shoot, Harry."

No reason to beat around the bushes, so Harry said, "Brian Boru."

"Brian Boru was our stable's main breeding source and will be sorely missed. I sent my personal condolences to Randle when I heard the news and promised our continued business when they replace him," Broderick said and seemed to mean every word of it.

"Pauly Broderick."

"My eldest son Paul runs the business now from California. He has been very successful with his string of horses and the overall stable has prospered under his guidance."

Broderick hesitated a beat as if measuring his words very carefully.

"Paul is and always was a free spirit, Harry. I'm sure you are well aware of his carryings-on and I can't say I approve of everything he is reported to have done. But, and mind this very carefully, he is the family business head right now and runs it with an iron fist. If there has been any wrong doing of a major proportion and Paul doesn't know about it, he may cease to run "my" business. And believe me, Harry, it still is "my" business."

"Matt."

"My youngest son Matthew is strong willed and full of himself. His success on the track with his modest string of horses has surprised some in the business, but not me. He has his grandfather's eye for a horse and instinctively knows what the horse needs and how to give it to him. He gets everything from every horse he has ever had. It's a gift few people have, Harry.

"On the other side, he is young. He is young and sometimes shows his youth in ways that I don't begin to understand. He hasn't fucked up to the extent it wasn't able to be fixed but, of my sons, he is the one that worries me. As was the case with his grandfather, his patience other than with his horses is sorely lacking."

"Micheal," Harlon began to interrupt.

Broderick looked at Weatherbay and Harlon said no more.

Prompted to continue, Harry said, "Davey Boy McGarry."

"I know David from the old country, Harry. Bad kid turned around in the public eye. He made himself into a fair horseman and an enterprising businessman."

Strange choice of words Harry thought.

"Mister McGarry's operations are far reaching and we come across him and his people fairly often in our dealings," Harlon contributed.

What the fuck does that mean Harry thought.

Broderick saw the doubt in Harry's face and said, "What Harlon is trying to say, Harry, is Davey Boy, as you call him, chooses to butt heads with us straight on and expects to supplant us here in the US while continuing his dominance in Europe."

"Will he?" Harry asked.

Weatherbay opened his mouth, saw Broderick look his way, and promptly closed his mouth without uttering a word.

"David and I don't see eye-to-eye on many things, Harry. When he crosses a line, I'll deal with him and his ways. Until now, he is on the other side of that line."

"Harry Mickey Shorts?" Harry said.

Broderick looked at Weatherbay and said, "Harlon, would you please inform Patrick that Mister Shorts and I would like another Harp. Then leave us for ten minutes to finish our conversation. You and I can conduct our business when Mister Shorts is gone."

"I'm sure I can be of continued assistance here, Michael," Weatherbay said in response.

"I said get us some beers and leave," Broderick scolded Weatherbay into leaving.

Weatherbay closed his folder and gave out the slightest hint of a "huff" before he rose and left the room.

Instantly, Patrick had two beers on the table in front of Harry and Broderick. A plate of Irish Soda Bread was placed in the middle of the table as well.

"Irish Soda Bread," Broderick said to Harry. "Put enough butter on it and it's almost edible."

An older guy stuck his head in the doorway and Broderick excused himself and left the room.

Harry tried the soda bread and agreed that "enough" butter might possibly make it edible.

Chapter 66

"Harry Mickey Shorts?" Harry repeated when Broderick was again seated across from him.

"You are an interesting young man, Mister Shorts, Harry. The fact you are actually sitting in my house sharing a beer with me is amazing of and by itself. It should also indicate to you the power of M. Randle Trundle and the respect he commands."

"You are preaching to the choir where Randle Trundle is concerned," Harry told him. "And thank you for allowing me into your home."

"Let's move on," Broderick said. "You have led a fairly full life for a man your age. And you are very good at what you do my sources tell me. But don't overstep your bounds, son. Don't tread in my family business and don't interject yourself into my family's personal lives unless you are prepared to pay the piper should he come whistling at your door. Do I make myself clear, Harry?"

"Crystal clear, Michael," Harry replied. "But also know that I've been warned before and I have to do my job or I'm out of the business. If someone or something in your family is dirty, I'm not backing down from you or anyone else. Your sources should have informed you of that or you need new sources," Harry concluded.

"They did and I respect that in a man, Harry. Just be dead sure before you come knocking at my family door. And one more thing, Harry, if there is dirt to be swept up involving my family, please allow me the opportunity to do the sweeping. I promise you it will be dealt with in the most extreme manner possible," Broderick said with emphasis.

"Fair enough," Harry replied.

"Any other questions?" Broderick asked.

"Rogers?" Harry asked.

Michael Broderick leaned back in his chair and thought on that one. He thought for a long time Harry felt.

"There was a Rogers with a ranch for sale near Board Room Farms' spread I believe I heard. If memory serves me, Harlon looked at it for us and took Matt with him, I believe. We turned down the opportunity to bid on it. Why do you ask?" he finished.

"Someone bought it and it remains unoccupied," Harry said.

"And?" Broderick asked.

"And nothing at this moment," Harry said. "I was just asking to see if the name meant anything else to you in any other way."

"No, can't say that it does."

If Broderick was playing straight with Harry, he wasn't part of the "flash" business going on at the old Rogers place. Since he had no reason to believe Broderick was lying to him about it, Harry would have to look elsewhere to find whoever was behind it.

"Thank you for your hospitality," Harry said. "One other question if I may?"

"Last one."

"I had the unfortunate occasion to run head first into a very large guy who knocked me into queersville a little while ago. He was big and spoke with a distinctive voice that pointed toward Irish descent. He yours by any chance?" Harry asked.

"Harry, if one of my people pays you a visit, we won't be talking again after that. You get my drift?" he asked.

"Clear as day," Harry answered.

"But, because I liked talking to you, I'll ask around about it. Give Harlon one of your cards and I'll be in touch should I hear anything."

Harry rose and shook Michael Broderick's hand. He again thanked him for his hospitality and followed Patrick out the back door the same way he entered Michael Broderick's house. Jones was waiting at the curb to open the door to the waiting car for him.

Harry wasn't sure what he had accomplished by his visit to Michael Broderick's house. If there was something dirty in the Broderick world, Michael Broderick either wasn't aware of it, or he wasn't giving it away.

A HMS QAS was lurking in the shadows. If not the Broderick's, then who? Look at the remaining prominent player in the equation. Time to acquaint himself with Davey Boy McGarry.

Chapter 67

"Harry," was what he heard when he finally answered the phone that had been ringing somewhere in his bedroom. He found it on the floor next to yesterday's clothes.

The alarm clock said 7:20.

"Who the hell," he thought before he recognized the melodious voice of Ms. Timmons, lovely assistant to M. Randle Trundle. There must be a good reason for waking him at 7:20 in the morning.

"Ms. Timmons," he finally got out.

"Morning, Harry. I didn't wake you, did I?" she asked.

"Of course not, Ms. Timmons. I've already had breakfast, did the wash and reorganized my underwear drawer. I've been meaning to do that for awhile now. Time is money you know and I just hate to sleep past seven in the morning," Harry answered with just the slightest hint of sarcasm in his voice.

"The world doesn't revolve around Harry Shorts time, Harry. Mister Trundle would like to see you. In fact, both Trundles will be present. Can you make lunch today?" she asked.

"I can make lunch but if the Trundles are having lunch and would like my presence, I'm there."

"You are a funny one, Harry. Charles will pick you up at eleven-thirty if you can finish with your drawers by then," she said.

"You could help me with my drawers…" Harry started to respond before he realized, as usual, he was speaking to dead air.

The phone was hardly back on the receiver when it rang again.

"Yello," Harry sing-songed into the phone.

"Is it still attached?"

Two second delay, then recognition.

"Yes it is, but just barely."

"It was fun," the voice said.

"Fun times three," Harry responded.

"They know," she replied.

"I know. So?" he asked.

"So, if I had balls, I would say I've gotten my balls busted unmercifully by both of them."

"Haven't heard a word," Harry said.

"Really?" she asked.

"Well, other than getting caught as I tried to sneak up the driveway; no, not another word."

"Was it worth it?" she asked.

"It was fun, especially since we hadn't planned it and it just happened."

"Some days I wish it had turned out differently. Some days I hate your fucking guts for how it did. Most days, well, most days are just days. You know what I'm trying to say?"

"Yes, I do. By the way, who is this?"

"Fuck you, Harry," she laughed.

"You did and quite well I might add," he said.

She laughed again.

"And I'm paying for it," she said. "But it was worth it, Harry. Thank you."

"Yes, it was. But really, who is this?"

"Why do I...?" Sherry started.

"Three times is why," Harry finished.

"Yeah. Now, who is this?" she said as she hung up the phone.

Ms. Timmons. Sherry. I gotta find somebody that won't hang up on me first Harry said to himself and laughed.

Chapter 68

"Charlie, you look damn good, man," Harry said as he came out of his apartment and rounded the corner.

Charlie was the personal chauffeur to M. Randle Trundle. He was sent to get Harry whenever he wasn't chauffeuring Randle around. Charlie was partial to Harry from transporting him around on a prior case Harry had worked for Trundle.

"Thanks, Harry. Feeling pretty good, too," he replied.

"The grandkids?" Harry asked.

"They're great, Harry. Thanks for asking. The wife spent a week with them last month and she says they're growing like weeds. I gotta get down there soon before they grow up without me seeing much of it."

"I hear ya, kiddo," Harry commiserated.

"Jump in, Harry. There's some traffic on the Long Island Expressway and I don't want to get you to lunch late."

"Then let's scoot," Harry told him.

"Your neighbor said to say hi by the way, Harry," Charlie said as he started down the driveway. "Haven't seen her in a while, but the daughter's turning out mighty fine," he continued.

"You hound dog," Harry said.

"Just looking and remarking is all, Harry. Don't figure I have to tell you though, do I, Harry?"

"Well, now that you mention it, Charlie, I may have noticed her growing up some recently."

Charlie looked in the rear view mirror at Harry and said, "And I'm the dog, Harry?"

They both had a good laugh together as Charlie turned onto Shelter Rock Road and headed for the L.I. Expressway.

~ * ~

Ms. Timmons met Harry at the entrance to the Trundle building and hustled him toward the private elevator that went directly to the executive dining rooms.

"Hey, slow down and wait for me," Harry said to her back.

He was admiring all of her back as she hustled in front of him. Those long legs pumping, ass swaying left and right, she made for a pretty entertaining sight if you had to follow behind someone.

He caught her as the elevator door opened and she stepped inside. She inserted her pass key in the panel and the doors closed.

"Why such a hurry?" he asked.

"Mister Trundle has a plane to catch and doesn't want to have to rush through lunch. He expected you here fifteen minutes ago."

"Make sure he doesn't go blaming Charles for that. The Expressway was a bitch and a truck broke down two blocks from here blocking the street. We had to go around and it added a good five minutes to the ride."

"I'll make sure Mister Trundle knows," she said.

"You look kinda cute when you're flustered," Harry told Ms. Timmons showcasing his patented smile as he did.

She looked at him and shook her head.

"And you know I love that little head shake you do. Sexy," he said.

She started to shake her head, caught herself and stopped.

"I am not flustered," she told him, head perfectly straight. "I'm trying to keep Mister Trundle on schedule and deal with his brother as well."

"Oh Danny boy," Harry sang.

"Don't, Harry," Timmons told him. "He's tough enough to deal with without you adding to the, to the, to the …shit, I don't know what," she finished.

"See, flustered," Harry smirked.

Timmons again started to shake her head, caught herself as the elevator doors opened.

"Walk this way, Harry," she said.

"You know I can't walk like you, Ms. Timmons. Love to watch you do it, but I can't duplicate it, no way, no how," he said knowing it would annoy the shit out of her.

She stopped, turned, and was about to say something when a voice from an open doorway saved her the trouble.

"Harry, come on in here and let's put the feed bag on. My ass is plain starving."

One Danny Trundle, brother of the distinguished M. Randle Trundle, had spoken.

"Ms. Timmons," Harry was about to say when he realized she was already gone. He was sorry he had missed her walking away from him.

Chapter 69

"Shake a leg there, Harry. R's got a plane to catch and I got me a big ol' lunch to eat. Chef up here makes a damn fine Chateau Briandie and I mean to get me one," Danny said as only Danny could.

Reluctantly, Harry headed for the door from which Danny was beckoning him. As he got to the door, a friendly voice brightened up things immeasurably.

"Please do come in, Harry," M. Randle Trundle said from inside the room.

Harry entered and was surprised by the room's simplicity. Only one window without a particularly interesting view and minimal artwork to speak of. Two tables were spaced about five feet apart in the room making it seem somewhat crowded. White tablecloth, plain china, and a waiter in a white shirt and tie—no tuxedo as Harry would have expected.

Randle sensed Harry's once over of the surroundings.

"We don't usually entertain corporately in this particular room, Harry. I use it strictly for myself and when I have friends in to visit for a casual lunch. Danny and I also eat here when he is in town."

Harry surmised it was the cheap stuff for Danny when Randle had to have a meal with him. He'd have to make it a point to get to the bottom of the Randle and Danny relationship next time he was alone with Randle.

"This is perfect," Harry lied to put Randle at ease.

"Gimme a martuni," Danny was telling the waiter while Harry and Randle exchanged their usual hellos. "Four olives on one of those little spear things, too," he continued.

"A *martuni* for Mister Trundle," the waiter repeated emphasizing the mispronounced "u" in martuni quite clearly for all to hear.

"Sir," the waiter asked Randle.

"Harry, what would you care for?" Randle asked Harry politely while scowling at Danny.

"A Paulie Girl would be great if you have one," Harry said to the waiter.

"Very good, sir, excellent choice," the waiter replied.

"Make it two," Randle told the waiter who promptly left.

"I have already ordered the Chateaubriand for Danny to give Marcel the necessary time to prepare it properly, so we can order whenever you are ready, Harry."

"Ms. Timmons said you have to catch a plane, so we can order immediately if you need," Harry replied.

"It's a plane, Harry. There are plenty of planes and I'll use the corporate jet if need be. With my current schedule I don't get the opportunity to indulge in what I want as opposed to what I need these days. I want to spend time with you right now and I will do so if I choose," Randle said with authority.

"What about me?" Danny rudely interrupted.

Randle closed his eyes, waited a blip, and then turned toward his brother.

"Danny, I was speaking to Harry. You, in case you have momentarily forgotten, are traveling with me when lunch is concluded. Did you forget that fact?" he asked Danny as if speaking to a forgetful child.

"Oh, yeah," Danny replied weakly. "But you don't always do…ah, we never…oh, never mind, R," Danny sputtered.

The waiter mercifully brought their drinks and the interaction between Randle and Danny subsided.

Having savored a sip of his St. Paulie Girl, Randle asked Harry, "What would you like for lunch, Harry. Marcel is quite a good chef and can prepare anything you would like."

"That's an intriguing offer, Randal. As Danny is having a somewhat heavy meal, how about a small Rib Eye steak, maybe a twelve ouncer. Medium would be great. Onion rings and some glazed carrots?" Harry said as if it was a question.

"That would be fine, sir," the waiter replied as if it was a normal lunch order on a normal day.

"I'll have the baked scrod, slightly singed as I like it, Paul. Mixed green salad and I think I'll also have some of those onion rings Harry is having," Randle told the waiter. "They sound too good to pass up. Ketchup, Harry?"

"Ketchup for the onion rings and some Worcestershire Sauce for the steak, please," Harry responded.

"Thank you, gentlemen," the waiter said and he was gone.

"To our health," Randle toasted as he lifted his glass.

"Down the old hatcheroo," Danny added as he proceeded to drain the remains of his martini.

Randle sipped his beer and shook his head.

Chapter 70

The Rib Eye was the best piece of meat Harry had ever tasted and cooked to perfection. Crispy onion rings were the size of a baseball donut. The glazing on the carrots had a hint of something extra added. Harry would have to get Randle to find out what Marcel had used to bring out the flavor more than he had ever experienced with plain glazed carrots.

All was going perfect until...

"So, what the fuck you been doing on our dime, Harry?" Danny blurted out, his mouth stuffed with food.

"I've asked you not to speak with food in your mouth before, Danny. Our guests don't, so why don't you try to reciprocate."

Danny was about to answer but stopped realizing at the last second he still had a mouthful of food.

He swallowed and then said he forgot what he was going to say.

"Harry, why don't you tell Danny and I what you have been doing since we last saw you. Catch us up with the Reader's Digest version, as you say, if you can."

Harry wiped his mouth with the linen napkin from his lap and started catching them up. Never knowing what Randle didn't know, which was probably nothing, and for Danny's benefit, Harry summarized his investigation from the start. He told them of his reacquaintance with Mueller and subsequent trip to the track, his Lee's Summit trip and his research on the Brodericks and Davey Boy McGarry. He then finished with his visit to Michael Broderick's home.

By the time Harry was done, Danny was cleaning his teeth with a tooth pick. Randle hadn't touched his food the entire time Harry spoke. If Harry wasn't eating, he would wait too. When Harry was done, Randle gestured for Paul the waiter to reheat their remaining food so Harry could continue enjoying his meal properly. No mention of him enjoying his meal as well.

"Nice tale, buddy boy. Where's the punch line?" Danny asked.

"Punch line?" Harry asked not understanding where Danny was going.

"Punch line. Finish to the what you found," Danny said. "What croaked the horse like you was supposed to find out?" Danny finished.

If he was originally distraught, he didn't sound overly distraught now Harry thought.

"The investigation is ongoing, Danny," Randle interjected on Harry's behalf.

"Meaning you ain't got shit, right hot-shot?" Danny threw at Harry.

"The investigation is ongoing as your brother has just correctly told you, Danny. Facts lead you to clues that show you the who, what, when and how of the circumstances surrounding the events in question," Harry told him.

Blank stare from Danny meant what Harry had just said had sailed far above Danny's head.

"If I may, Danny," Randle said to attempt to bring the conversation back to a level of intelligence somewhere above the moron stage.

"Michael Broderick is a shrewd man, Harry. People don't get into his business very easily, never mind into his house. He took away as much as he gave from your visit, you can bet on it."

"Thank you for that by the way," Harry said to Randle as a test.

"I have no idea what you are talking about, Harry."

Harry passed.

Paul brought their food back in and a plate of éclairs for Danny to amuse himself as Harry and Randle finished their lunch. By the time they had finished, Danny had cleaned off the plate of éclairs.

Danny had finally managed to royally piss off Harry.

~ * ~

Randle and Danny got into the waiting car in the underground garage with Charles nowhere in sight. Harry wished them a good flight and walked over to the other waiting car that would take him back to Manhasset.

"Afternoon, Harry," Charles said as he stepped out of the front seat to open the car door for him.

"Hey, Charlie. Why aren't you driving the Trundles to the airport," Harry asked.

"Mister Trundle asked me if I would drive you back home this afternoon, Harry. He said if you had to spend that much time with Danny you deserved a friendly face for the ride home."

"Well I'll be," Harry replied.

"The Girls are cooling in the back seat waiting for you, Harry. Pop one and I'll have you home in no time," Charlie told him.

Harry settled in, popped the cap off a St. Paulie Girl, and they were on their way.

Chapter 71

"Welcome back to Board Room Farms. It is a pleasure to see you again, Mister Trundle. Danny," J'Orr said in greeting as they exited their car.

"J'Orr, it's been much too long," Randle told him as they shook hands as only true friends would.

"How was your flight?" J'Orr asked.

"Flight sucked," Danny answered first. "Fucking people crowding all over you and you can't get a drink for shit on regular planes. Company plane was just sitting there…" he trailed off.

J'Orr seemed to shrug off Danny's comments and turned back toward Randle.

"The flight was smooth and right on time," Randle said. "I prefer to travel commercially every so often to remind myself of where I've been and where we all are in life."

J'Orr looked at Randle and, while not fully understanding where he was coming from, understood where he was trying to go.

"Should of taken the jet," Danny groused again to nobody that was listening.

~ * ~

J'Orr, Randle, Danny and Stu were seated in the small conference room that adjoined J'Orr's office. Stu had just finished running down the condition of the ranch grounds and the completion of the new storage facility.

"That's good, Stu," Randle said. "The place continues to be in good hands and we appreciate your efforts and the hands under you."

"Thank you, Mister Trundle," Stu told him.

"So, J'Orr, let's get to the meat of why we are here. What's the news on our new addition to the stable?" Randle asked.

Danny got up and got himself another beer failing to offer to get anyone else a refill.

"Before you start, J'Orr, I'm going to have another long neck. Can I get you guys one?" Randle asked J'Orr and Stu.

Danny remained clueless.

"Sit, Mister Trundle. I'll get us some beers and J'Orr can start telling you and Danny about the stable's newest addition," Stu said.

"Thanks, Stu. That's very nice of you to offer," Randle said as he looked directly at his brother.

Danny continued to remain clueless.

As if on cue, the door opened and Doc entered the room.

"Kate," Randle said as he jumped from his chair and went around the table to give her a warm hug.

"Mister Trundle," Doc said returning the hug earnestly.

"It's Randle, Kate. When are you going to learn to stop with the "Mister" business and call me Randle?" he said.

"I forget, Mister Tru...I mean Randle. It's good to see you again," Doc said.

"Hi there, Doc," Danny said to her smiling broadly as he spoke.

"Danny," she responded coldly.

Randle noticed but still didn't know why. It had been that way for some time now.

When they were all seated, J'Orr continued.

"The stable's new star arrived yesterday and showed no ill effects from the trip. The driver told me it took them about ten hours, clear sailing all the way. He's taken to his new stall like he's been living there all his life. A beautiful animal he is, Randle."

"What do you think, Kate?" Randle asked.

"As J'Orr said, he came through the trip just fine. I checked him out from top to bottom and had the vet from the hospital do the same. He's as fit as he looks and he looks great!" she said excitedly.

"Well then, looks like we are in business again," Randle said. "Let's put a full page spread in the Racing Form announcing our new arrival and welcoming all comers. We can pick and choose once the requests start coming in. What's the waiting list look like right now, J'Orr?" he asked.

"When word got out who we had coming to Board Room Farms, the phone rang off the hook. We probably have six months worth of stud cover services already lined up and the phone still hasn't stopped ringing," J'Orr told the group.

"That's great news, but let's advertise anyway," Randle said. "Doesn't hurt to trumpet our barn's power in the industry and resecure our spot as the number one breeding stable in the United States." Randle beamed at the group.

~ * ~

The meeting broke up and the group headed out in different directions to get on with the business of running a thriving horse farm. Randle and J'Orr hung back to "handle a few things" as he said to J'Orr when the meeting ended.

Doc was headed for the door when she sensed a presence behind her.

"Hey, sweet cheeks, what's your hurry?" Danny said to her back.

Doc whirled and jumped up in Danny's face so quickly he almost fell over backwards.

"Danny, I told you the last time you said something of that nature to me, if you ever tried it again, I'd rip your tongue out and shove it up your ass. Say one more word, any word, and it will be your last word ever spoken."

Danny could see the fury in her eyes.

"Hey, I'm only playin' with ya here, Doc. Just having a little fun," Danny said trying to sound apologetic

It didn't sound apologetic to Doc, and it didn't work.

Doc glared at him, then turned and left the building.

"Bitch," Danny said as he flipped her the bird.

Luckily for him she was already out of earshot and couldn't hear him, or see what he did.

Randle was standing in the doorway to the conference room. The door was open barely an inch, but far enough for him to catch the exchange between Doc and his brother.

Now he knew, and he also knew he'd have to do something about it. One way or another, it was finally time to deal with Danny, even if he was the President of one of his corporation's entities and his younger brother.

Chapter 72

"Two weeks from Saturday," Max was saying to his father over the phone. "Two weeks from this past Saturday is our day and you better not get caught sneaking down some driveway and getting your ass thrown in jail," Max finished with a hearty laugh. "Or shot," he concluded.

"You think you're pretty funny you little runt?" Harry retorted.

"I am what I am," Max replied and laughed even harder.

"If you don't watch your butt, you're gonna get a swift boot up your ass is what you am," Harry said as he laughed along with him.

"You cool for then?" Max asked.

"Yeah, all's cool," Harry told him.

"Mom said to say hi," he let hang in the air.

Harry hesitated, and then he said, "Tell her I said hi right back."

Max hesitated himself and then he said, "Gotta split," and he was gone.

~ * ~

Harry often went over the facts of a case in his mind until numbness set in. He would go over and over the facts as he knew them trying to wiggle some sense out of them. When he was done, he started the process over again.

When he found himself stymied, it did him good to write down everything he knew about the case and try and look at it from every angle. Harry looked down at the pad of paper sitting on his table, the words looking familiar but not telling Harry anything. They weren't singing a song or conjuring up a story. Words will talk to Harry when he gets a revelation during a case. They do a little dance and jump up off the page.

No Mexican Jumping Words, no singing, no storytelling.

Here's what he had written:

Initial Connection—M. Randle Trundle calls Harry and tells him during a private meeting he believes a horse (Brian Boru) was killed. He wants Harry to find out if his feeling is right.

Pieces to the Puzzle—not necessarily in any order:

• EBIL hooks him up with a local horse connection and Harry meets him for breakfast

- Harry leaves the meeting and gets knocked into yesterday by a big burly Irish bloke
- The local connection Harry had just met disappears
- Harry begins to look at two prominent racing stables—the Brodericks and Davey Boy McGarry
- Harry makes a trip to Board Room Farms in Lee's Summit, Missouri
- The personal groom to Brian Boru is hit by a truck
- The top bug rider for Board Room Farms is kicked off the premises
- There's something going on at the spread next to BRF that belonged to a guy named Rogers
- A computer generated investigation of both stables in question is undertaken; large amounts of information are found and printed
- Harry meets with Michael Broderick after the local source (Mueller) puts word out on the street Harry would like to meet with him
- Harry meets with Randle and Danny Trundle on two separate occasions showing two totally distinct individuals
- As an aside, Sherry spent some time with Matt Broderick

All of which leads Harry to the undesirable position of knowing jack shit where this case was going. Reading it fifty times wouldn't give him any more insight—he must know more than he's seeing on the piece of paper in front of him. At least that's what he is telling himself at that very moment.

There are clues staring him in the face and he can't see them. At least there should be clues staring him in the face. He's followed the same procedure he always uses and it's proven to be rock solid in the past.

Where did he go wrong?

What's he missing?

Is it there for him to see?

Why is he asking himself all these questions?

When in doubt—drink heavily has worked at this stage in an investigation in the past. So, he walked into the kitchen, opened the fridge, and extracted a bottle of Sierra Nevada Pale Ale that was left over from past sessions like this one. Just because one chooses to move on to another beer of choice doesn't mean the old one should go forgotten.

Let's see, one more time, point one...

Chapter 73

When one is awoken the morning after a "When in doubt—drink heavily" work related incident, one is normally not overly pleased. Especially when that wakeup call comes at seven-fifteen in the morning.

"Fuck do you want?" was what Harry got out when he finally engaged the phone to his ear.

"Not right now, Harry," Ms. Timmons responded merrily.

Silence.

"Huh?" was all Harry could get out. It probably would have helped if he knew who he was speaking to.

"I do not want Fuck at this moment, Harry. You did ask me the question," Ms. Timmons explained.

"You playing with me, Timmons?" Harry replied as he started to regain consciousness slowly.

"Harry, if I had said I wanted Fuck, I would also probably be playing with you as well, wouldn't I?"

Harry had to let that sink in for a second, then said, "How about you tell me why you called, Ms. Timmons. I'll listen and continue to clear the cobwebs from my brain while you talk."

"That will work just fine, Harry. Mister Trundle would like you to join him for the Yankees vs. Kansas City Royals game tonight in Kansas City. Charles will be there to get you at eleven and you will fly out on the corporate jet. Can you get yourself together by then, or should I tell Mister Trundle we were too busy playing word games for you to make the flight?"

His head now semi-clear, Harry said, "Word games?"

"Never mind, Harry. Shall I tell Mister Trundle you will be joining him and J'Orr for the game tonight? Oh, Mister Trundle's brother Danny will also be attending the game as well," she finished.

"Um, of course I'll be there," Harry told Ms. Timmons. "It's a Yankee game. Is there some reason other than the sheer joy of my company that compels him to invite me to join him to watch the Yankees annihilate the K.C. Royals?"

"Sheer joy, Harry? That remains to be seen," Timmons replied.

"And if you would come to your senses and realize the inevitable, the sheer joy could be all yours as well," Harry told her.

Ignoring his last comment, Ms. Timmons said, "I take it your answer is affirmative and Charles will be there at eleven as I previously stated."

"What about the sheer joy…" Harry was starting to say.

Dead air. How the hell does she manage to do that every damn time.

~ * ~

Sufficiently humanized après the three S's, a piece of toast with a slice of American cheese and strawberry jam in his tummy, Harry was ready at eleven for Charles' arrival.

That "piece of toast with a slice of American cheese and strawberry jam" is another Harry fave you should try. No chips on this one though.

"Charlie, good to see you so soon. Didn't think I'd spy you again for awhile," Harry said to Charles as he got out of the car to open the door for Harry.

"Always good to see you, Harry," Charles replied with a broad smile. "Let me have your bag and I'll put it in the trunk."

"Don't trouble yourself, Charlie. I'll toss it in the back here with me to make it easier to hop out when we get to Teterboro. I assume we are headed to Teterboro?" Harry asked.

"Teterboro it is, Harry. Coffee is on the arm rest for you plus the papers you like. Can I get you anything else for the trip?" Charlie asked.

"Charlie, you're the best. This should keep me for now. Let's hit it," Harry said.

As Harry was about to get in the car, his neighbor Sandy called out to him.

"Hey, Harry, you off somewhere?"

She's a good one, Harry thought, *but not the brightest bulb at all times.*

Even Charlie gave Harry a look after her comment.

"Yes, Sandy, I'm taking a quick trip. Be back in a few days, I think," Harry told her. That's why I'm getting into the limo he didn't say to her.

"Oh, my kid is out of town for a few days and I was hoping to stop by and see you," she said with that look she gets when she wants Harry to bang her brains out.

Charlie had seen that look before and, from the look on his face, Harry had the feeling Charlie was wishing Harry would drive himself to the airport so he could "accommodate" the lady.

Charlie caught Harry's eye and sheepishly ducked into the driver's seat.

"Sorry, Sandy. You know I'd love nothing more, but it's business. I'll call you when I get back and maybe you can rustle up one of those lasagnas we've enjoyed together. I'll handle dessert if you know what I mean," he finished.

It almost looked like Sandy blushed a bit.

"That's cool, Harry. Give me a day's notice and I'll be ready," Sandy said.

"I'm sure you will, Sandy, I'm sure you will," Harry replied.

With that comment Harry was sure she did blush more than a bit.

"Hit it Charles, you old hound dog, you. The quicker I get to K.C. and back, the quicker I get lasagna and Sandy for dessert," Harry said with a smile.

"I'm flying, Harry. And I'd be in a hurry if it were me, too," he said with a smile of his own.

Chapter 74

The jet touched down at a secure private airport outside of Kansas City. Harry later found out it was built by a consortium of wealthy executives from the K.C. area specifically for their use.

Pretty cool Harry thought.

The limo was waiting when Harry disembarked and whisked him out of the airport without anyone asking any questions. It was as if he was never there. He couldn't see it, but there was no doubt in his mind security was tighter than an eighteen year old virgin.

The plane ride had given Harry time to let his mind wander free form. It was something he very rarely had the luxury to let happen or wanted for that matter. When he did, thoughts came to him in random fashion with no rhyme or reason tying them together.

Why couldn't he get a thread on this case? Just one small sniff and he'd know where to follow it right to the end. Why was it so blank, so nothing there?

Sherry. Was the time he spent with her increasing? Was it his imagination? Did she seem to actually like spending time with him, and he with her?

The sex.

The kids.

The complications.

The sex. That's twice on the sex angle—it was dynamite, but it always had been. If marriage was nothing more than sex and work, Harry would be Chief of the husband tribe.

It wasn't, not even close, and that's where Harry fell off the pedestal. He just wasn't good at the rest of what normal people did together. At least not up until now.

Could he?

Would he?

Did he want to or was his hit and miss life what he actually wanted?

He did love his kids more than anything.

Doc. Another hit and miss or was there something different about this one. She was good; man was she good. And strong. Didn't back down and could handle the world she lived in like it was hers. At least that's what Harry saw and it made him more interested and more scared.

Could she be the one? Or was she just one more in a long line of ones.

When this case was over, he had to right the ship and figure out what direction it was sailing. Or, if there was still doubt in his mind—drink heavily and get the doubt out of his mind.

The case. It always came back to the case. His mind never let the case slip out of immediate reach for more than a few minutes. Cases were obsessions. Cases were what he lived for these days to prove to himself he was good at this. To prove he was good at something and his life of past failures was the past. Other than sex—he knew he was good in that department. That didn't count.

Random thoughts with nothing to tie them together but him—Harry Mickey Shorts—shitbum private investigator extraordinaire.

Harry grabbed his bag and thanked the driver. He had an hour to kill before they were going to pick him up for dinner prior to the game. Hot dogs and beer at the park would have been his choice but you have to go with the flow when the boss man is dictating the show and picking up the tab.

The Heinie he had snatched from the mini-bar was half gone when the talking sports head on the local TV station came on reporting from the stadium. Kansas City this, the Royals that, gonna be a tough battle, yada, yada. What he meant to say was, "*The New York Yankees will come into town and bash the living shit out of our Royals and leave having swept the four game series.*" Then yada, yada sports speak to fill the remaining time he was allotted.

Harry shut off the TV. With Heinie in hand, he went for a quick shower before he had to leave to watch his beloved Yankees do some bashing, New York kick-ass style.

Chapter 75

The elevator door opened and Harry instinctively scanned the lobby. Old habits never die. He spotted who he was looking for immediately.

"Harry, glad you could make it," Randle said as he walked up to him, hand outstretched.

"Randle, I wouldn't have missed it for the world. Thank you for inviting me," Harry responded.

Harry and J'Orr shook hands as well.

Danny stood right where he was when Harry got off the elevator. Never moved a muscle and looked royally pissed-off at the world

After a minute with Randle and J'Orr, Harry walked over to Danny and extended his hand.

"Good to see you again, Danny," he offered.

"Yeah," was all he got in response.

"Never mind him, Harry," Randle said as he came up behind Harry. "Let's head on out and have ourselves a fine dinner before we go over to the stadium."

"You fellas are gonna need a good meal in your bellies to stomach the thrashing the Royals are gonna lay on those fat-cat Yanks," J'Orr piped up.

"That so," Harry said. "Care to wager a few of those hard earned dollars of yours on those loser Royals of yours?" Harry chided him.

"Got our ace going tonight, Harry. Kids pretty tough if you haven't seen any of him yet."

"I know who he is, J'Orr. Good for a kid, but this ain't kiddie time, it's the big boys coming to town," Harry informed him.

"Okay, big shot. How about a twenty spot on the game?" J'Orr offered.

"I'd be pleased to take twenty dollars of your money, J'Orr," Harry agreed.

"Twenty it is then," J'Orr said. "Let's eat and, since I'm gonna be flusher by twenty smackers in a few hours, I'll buy.

"Fuck this twenty bucks shit," Danny said when he finally spoke up. "A hundred says your Yanks don't even score against that kid, Harry.

How's that for you, Harry? Care to put a hundred where your mouth is, Harry?" Danny said getting more excited with each word.

"A hundred on the Yankees scoring one run. I believe that's a wager I can't refuse, Danny," Harry said. "And since I'm now going to be a hundred-twenty bucks flusher in a few hours, I'll definitely buy dinner," Harry finished.

"The fuck you will…," Danny said before Randle cut him off.

"Gentlemen, gentlemen. As I am the one who set up this evening's activities, I'll be the one to pick up the dinner tab. No questions from any of you—do I make myself very clear?" Randle said authoritatively.

As there were no objections from anyone, the matter was settled.

"Now that we have that taken care of and before the game is over and we don't even get to see any of it," Randle told them, "why don't we adjourn to dinner and begin the festivities."

~ * ~

The steaks were prime Mid-Western beef, the baked potatoes the size of softballs accompanied by a garlic butter that was outrageous. Randle ordered a wine that must have been extremely expensive judging by the way the waiter ran off to get the bottle before Randle had a chance to change his mind.

Beer was the drink of choice for the rest of the group. Not Danny Beer, but beer that was fit for human consumption. A local micro brew that actually tasted pretty good from the first one right through the third one Harry tossed down.

Dinner conversation revolved around Board Room Farms and their new stud horse. The general tone was very upbeat except for Danny who said very little and answered questions with one word answers.

Dinner done, it was time to "Play Ball!"

Chapter 76

Sitting in a luxury box to watch a baseball game was something Harry had done very few times in his life. Sitting in the Owner's luxury box hadn't been a pleasure to hit Harry's "done that" list before tonight. Turns out a minority owner in the Royals was also a minority owner in Board Room Farms.

"This okay, Harry," Randle asked as they sat enjoying a beer before the game started.

"It will do if it's all that's available," Harry said with a straight face.

"There are a few bleacher seats still available if that suits you better, Harry?" Randle asked.

They both smiled.

"Nah, I'll hang here to keep you company," Harry replied.

"Very kind of you, Harry. You do sacrifice so much for me," Randle said.

"He's here, R," Danny said from the back of the box in a very nasty tone.

As Randle stood and started to move to the back of the box, Harry turned to see who Danny was referring to.

The two men were shaking hands and Randle gestured for Harry to come and join them.

George Steinbrenner in all his Yankee splendor was standing next to Randle.

"George, this is Harry Shorts, a very trusted associate of mine. Harry, George Steinbrenner," Randle completed the introductions.

Harry shook George Steinbrenner's hand as George said, "A pleasure to meet you Harry. I hope you enjoy the game."

"Mister Steinbrenner, the Yankees are playing. What's not to enjoy," Harry replied.

"I like this guy," George said to Trundle. "And Harry, here's something for Max," Steinbrenner said as he handed Harry an authentic Yankee hat autographed in silver Sharpie by Derek Jeter and Alex Rodriguez.

"Oh, man, Max is gonna flip when he sees this," Harry said. "I can't thank you enough, Mister Steinbrenner."

"Please, call me George, Harry. I've known Randle for more years than either of us cares to admit to and, if you're one of his guys, you are good by me as well. If I can help you in any way while you are in town, let my people know and it's done."

"Gotta run, Randle. See you in New York when you get back," he said as he left the box.

Danny he ignored completely.

"I'm totally blown away," Harry said to Randle when Steinbrenner was gone. "And the hat for Max, how'd he know?"

Harry knew it was a stupid question as soon as it left his mouth.

"As George said, we go way back," Randle replied. "Let's have another beer and enjoy a Yankees victory, shall we?"

"We shall," Harry agreed.

~ * ~

Jeter led off the game with a single up the middle and promptly stole second on the next pitch. Rodriguez lined a low slider up the gap in right center and the Yanks were on the board.

"That's a hundred, Danny," Harry yelled to Danny sitting by himself in the back of the box.

"Fuck you, Shorts," he replied as he crushed a beer can and tossed it in the corner with the other empties he had disposed of in the same way.

Harry smiled, as did Randle.

"Getting to be a bigger asshole every day," Randle remarked.

"An asshole who happens to be a hundred bucks lighter," Harry added.

The Yanks put a whipping on the Royals and finished the game up 11-1. Harry collected his one hundred and twenty dollars and handed it to the young gal that had handled the box during the game.

"Thanks, Cathy, you were great," Harry told her.

"And thank you, Harry, that's very generous of you," she said back as she shook his hand in appreciation.

Harry discreetly pocketed the napkin she surprised him with as they shook and he was sure it would have her phone number.

"J'Orr, you drop Danny off at the hotel, okay? I need to talk to Harry for a bit and I'll get him back to his hotel," Randle said to J'Orr as they got to the reserved parking lot.

"No problem, Mister Trundle. I'll see you tomorrow at the ranch," he replied.

"Why do I have to…," Danny was starting to say before Randle put up his hand to silence him.

"Because it is what I want and what I need right now, Danny. Do it and we will speak tomorrow when I get to the ranch," Randle said to Danny. His look said challenge me if you dare.

Danny was about to say something back to Randle but obviously thought better of it and walked away.

"Sorry, J'Orr," Randle told him.

"Not a problem at all, Mister Trundle. See you tomorrow. You too, Harry."

"It's been a long day, Harry," Randle said. "Let's get the fuck out of here."

Chapter 77

The limo pulled away from the gate and inched out into the post-game traffic. Randle handed Harry a long necked beer and poured himself a glass of wine in a crystal goblet.

Man travels with class wherever he goes Harry thought. A reminder he really didn't need.

"You look troubled," Harry said to Trundle.

"I don't know if I'd say troubled is the right word, Harry. But you are correct, there is something on my mind," Randle told him.

Harry had seen this look before and it confused him every time.

"I've spent some more time with Doc and she is one hundred percent convinced she didn't miss anything when she examined Brian Boru after he died. She also is convinced the vets we brought in to do the autopsy on Boru couldn't have missed anything either. I'm beginning to think maybe I was mistaken and it was just a terrible loss for Brian Boru to go before we all wanted him to."

Randle sipped his wine and looked at Harry as if he might have the answers he was searching for.

After a long pull on his long neck, Harry said, "Your instincts have carried you a long way in this life, Randle. I can't say I've found anything definite to say your original feelings were correct, but I keep feeling there is something there to grab hold of and I can't quite reach it. Little things combined with the Shorts feeling. Same as you, Randle," Harry answered him.

"Still, we could be chasing ghosts here, Harry. The ghost of Brian Boru only because I don't want him to be dead. I want him to be alive and patrolling Board Room Farms."

"Let's give it a bit more time, okay. I'll finish up what I'm looking at and then we can decide if we are looking for answers that just aren't there. Deal?" Harry asked.

"Deal," Randle agreed.

"Anything else bothering you, Randle?"

"You are perceptive, Harry, I'll give you that."

Trundle thought for a minute and sipped his wine.

"Doc and Danny," Randle started. "Doc is a wonderful woman and I value her a great deal, Harry. You and I have spoken about a particular woman once before and I appreciate you heeding my wishes. I care for her and she seems to care for you, Harry. If it is reciprocal, I wish the two of you all the luck in the world. But, if she is just another of your conquests, Harry, beware. Do not lead this lady on and do not incur my wrath for doing so."

Rather harsh words Harry thought to himself.

"I don't mean to be so harsh, Harry. I just don't want any ill will to come upon Kate," Randle said like he meant it sincerely.

Kate, Harry thought to himself.

Gathering his thoughts first, Harry replied, "Doc is an amazing woman, Randle. The short time I spent with her, I was blown away. She grabbed me like no woman has grabbed me before. I'd like to spend more time with her and I intend to do so."

Harry stopped and took a pull on his beer. Also gave him time to construct what he was about to say.

"I want her to be the one, Randle, I really do. In my heart I want a woman to love and nobody has touched me like she has. But, and there's always a but with Harry Shorts, I know myself. Or at least I thought I did. She's different and I wouldn't hurt her for the world. You have my word on that, Randle," Harry finished.

"Good enough, Harry. Now to my second problem child—Danny. A little Trundle history very few people are privy to, Harry. My parents split when we were young and I stayed with my father in New York. Danny went to live with my mother in Lexington, KY. She was from there originally. Danny wasn't the brightest child God ever created and I sometimes wonder how two brilliant parents could produce, well, Danny.

"He flunked out of a few high schools and eventually started working for a horse auctioneer my mother took up with. I believe they knew each other as youngsters. Anyway, Danny had an amazing proclivity for the thoroughbred horse business and climbed his way up the auction sales ladder very fast. He eventually owned his own company that Trundle Industries bought about ten years ago. Danny continues to run that entity for me and started Board Room Farms with the capital partners I was able to put together for him. He really does know the horse business and horses, Harry."

"I've noticed the dissimilarity between the two of you," Harry said as tactfully as he could.

"Thank you, Harry. Well put. My problem is that he has gotten too big for BRF in his own mind. He's lost sight of what we created and why. He wants to be bigger than life; he wants to be bigger and better than his older brother."

Randle paused and refilled his glass.

For something to do, Harry grabbed another long neck.

"As you know, Harry, that isn't going to happen. I'm going to remove him from the role of controlling partner and bring in someone else to run BRF. Danny will continue to run his original company for Trundle Industries if he so chooses. If not, I'll buy him out and be done with him. He won't embarrass me again as he has recently.

"Danny's demeanor since you have been here was caused by my telling him what I have decided. He is dealing with it as he has always dealt with adversity—like a child. Please ignore him for now and he will be out of our hair very soon," Randle concluded.

"I'm cool with that, Randle. And thank you for giving me a peek at the Trundle history. You didn't have to and I appreciate it. If there's something to find concerning Boru, I'll find it, and soon. I won't drag it out for my own selfish concerns. I don't want to fail or disappoint you and I won't," Harry told him.

"As you would say, I'm cool with dat," Randle responded.

Harry laughed and Randle joined him.

A clink of long neck to crystal goblet and they drank as friends would.

Chapter 78

The conference room was full at 9:00 am the following morning when Randle walked in and said good morning to each person separately: J'Orr, Stu, Doc and Harry. A man Harry had never seen before accompanied Randle.

"I'd like to introduce Todd Mitchell to all of you. Todd is a trusted friend who has done all of my recruiting work since I have been involved with Trundle Industries. He is the best there is at his trade. His role here will be understood momentarily."

Hellos were exchanged and Todd sat in a chair against the wall.

"Let's get started," Randle began. "Board Room Farms has been one of, if not the leading breeding farm in the United States for the last five years or so. There can be no denying the death of Brian Boru is a devastating loss on several levels."

The door to the conference room opened and Danny entered.

"Ah, there you are Danny. Please come in and sit here next to me. Would you like some coffee perhaps?" Randle asked him.

"No," was all he said.

"All right then, let's continue. While Brian Boru was the number one stud money earner last year nationally, we can't bury our heads in the sand and cry boohoo. We have replaced Boru with what we believe is a fine stud horse and one that will keep us in the national spotlight for many years to come. That being said, we will all miss Boru.

"The running of this farm will not change. I have every confidence in the management team we have assembled and you will continue doing exactly what you have done before—make us number one. Our results on the track the past six months have been a major success and the yearlings we have on the farm look to be our best crop ever. On all fronts we have proven to be a top notch racing stable."

Randle stopped to take a sip of his coffee and let the room bask in the congratulatory comments they richly deserved.

"The one change we will be making at this time is a very significant change. Danny Trundle has served as President of Board Room Farms since its inception. The board of directors has decided at this time new leadership is in order and Danny will be stepping down as President. He will concentrate one hundred percent of his efforts on other Trundle Industries' businesses. The board wishes to thank Danny for the leadership he has provided to date and wishes him nothing but success in his future endeavors."

Randle stood and led the group in a round of applause for Danny.

Doc couldn't help but smile.

In his inimitable fashion, Danny said, "Yeah, whatever."

When the group was seated and quiet, Randle said, "The reason Todd is with us today is I have entrusted him with the task of finding a successor for Danny as President of Board Room Farms. And let me make it perfectly clear, the number one job requirement for the new President is to keep the entire staff at Board Room Farms intact for a period of one year. Any changes to the management staff after that one year period will require the approval of the board of directors."

A collective sigh of relief could be heard throughout the room.

Danny mumbled something that was indistinguishable. Randle gave him a look and Danny turned away.

"Todd understands the seriousness of this requirement and has provided the board with three excellent candidates for us to review. I expect to have the new President of Board Room Farms onboard within the month."

Randle smiled and said, "Onboard at Board Room Farms. I'm surprised you didn't ding me for that one, Harry."

The entire group smiled and the mood lightened considerably.

Danny made a "harumpy" sound that clearly pissed Randle off.

He ignored it.

Randle continued. "Todd will accompany the new President when he arrives here at Board Room Farms and ensure he gets acclimated as quickly as possible. His people are scouting suitable housing for the new President and his family and they will be moving here immediately. Todd, anything you would like to say?" Randle asked.

"I'd just like to say it's a privilege to assist Board Room Farms in this difficult time. My entire staff and I are at your disposal twenty-four seven from here on out. If you need anything, just call and I'm here to take care of it. The three candidates are all excellent horse people, they all know how to run a business, and they are people you all would want to be associated with. Trust me, before long it will seem as if nothing has changed. Any questions?"

Scanning the room, Todd said, "No, that's great. Again, twenty-four seven and I mean it. The phone rings and we jump and don't stop jumping until whatever you need is taken care of. Randle," Todd said turning the room back to him.

"As you can see, that's what makes him the best at what he does. Some day he'll realize where he should be and come work for Trundle Industries full time. Okay, any questions at all?"

The group was quiet.

Harry had questions, but he had been instructed by Randle to hold them until after the meeting was over.

"If there are no questions, I will speak with each of you separately as the day progresses. Harry and Doc, would you mind staying behind for a few minutes? The rest of you can go with Todd and ask him all the questions you didn't want to ask in my presence."

A relaxing laughter filled the room as they exited.

Chapter 79

After the rest of the group left the room and those remaining got a fresh round of coffee, plus another éclair for Harry, Randle addressed the two of them.

Looking directly at Doc, he said, "First, and perhaps most important, you will be at Board Room Farms for as long as I am alive and, of course, you choose to stay at BRF. If you should waiver at any time, I only ask that you come and see me before you make any decision. No one will ever circumvent my wishes in this matter."

"Thank you, Randle. You can't begin to know how much your confidence in me means at a time like this," Doc replied.

"Excellent, then let's move on."

Randle turned so he was facing both Doc and Harry.

"The next order of business, sadly to say, is Brian Boru. Kate, I have accepted your professional opinion as to the circumstances surrounding Boru's death. I don't like what you have told me, and I don't want to accept it as fact, but I have found no reason to doubt your findings. For your edification, I have had Harry looking into his death behind the scenes. To date he has found nothing to alter your view of Boru's death as nothing more than natural causes.

"Harry, is there anything I am missing up to now?"

"No, Randle, nothing has changed from our last discussion on the topic," Harry added.

Doc flashed Harry a *"We will talk soon"* look.

Harry knew it was coming and had actually expected worse.

Randle observed the byplay and moved on.

"That being said, Harry has convinced me to allow him to continue his investigation based on other "occurrences" he has come across while looking into this unfortunate matter. While I can't say I am one hundred percent sold on prolonging the investigation, I trust Harry as I trust you, Kate. Thus, I shall defer to his wishes and let him detect on for a period to be determined."

Randle stopped for a sip of coffee, put a finger to his cheek to indicate to Harry he had chocolate from the éclair on his face, and then continued.

"I will be staying here at BRF for the remainder of today through tomorrow noon. The corporate jet will be here to take me back to New York and you are welcome to join me if you would like, Harry.

"As for the two of you, I have taken the liberty of reserving a suite at the best hotel in Kansas City for this evening and a car is waiting to take both of you there right now. No need to take anything with you as I have seen to anything you might need. We will convene here at nine am tomorrow morning and you and I will conduct some business before we leave for New York, Harry."

"Business?" Harry interrupted.

Clearly disturbed by the intrusion, Randle continued, "Yes, business, Harry. Business that I will explain to you tomorrow at nine am when we meet here as I just said. Now, get lost, both of you," Randle said as he stood and walked out of the room.

Not knowing what else to do, Doc and Harry got lost.

~ * ~

"Yes, sir. Like I told you yesterday, there's lots of commotion down there and a whole bunch of people showed up this morning real early. Fancy cars brung 'em in. I can see it clear as day from up here where I've been watching the ranch like you been telling me to do."

"People you have seen before?" the other person on the call asked.

"Some yes, some no. They must have been meetin' this morning cuz the usual hands like J'Orr and Stu been back out tending to things while the new folks are still inside. A big black limo-like car just left with that Doc lady and the guy been here maybe couple of weeks ago. Not a new hand like I told you first time he showed up."

"Okay. You're doing a fine job. Now you're sure they aren't on to you?" the caller asked.

"No, sir, not so's I can tell. Nobody been up here to hassle me and I been real clever in hiding what I been doing. Not that I been doing anything illegal or nothing like that. Just watchin' the spread like you asked."

"Good, keep at it and call me tomorrow if anything interesting occurs."

"Yes, sir. I sure will."

Chapter 80

"Yes sir, Mister Shorts. Your reservation for this evening has been previously taken care of and the bellman will be pleased to assist you and the lady with your luggage," the person behind the counter informed Harry.

Nice hotel and great service Harry thought.

"That won't be necessary," Harry told him. "I'll just take the key."

"Oh, it's no trouble at all," he responded. "Henry, assist these people with their bags, please," he called out.

Slightly flustered, Harry said in a low voice, "We don't need Henry's assistance. We have no bags. Just give me the key, please."

Not knowing quite how to respond to Harry's statement, the desk clerk said in a voice loud enough for most of the people in the hotel lobby to hear, "Oh, no bags? Very well, then. No need to assist them, Henry. They have no luggage. Here is your key, Mister Shorts, and please enjoy your stay."

Harry and Doc walked over to the elevator bank and stepped into the waiting elevator. Harry pressed the button for the top floor and turned toward Doc as they both burst out laughing hysterically.

~ * ~

The car ride to the hotel had been a quiet ride and rather uncomfortable from Harry's perspective. Now that they were in their rooms with an "s", Harry wanted to get off on the right foot.

"There seems to be a bottle of champagne here. Would you like a glass?" he asked.

Doc looked at him, carefully measuring her words before she spoke.

"What the fuck are you doing, Harry?" Doc finally said.

"Um, offering you a glass of champagne," he replied.

She 'humphed.'

"Not that, Harry. What are you really doing here at Board Room Farms? What did Mister Trundle mean when he said you're 'looking into Brian Boru's death behind the scenes...'?"

"Well, just that, Doc. I'm a private investigator and that's what I do.

I help people figure stuff out and I've been working for Randle, Mister Trundle, for a few years now," Harry told her.

"And now? Me?" she asked.

"You what?" Harry replied looking somewhat confused by her questions.

"Are you investigating me, Harry? Is that what you were doing at my house, in my bedroom, in my bed? All part of the investigation?" she continued.

"What the…," Harry started to say. He caught her meaning and put both of his hands up in defense.

"Whoa there, Doc. Let's jump back a few steps here," he started. "I came to you because you were a natural extension of my investigation. An important piece in the chain of events I needed to look at. You weren't singled out for any other reason and what happened in your house, in your…, ah, in your," Harry stammered.

"In my bed, Harry. You fucked my brains out in my bed. Was that part of a planned investigation to throw me off and get me in a vulnerable position so you could grill me?" she finished Harry's thought for him.

"Doc, what happened in your bedroom just happened. And if I remember correctly, it was you who took a fairly active role in us ending up in your bedroom. As far as who did what to whom, I'd say it was a mutual exchange when it came to positions.

"And as to what my intentions were, I needed to get some information from you. I still need to get some information from you. The rest was something that has been riding in my mind ever since. I enjoyed every minute of it and was hoping we could continue enjoying it in this fine set of rooms we find ourselves in."

"Oh you do, do you? You're pretty cocky for a guy whose ass I should kick for the next hour. You could have told me what you were doing, Harry. You could have trusted me," Doc told him.

"Doc, you trust nobody until you know who you're dealing with and who you can put your trust in. It's the nature of my business," Harry explained.

"That sounds like a lonely business to be in, Harry," Doc said.

"Can be. Isn't now," he tried.

"Harry, what's a girl to do with you?" Doc said.

"Oh, I think you did pretty well last time we were together," Harry replied while flashing that famous HMS smile.

"I'm still gonna kick your ass for not telling me what you were up to, Harry. But for now, you're right. No sense in wasting fine digs like these. I'll take some of that champagne now."

"Ms. Martin, it would be my pleasure."

Chapter 81

The bed was the king of king size beds and Harry and Doc had used every inch of it. Covers, sheets and pillows littered the floor and Harry found himself fully spent when they were done getting reacquainted. Even Doc was breathing slightly heavy as she sat propped up against the headboard, champagne glass in hand.

"I'll take a bit more champagne if you can manage to get yourself over to the bureau and fetch the bottle, Harry," she said.

"Let me make sure everything is still attached and in working order," he replied.

Confident he could make the trip across the room and back, Harry fetched the bottle as instructed.

"So, now that we are properly reacquainted, and you have had your way with me again, what's the real story?" she asked.

"Who had their way with whom would be highly debatable, I would think. But I would have to say it was a fairly enjoyable way whether I was the hader, or the hadee," Harry said once he was back in bed after having retrieved the bottle of champagne.

Glasses properly refilled, Harry started in.

"Randle asked me to look into the circumstances surrounding Brian Boru's death. I think that much was clear when I came out to Board Room Farms the first time."

"May have been clear to you," Doc interrupted.

A sip of bubbly while ogling Doc's exposed breasts, which she caught, Harry continued, "As I was saying, Randle asked me to look into the circumstances surrounding Brian Boru's death. It is what I'm good at. It's what I do. I don't advertise what I do and I don't announce what I'm doing. I just do it and, as you have seen, I do it well."

"It's not all you do well," Doc said. "But that doesn't excuse the fact you came into my home and under false pretenses no less. I was stupid," she spouted out.

"False pretenses?" Harry asked.

"Yeah, false pretenses. What is it about the two words 'false pretenses' you don't understand, Harry?" Doc asked.

"Doc, I'm a private investigator. I don't carry a sign around announcing who I am and what I do. I do my thing undercover and it's what sets me apart from many other P.I.'s."

"Undercover being the optimum word for you, Harry? You lead women on and charm them into bed to gain their confidence and then interrogate them. Get 'em off guard so you take advantage of them. Is that what you do best, Harry?" Doc asked obviously gaining steam. "Is that what gets you off, Harry? Makes you feel like a big man?"

Before she could go any further, Harry grabbed Doc and kissed her. Kissed her hard. Kissed her deep. Kissed her like it meant something.

When he let go, Doc remained in that exact position, eyes closed, not moving.

"That's what I do when I care about someone, Doc. That's what I do when I'm not working and when I'm trying to show a woman I care for her. That's what I want to give to you, now, and hopefully more in the future."

Doc opened her eyes and cried.

"Why do I always get the criers," Harry said softly.

~ * ~

They were in the sitting room dressed in the complimentary bathrobes, eating room service. Harry said his steak was excellent and Doc proclaimed her salmon superb.

"So, now that we have the hysterics over with, what now?" Doc said between bites.

"I'm sorry I got so hysterical," Harry joked.

"Fuck you, Harry," Doc answered.

"Can it wait until after I'm done with my steak," Harry replied, mouth full. "It'll get cold and it's too good to waste on a mere roll in the hay with the likes of you," Harry finished.

The roll hit him square in the forehead and dropped down on his plate.

"Ah, a roll. Thank you, dear. Pass the butter, will you?" Harry said with an absolute straight face.

"Please tell me this isn't what I have to look forward to? Please tell me this, this...this 'you' isn't real?" Doc finally got out.

"All me, all the time. Ain't it just the cat's meow?" Harry replied.

The only thing Doc could do was shake her head. Unfortunately, Harry's 'you' made her hornier than hell.

"Now that you've made the mistake of introducing cat into the conversation, screw your steak, and screw me. This meat's plenty hot and ready to be eaten."

Harry chased a long drawn out *meeeeow* into the bedroom.

Chapter 82

At nine the following morning, Harry and Doc were sitting in the conference room at Board Room Farms. M. Randle Trundle was late.

"Good morning, Harry, Kate. I trust you two had an enjoyable afternoon and evening in Kansas City?" Randle said as he swept into the room.

"Yes we did," Harry answered.

Doc colored.

"I take your rosy cheeks for an affirmation of Harry's proclamation of a good time had by all?" Randle said to Doc.

"Yes, Randle, it was a very nice day, and evening," Doc finally chimed in.

"Good, then let's get today started. The two of you missed our six-thirty briefing this morning and the eight am follow-up meeting as well. There you are," Randle said as J'Orr and Stu came into the room.

"Morning all," they both said in unison.

"Morning," came in return.

"In three minutes a gentleman will be joining us that should prove to be most enlightening for everyone here. I know you have a full day ahead of you, Kate, so we will let you get to it as soon as we are done with our guest. I want you here to corroborate a piece of my thinking on what we will hear. Okay?"

"Of course, Randle. Whatever you need," Doc responded.

"Harry, I've set it up so J'Orr will handle the initial questioning with Stu as his bad guy counterpart. You will observe until you have questions of your own, but not before I ask a question. Is that understood?"

"Got'ya, Randle. May I ask where our guest is coming from? Why he is here in the first place?" Harry asked.

"It will be quite evident early on, Harry. Trust me on that," Randle told him. "J'Orr, are you and Stu ready?"

"We're set, Randle. Let's get it on with the sumbitch," he answered as Stu nodded his head in agreement.

"Good. Then, if we are all ready, let's get it on," he parroted.

Randle picked up the phone by his side and said, "Now."

Less than a minute later, the door opened and a smallish cowpoke of a man came in followed by Randle's personal assistants for this type of work—two giants dressed in matching black suits. They stood against the wall and took up watch.

"Good morning, Hutch. It is Hutch, isn't it?" Randle asked.

"Um, sure enough is," he responded.

"I trust you understand that if you as much as twitch without me asking you to, the two gentlemen that brought you here this morning will be required to deal with you. And Hutch, they have been instructed to subdue you with *due force*. Do you know what that means, Hutch?" Randle asked.

"Don't know no due force," he said, "but I gets the picture right clear."

"Excellent," Randle said. "Then, shall we begin?" he said to everyone in attendance.

As planned, nobody moved or said a word.

Stu reached over and slapped Hutch behind the head almost causing his head to hit the table. Surprise works wonders in these circumstances.

"Hutch," J'Orr began immediately, "I'm going to ask you some questions and you are going to answer them truthfully. If I think you are lying, God help you. You got that?"

Hutch rubbed the back of his head and said, "I hear ya good enough. What questions you got and you got no reason to be holdin' me here noways."

"We aren't holding you here, Hutch. We're just having a friendly talk and having some coffee. You want coffee, Hutch? No, then let's go on. What's your full name?"

"Ah, people call me Hutch," he responded.

"Your full name, Hutch, first and last."

"It's James, James Hutchinson."

"Where you from, James?"

"I was born in Jackson but moved here when I was young. Lived in the next town over my whole life, mostly."

"That's good James…"

"Ah, people call me Hutch," Hutch interrupted.

"And he's calling you James. You got a problem with that?" Stu asked forcefully.

"No," Hutch said hesitantly. "You can call me James if you wants to."

"Good, Hutch," J'Orr said. "Now this is an important question, Hutch, so listen to it very carefully. Are you listening, Hutch?"

"I'm listening," he said.

"Who do you work for?" J'Orr asked.

"Work for?" Hutch replied.

Stu leaned toward Hutch, but J'Orr waived him off.

"No need to persuade him, Stu. I'm sure James will answer the question, now won't you James?" J'Orr asked him.

Hutch looked at Stu and the two guys leaning against the wall, then back at J'Orr.

"Don't know," Hutch said.

"You don't know?" J'Orr repeated what Hutch had just said. "You don't know who you are working for? And what was it you were doing up on the hill?" J'Orr continued.

"Huh?" Hutch grunted out.

"James, listen carefully. My men saw you up on the hill overlooking our ranch, watching what was going on. Spying you might call it. You'd call it spying, wouldn't you, Stu?" J'Orr said.

"Damn right I'd call this here sidewinder a freakin' spy. And you know what we do with people we catch spying on our operations here, J'Orr?" Stu said.

It was time for Randle to step in.

"Mister Hutchinson may need to gather his thoughts for a minute, J'Orr. Why don't we get a breath of fresh air and leave Mister Hutchinson here to gather his thoughts. J'Orr, Stu, why don't you join me and we can leave Harry here with Mister Hutchinson. Sound okay, Mister Hutchinson?" Randle asked.

"That be good," was all he said.

Randle, J'Orr, Stu and the two human monuments left the room.

Chapter 83

When they had left the room, Harry looked at Doc and let out a long *phew*. Then looking at Hutch, he said, "Those boys can be pretty intense, can't they? Shit, they scare even me and I didn't do nothing wrong."

"Had me practically pissing in my drawers for you, Hutch," Doc threw in.

Harry gave Doc a look that said, *What the fuck was that?*

"You want me to get you something, Hutch? A soda or bottle of water, maybe?" Harry asked him.

Feeling Harry kick her under the table, Doc figured out Harry wanted a shot at Hutch alone.

"A soda 'bout now be mighty good," Hutch responded.

"Why don't I get it?" Doc said.

"That would be great, Doc. I'll just stay here and keep Hutch company 'til everyone gets back," Harry offered.

Doc got up and left the room. As she closed the door she saw Randle and the rest of the boys across the hall doing of all things, watching TV. When she came up to them she saw why they were gathered in front of the television screen. There, clear as day, sat Hutch and Harry—the room had a surveillance camera trained on Hutch. The audio was equally as good.

"Seems to be a pretty tough spot you're in, Hutch. Anything I can do to help?" Harry asked him.

"That guy ain't got no cause to smack me upside my head," Hutch started. "And the other guy, he be jumpin' all up and down towards me and I don't know what fur. I ain't done nothin' wrong; done nothin' but use the glasses they gave me and watched the boys down at Board Room Farms doing their normal chores."

Hutch went to stand, but Harry suggested he stay seated unless he wanted the two goons to come in and keep watch over him.

Seated again, he said, "I'm cool."

"Who is they, Hutch? And what did they ask you to do?" Harry asked.

"They, ah them, ah…I don't know who they are like I said before.

Guy calls me up on the phone and offers me money to go up on the hill and report what's going on down on the ranch. Don't ask me to do nothin', just watch. Can't be nothin' wrong with that I figured, so I says sure, I'll do it—lot a money to do nothin' but watch."

"How did they come to call you, Hutch? Why you?" Harry asked.

"Man says guy told him 'bout me and he calls me. Says he heard I did good work for this guy before."

"Do you know who he was talking about, Hutch? Who it was you did the work for previously?"

Hutch had a look on his face like he was trying to figure out a very complex problem. Looked to be quite a struggle.

"Nope, can't say I actually do. I do lotsa odd jobs for lotsa people. It's how I get by mostly. Musta been one of them folk, I guess," Hutch said.

"What did he sound like, Hutch? Did he say where he was calling from?"

"Older soundin' fella, not from around here, though. Talked a little funny like a kid my niece married few years back. From overseas she tole us. Can't tell ya where, but funny soundin'."

"Okay, now this is important, Hutch. Exactly what did he tell you he wanted you to do?"

Thinking hard, Hutch said, "Just wanted me to sit up on the hill inconspicuous like and watch what goes on down at Board Room Farms. He used that word and I liked it. I was doing inconspicuous real good 'til them boys snuck up on me and brought me down here. Didn't do nothin', I was just watchin' like I was tole to do," Hutch finished.

"And what did you do after you watched inconspicuously, Hutch? And how long did you do it?" Harry asked.

"Man, I gotta hit the head bad," Hutch told Harry.

"Just a bit more, Hutch."

"Nah, man, I gotta go, now," Hutch said with some urgency.

"All right, Hutch. Let's get that out of the way and we will continue afterward.

Okay?" Harry said.

"All right," Hutch replied and Harry led him out the door as the group watching on the television scrambled for cover.

Chapter 84

Harry led Hutch back into the conference room which was now filled with the entire original group that was there when the conversation with their guest started.

Hutch took two steps into the room and pulled up short.

"Come on in, Hutch. Please take the same seat you were in before and let's continue our discussions," Randle said to the wide-eyed Hutch.

"Y'all come back," he finally got out.

"Very observant, Hutch. Now please be seated so we can move this along," Randle said with a bit of authoritativeness in his voice.

"Grumbely-mumbly pishaw," is the best description of what came out of Hutch's mouth as he reluctantly sat.

"I believe Harry asked you '*What did you do after you watched inconspicuously, Hutch? And how long did you do it?*' just before you left the room to relieve yourself, Hutch. Please answer those two questions for the group if you would," Randle instructed him.

Hutch was startled to say the least.

"How you know what he asked me?" Hutch said.

Smiling, Randle said, "Mister Hutchinson, I know everything that happens at Board Room Farms. I know what each person here does and everything that goes on here twenty-four hours a day, seven days a week, every week of the year. It's who I am and what I do. If you continue to choose to fuck with me, you will be one very sorry cowboy. Do I make myself one hundred percent clear, Mister Hutchinson?"

Hutch hesitated which proved to be a huge mistake.

"DO I MAKE MYSELF ONE HUNDRED PERCENT CLEAR?" Randle screamed at him.

If he hadn't just hit the head, Hutch would have pissed himself right there and then. Harry was pretty happy he had gone as well.

"Yes, sir, very clear, ah…perfectly clear, sir…a hundred percent sure enough clear, sir," Hutch stammered out.

"Good, then please answer the two questions I just posed to you, Mister Hutchinson," Randle practically whispered.

"Okay man, I'll tell ya right off now. I watched on the days I was supposed to and then called them on the cell phone they sent me. Just had to push a button and they answered—don't know no number or who they were. I swear I don't," Hutch said.

"Good, Hutch," Randle told him. "Continue, please."

"I was watching from before that horse died and called each time and tole them what happened that day. Who was near the big horse and where he went and when."

"The big horse?" Randle asked.

"Oh, I's sorry. The horse that died, Brian Boru. Everybody worked a horse ranch these parts knows Boru. Proud to have him here in our parts. I watched him and everybody 'round him. Mostly supposed to pay attention when he was up in the north pasture and how long he be up there each time he be let out. Who go up there with him and anybody stay nearby."

Hutch reached for the can of soda Doc had brought him when she had returned to the conference room. He took a long drink and looked slightly calmer now.

He continued.

"End of each day I watched, I'd press the button and report what I'd seen. Mostly the same thing every day 'til he didn't come up one day. Heard later he passed on that night before. Damn shame it is. Prettiest horse I ever laid my eyes on and woulda loved to have cared for that animal. I damn sure would have," Hutch said.

"What are you watching now that Brian Boru isn't here any longer?" Harry asked.

"They tole me to keep watchin' 'til a new stud stallion be coming. See what happened around the ranch every time I watched and report when the new horse get there. Any 'change in routine' they tole me to watch for. Had to explain to me what that was, but I did it after they explained it to me. I tole 'em the routine always the same no matter what's going on. Ranch got certain things gotta get done and the hands do 'em real good at Board Room Farms. Tole 'em that pretty Doctor lady still tended to the animals like they asked me to watch for."

"That all of it, Hutch?" Randle asked. "You still saying you don't know who hired you or who you reported to?"

"Sure enough right," Hutch replied.

"May I have the cell phone?" Harry asked Hutch.

"I won't be doin' no more reportin'?" Hutch asked.

"No, Hutch, your reporting days are over. We'll handle it from here. One last question though—how did you get paid?" Randle asked.

"Come to the post office in what they called a Post Office Box they sets up for me early on. Once every two weeks an envelope showd up with the same money inside—five hundred dollars. Lota money to sit and watch hands do their jobs. Got one right here with me now," Hutch said. "You ain't gonna take my money, are you, Mister?" Hutch said to Randle.

"No, Hutch, I'm not going to take your money. But I would like the envelope if you don't mind," Randle replied.

Hutch ripped the bills from the envelope and thrust it at Randle as fast as he could.

"Thank you, Hutch. Now, the two gentlemen by the door are going to take you to the county border," Randle told him. "If I ever hear of you setting one foot in this county again, you will be a very sorry cowboy. You get my drift, Hutch?"

"I'm gone like the wind, you bet I am," Hutch said. "You ain't never gonna see my sorry ass near a hundred miles of this place ever again. You can count on it, Mister."

"Oh, I am, Hutch, I truly am," Randle replied.

~ * ~

When the room was emptied except for Harry and Doc, Randle picked up the phone and dialed.

"Ms. Timmons," he said into the phone, "I want our best telecommunications person in my office when I return and the forensics team as well. We have some work to do," and he hung up the phone.

A man who truly does not waste words when someone, or something, has royally pissed him off.

"Harry and Kate," he said to them, "I have some work to do here before the plane leaves at noon. I have what I need and won't need your confirmation, Kate, but thank you for attending our little meeting.

"Harry, why don't you accompany Kate while she looks after BRF's newest arrival and I'll see you at noon for our departure. Does that sound okay to the both of you?" Randle asked.

Harry looked at Doc, she looked at him, then they both smiled and nodded in agreement

Chapter 85

Having an hour or so to kill while Doc looked in on Board Room Farms' newest arrival and the rest of the string of horses, Harry decided to do a little exploring. He borrowed a truck and headed over to the adjoining ranch, the old Rogers place.

Never know what you're going to find until you look for it.

The place looked as deserted as it was supposed to be as he came up the road to the main house. The usual corrals and barns dotted the property that Harry could see from where he was. A straggly looking stray dog was sleeping on the porch of the main house. A guard dog he wasn't.

Harry got out of the truck and walked around the side of the main house to get a look at the rest of the spread. Big place was his first impression, but they were all big in this part of the country. Hard to run a horse farm on a half acre lot he thought to himself. Since he was alone, with nobody to tell his thoughts to, himself would have to do.

He wasn't sure what it was about it, or why it caught his eye, but something about the big barn on the east side of the grounds was calling him to come on over and take a look. Harry was a man who had learned to trust his instincts, so he moseyed on over to the barn and opened the right hand door.

In the city he would have hustled on over; when you're in horse country, you mosey.

The inside of the barn was just what Harry expected to find—big, musty and unused for some time. Whoever had bought the place surely hadn't been around recently, at least not in this building. The floor was covered with straw and an assortment of farm tools were scattered on the floor toward the back wall. Additional tools were hanging on both side walls. Harry had no fucking clue what any of them were for and he had no desire whatsoever to find out.

Harry practically jumped out of his shoes when the mangy-assed mutt rubbed against his leg.

"What the fuck is the matter with you, you mangy-assed dog?" he yelled at the dog when he started breathing again.

An incredibly sad face looked up at Harry with help-me eyes.

"Ah, man, don't look at me like that," he told the dog.

It was a distant memory in Harry's varied past. It was six or seven years ago the best Harry could figure. Her name was Colleen. He met her at a college bar in Boulder, Colorado while he was working at a ski resort and learning how to be a mediocre skier. Two weeks later they were sharing his one bedroom apartment; Harry, Colleen and her mutt.

Colleen had graduated from the state university with a major in theater. She didn't need the degree—her acting skills were inborn and she was marvelous at anything she tried. She even got Harry to take a small part in one of the local theater plays she starred in and he wasn't half bad. He actually kinda liked it.

For a few months they had a blast and Harry enjoyed the hell out of his time with Colleen and Flops. The dog—Flops. It became clear to Harry she wouldn't be in Colorado long, though. Turns out her dad was a big muckety-muck in Hollywood and Colleen was whisked off to California to begin her screen career on her way to stardom. Took two years, but she got there.

Harry stayed and became an excellent skier. The dog stayed, too.

The dog walked past Harry, deliberately rubbing up against his leg again, and headed for the back left corner of the barn. When he got to a spot about two feet from the back wall, the dog started pawing the straw like he was intent on digging his way to China.

Harry followed and, when he caught up to the dog, he saw what the mutt was trying to get at. What looked like a trap door had been built into the floor. With the straw covering you'd never find it if you didn't know it was there. Or, your faithful companion didn't find it for you.

"Good boy," Harry said to the dog and rewarded him with a pat on the head and a scratch behind the ears. After clearing away the rest of the straw and pulling up the door, Harry took out his cell phone and called over to Board Room Farms.

Chapter 86

It would have been easy for Harry to allow Trundle Industries and its vast array of everything under the sun to track the Rogers ranch sale. Who owned it three owners ago, two owners ago, and who just recently purchased it. Easy, but not the preferred Harry Mickey Shorts way. When he needed something done during an investigation, he preferred to do it himself.

"Jaxy, my main man," Harry said into his cell phone. "How the jewels be hanging, dude?"

Jaxy was Harry's contact at the Web Dudes and, as far as Harry knew, the main Web Dude. If you needed some intergalactic web intelligence, no better source than the Web Dudes.

"Yeah, Jaxy, Sherry's cool. She was asking about you," Harry told him.

Jaxy liked to hear people were asking about him. It wasn't that he needed his ego pumped up; he just liked to know people were talking about him which might someday lead to his favorite thing in the world—more money.

"Do me this solid fast, okay, Jaxy? The burners are up high on this one and my ass is gonna get scorched if I don't know the low down pronto," Harry told him.

Harry listened a minute, then said, "Cool, man. Usual contact when you're down. Later."

~ * ~

Doc was standing at her front door when Harry came around the corner. That smile of hers got Harry every time.

She pecked him on the cheek while pinching his ass at the same time.

Johnson sighting.

"How long before you have to go?" she asked.

"Randle is on a conference call and then he has to go over some papers with J'Orr before we split," he told her. "We were due to leave at noon but it's looking more like one now."

"Hm, that's an hour and fifteen minutes from now, isn't it?" she said.

"That it is," he replied. "My bags are packed and sitting in the car. I've got nothing but time on my hands right about now."

"Time's not the only thing you're gonna have your hands on. Get in here and let's give the boys something to howl about when you're gone," she said as she grabbed his shirt and yanked him through the door.

~ * ~

They had driven in silence for about five minutes after leaving Board Room Farms. Randle was quietly studying some papers and Harry had checked his voice mail at home to see if anything important had come in over the last two days.

"Lilac," Randle finally said out of the blue.

"Lilac?" Harry repeated as a question.

"Yes, lilac. You smell of lilac, Harry."

Taking a whiff of himself, Harry guessed it could be Lilac he smelled of.

"On Kate it's most enticing and attractive. On you, Harry, too girlie," Randle said still not looking up from his papers.

They rode in silence for another five minutes.

"But knowing you as I have come to do, Harry," Randle said, "I'm sure you're finding a day smelling like lilac will have been well worth it. Right?"

Without much thought, Harry said, "Right you are, Randle. Oh how right you are"

~ * ~

As Harry and Randle boarded the Trundle private jet for their trip back east, Flops was lying in the sun on the back porch of his new home, Board Room Farms.

Chapter 87

The wheels touching down caused Harry to wake from a sound sleep. You know your ass is dog-turd tired when you go off to beddy-bye land the instant the plane leaves the ground and you don't wake until it hits terra firma again several hours later.

"You're becoming better and better company every time I'm around you, Harry," Randle teased.

"Sorry, Randle. I guess I was more tired than I realized," Harry responded.

"When you leave a beer sitting in front of you untouched, I know you're dead tired," Randle said.

"Did I miss anything?" Harry asked.

"We were in the air, Harry, from Kansas City to New Jersey. What is it you could have missed? We left the dancing girls at the airport and I worked the entire way east. So, I say again, Harry, what is it you could have missed?"

"Ohio?" Harry said.

Randle smiled.

~ * ~

"What do you mean he isn't there anymore? Where is he? What the fuck is he doing if he isn't there anymore? What kind of putz pisses away easy money like we're paying him to do nothing but sit on his ass and watch ranch hands doing what they always do? What kind of moron did you hire to do this simpleton job a fucking monkey could do? What kind of idiot putz are you?"

"Are you done?" was the only reply he could think of in response to the cell phone caller.

"Am I done? What the fuck kind of question is that—'*Am I done*'?"

"Just what it sounds like, are you done. Are you done, or do I have to listen to more of your bullshit questions I obviously don't have the answers to? If I had the answers, don't you think I'd have already given the answers to you?"

"What happened? He was supposed to be there through the end of this week," the voice on the cell phone asked.

"Simple. He didn't call in yesterday as he was scheduled to do. When we sent someone to check on him, he couldn't be found. We got word from our guy inside that some boys from Board Room snatched him up from his spot up on the ridge late yesterday afternoon and brought him down to their spread. From that point on, nothing."

"Nothing. What's nothing? This is not good, you know that. I'll have to call the man and let him know what's developed. You better get a handle on this situation, and fast. The man is going to want this fixed. There is too much to be lost if one small piece like this destroys the entire plan. You understand; while he doesn't know much, we have everything riding on that putz keeping his mouth shut. If you have to, shut it for him, as permanent as need be."

"Done."

~ * ~

They deplaned at Teterboro Airport and Randle started for his limo to take him directly to Trundle Industries. Harry was at his side but would be taking a second limo back to Long Island.

They stopped before either got into their respective cars.

"Are you absolutely sure you don't want any assistance with the Rogers property research?" Randle asked him.

"I've got it covered," Harry responded. "My guys are as good as they come and equally as expensive. I'll have the information in a day or so, and as soon as I get it, I'll forward it to you immediately."

"Good enough, Harry."

"We still set for next Saturday?" Harry asked.

"Everything is in place, Harry. I'll be there myself and even Ms. Timmons will be attending," Randle confirmed.

"Cool. Thanks again for the joy ride," Harry told him. "It sure beats commercial travel any day."

"That it does, Harry, that it does."

Chapter 88

Harry was just walking up the stairs into his apartment as the phone starting ringing. He jumped over a pile of dirty clothes he had left on the floor when he took off for Missouri and hit the speaker button just before it went to voice messaging.

"Shorts," he blurted out.

"Harry, its J'Orr. You sound out of breath. Are you all right?" J'Orr asked.

"I'm good, J'Orr. I just walked in the door and had to hustle to get the phone before it went to voicemail. I didn't expect to hear from you for a few days. What's up?"

"Unofficial like, 'cause it wouldn't be legal to be trespassing on another person's property, Stu and one of the boys went over to the property we discussed when you were here. Wanting to be neighborly, Stu went to tell them one of the fence posts was down along the property line between their property and Board Room Farms. He was gonna tell them we'd be fixing it and not to get alarmed if they saw our boys on their land."

"Sounds neighborly enough," Harry replied.

"Problem was nobody seemed to be around. Just to make sure there wasn't anybody hurt or nothing on the property, Stu took a look around and checked the outer buildings as well. Surprising as it might sound, he found a trap door in a barn and yelled down to see if anybody had fallen in. Nobody answered, but you can't be too careful, you know, Harry?"

"Yeah, you can't be too careful when somebody might be hurt," Harry agreed.

"Anyway, since Stu couldn't see proper down in the trap door, I'm sending a few boys over there to help out and check out what's down under the barn through that trap door. I'll let you know what we find."

"Thanks, J'Orr. Be sure and let me know if there is anything there to be concerned about," Harry said as they disconnected.

J'Orr was on the case and would find out what, if anything, was going on at the Rogers place. It took Harry several minutes to put his things away and toss the dirty stuff in the washer. He didn't turn it on, but it was the beginnings of a load at least.

Engaging the speaker phone again when he went back into the living room, Harry hit speed dial number one on his phone.

"Hey, pops," Max said in greeting.

"Max, my favoritest of all sons, how is a big time private investigator like me supposed to remain incognito if I can't even make a phone call in secrecy?" Harry asked.

"Caller ID your BTPIness," he replied.

"Ah, the pains of modern technology foil me again. BTPI-ness?" Harry asked.

"Sounds cool, doesn't it—Big Time Private Investigator-ness? It's pure bullshit, I know, but somebody's gotta prop up the old man's ego every once in a while," he said.

"I'll prop you up, you little shit."

They both laughed.

"What's up?" Max asked. "You aren't bailing on us for next Saturday, are you?"

"No, we're solid for Saturday, but change of plans. Instead of you two guys doing all the planning, I'm gonna be in charge this time. You haven't put everything in place yet, have you?" Harry asked.

Max hesitated a few beats.

"Max?"

"Yeah, I'm still here," Max said into the phone.

"So?" Harry asked.

"Me and Briande sorta had things in line, but we hadn't finalized anything yet. Nothing was confirmed and we haven't spent any bucks yet," Max said.

"Good. This is just a onetime thing and you can use the plans you had set up for this month next month. Trust me short-stuff, it's gonna be cool," Harry tried to assure him.

"Briande gonna be cool with it, too?" Max asked tentatively.

"Oh yeah, it's gonna be way more than cool for her. More than she can imagine and pretty cool for you, too. Don't you trust me, short-stuff?" Harry asked.

When Max hesitated again, Harry said, "Just get you and your sister ready for the usual nine am pickup and plan on some fun."

"Okay," Max said tentatively.

"Relax, will ya, and put your mom on," Harry said.

Chapter 89

Being back in town again, Harry planned on doing what he normally did when he was in town. First thing in the morning he headed up the street to visit with his favorite EBIL—Big Mel. Hopefully he'd be able to hit on Mel's able bodied assistant, Ms. Bunny Malone, for a little romp in the hay at some point during that day or night. Able bodied was a key phrase when discussing Bunny Malone.

Also on the agenda was lunch with his ex-wife, Sherry, that he had set up on the phone the day before. Something was nagging him about one of their previous conversations and he wanted to see if he could flush it out. If he didn't get lucky with Ms. Malone, he could always ply the ex with booze and try and coax her into a little mid-afternoon hoochy-miscoochy.

Their last encounter was still fresh in his memory bank and the memory was quite pleasurable.

As Harry entered Big Mel's office he quickly came to the realization that this was going to be a great day. There, leaning over to get some supplies out of the filing cabinet bottom drawer was one Bunny Malone, her splendiferous view for all to see. Well, at least for Harry and Big Mel to see. Her slightly turned side view showed off her longer than legal legs right up to the edge of her butt cheeks and her generous bazooms as gravity pulled them toward mother earth.

Gracias mama earth, Harry thought. And as he often does, Harry thanked the God of fashion for his continued support for miniskirts.

"Big Mel," Harry said to EBIL to establish some decorum within the business establishment.

After lingering for just a few more seconds of visual bliss, Mel said, "You're back?"

"Nope, an apparition is all I am," Harry responded.

"Asshole," Mel replied.

Bunny straightened up to the dismay of all in attendance. She thought about what Harry had just said and broke into a big smile.

Takes a while, but she usually gets them sooner or later.

"Of course, if we were to find ourselves at my place sometime today, you wouldn't think I was an apparition, Ms. Malone," Harry said as he walked by her heading for the back of the office.

Again, momentary thought, knowing smile following.

To his back Bunny said, "My dad's out of town and I promised my mom I'd take her shopping and have an early dinner with her tonight. Girly stuff, you know. I could stop by for dessert."

Harry turned to face her.

"Our usual dessert?" he asked.

"I'll bring all the sugar you'll need, Harry," Bunny cooed.

"You're on," Harry said.

"I like it that way," Bunny replied.

Mel got up and walked out of the office shaking his head and mumbling "You have got to be shitting me" as he left.

"How's eight-thirty sound?" Harry asked Bunny.

"Great, I'll be there with bells on," Bunny said.

"Not for long if I have my way," Harry smiled.

Chapter 90

It took a full two hours for Harry to bring the case file up to date. As he did, Harry realized there was one gaping hole in the investigation that needed to be plugged. It was on his priority list and had been for some time. He just hadn't gotten to it and it pissed him off he had let an integral piece of the puzzle go unexplored to its fullest for this long.

Davey Boy McGarry.

Why had he let it go untouched for so long. There wasn't really much available information to latch on to. Get over it and do what you do—dig for it or make it materialize.

A Harry Mickey Shorts QAS that needed attention badly. But not before lunch with his sweetie of an ex that happened to be next on his agenda.

~ * ~

The local pub was semi-hopping for a mid-week almost past lunch time afternoon. Why was it almost past lunch time—maybe it was because his sweetie of an ex happened to be over a half-hour late for their lunch appointment.

"Car this and drop something off that," she had said when she called him on his cell as he sat at the table waiting for her.

Real reason—she was almost always late when she was off doing shit for somebody else that she did way too often.

Not my problem was how Harry rationalized it. Plus, he was on his second cool one, relaxing and enjoying the music and pleasant atmosphere of people enjoying people. The case was on the back burner of his mind and would stay there until he summoned it to the front.

He could do that. Van Morrison singing the praises of one Brown Eyed Girl was helping.

Sherry swept in moments later and could still turn more than a few heads when she came into a room. Harry had looked up immediately and had been staring at her the entire time.

Yep, you can call me Johnson…

"I'm so sorry, Harry. The traffic was crazy and I couldn't find a spot to…," Sherry was saying before Harry stood, reached over and kissed her on the cheek.

She seemed to lose track of what she was saying and slumped down in the booth.

"Thanks, Harry. You always did know exactly what to do when I needed it," Sherry said.

"Yeah, it was all the other things I did when I happened to be around that got in the way," Harry said somewhat glumly.

"Screw that for now, Harry. We drinking here?" she asked.

"I'm way ahead of you sweetie," Harry said showing her his half empty glass. "What will you have?" he asked.

"I parked the car at home and walked over, so…," she finished.

Harry waived for the waitress to come over and ordered Sherry a Black Russian.

"Everything good with the kids?" Harry asked her.

"They're great, Harry. It would be good if they could see you a little more, but they appreciate the time you spend with them," she replied. "Next Saturday something special?"

"A surprise is all. You wanna come along; it could be a blast?"

Sherry thought about it, then said, "Nah, Harry, it's your time with them. You enjoy it and they look forward to these special Saturdays just with you."

"All right, but if you change your mind, you're welcome to tag along," Harry told her.

"Speaking of the kids, they're off on a school trip this afternoon and won't be home until after six," Sherry said as her drink was placed in front of her.

"After six you say?" Harry repeated with an upturned eyebrow to emphasize the possibilities.

Sherry took a healthy sip of her drink and said, "Yep, not gonna be home before six at the earliest."

"Hm," Harry hm'd.

"Yep, hm," Sherry almost hummed.

With another wave of his hand as he proceeded to finish off his beer, Harry summoned the waitress and gave her a twenty dollar bill. He and Sherry were headed for the front door before the waitress could even produce a check.

Chapter 91

Their naked bodies resting on pillows propped up against the head-board, Harry and Sherry were sharing a bowl of ice cream with whipped cream and chocolate sprinkles.

"I bought the multi-colored sprinkles one time, but Max threw them out before I could even put them on the shelf in the cupboard," Sherry said between bites....of ice cream.

"That is a very intelligent son you have there, my dear," Harry said.

"I know," Sherry agreed. "He was taught by the best or so he keeps telling me," she chided him.

As Harry was scooping the last bit of ice cream out of the bowl with his spoon, he gestured with his head toward the window and said, "What kind of bird is that?"

Sherry turned toward the window to look and Harry proceeded to drop the ice cream on her chest right between her breasts.

Sherry squealed in surprise when it hit. Being the gentleman that he is, Harry quickly moved his head between her breasts to clean up the mess.

~ * ~

Safely propped up against the headboard again and no more ice cream in sight, Sherry asked, "So, what was it you wanted to talk to me about, Harry?"

Glancing at the bedside clock to make sure he had plenty of time to vamoose before the kids got home, Harry said, "Your dates."

"My dates?" she said somewhat confused.

"Yes, the dates you had with Matt Broderick. There was something you said, or didn't say, when we discussed you seeing him that has been sitting in the back of my feeble mind, gnawing away at it. I'm sure it's relevant to what I've been working on, but I can't put my finger on it," Harry told her.

"Any hint what it was?" she asked.

"It was something like 'about breeding' and a 'partnership with some-thing, or somebody' I think you said. Maybe it wasn't exactly that, but it was close I think. Do you remember us discussing that?" Harry asked her.

Sherry folded her arms over her chest and thought about what Harry had just said for a few seconds. For some reason her concentration caused her nipples to harden on breasts already pushed up and out under her folded arms.

Fully noticing the new development before him, Harry slunk down in the bed while saying, "Keep concentrating," to Sherry. Quicker than you could say *mouth full of luscious tit* Harry had his lips locked on one of Sherry's firm and inviting nipples.

A quick smack to the side of his head put a damper on his anticipated activities.

"Get a grip on yourself, Harry. We're talking here," Sherry told him firmly. "Talk first and, if you're a real good boy, they'll be another round of sucking and fucking to follow. Can you handle that?" she asked him.

Giving her his best scolded little boy look, he nodded his head to say he could.

"Good. Now where were we? Yeah, Matt. He did say something about a partnership and some breeding deal. That's why I looked up breeding later on. He talked about another guy like he was important and he was going to get him away from "them," whoever them was."

"Them?" Harry repeated.

"He was kinda drunk and rambling on by then. I think that was when that big scary guy that was always by his side suggested they leave…"

"Whoa," Harry said. "What big scary guy? You didn't mention a big scary guy before. What'd he look like?" Harry asked already thinking he knew the answer.

"He was a big guy, Harry, what you'd refer to as a brick shithouse I think. And if you can look Irish, he was all Irish. Talked with a brogue I believe you call it, like he was right off the boat," Sherry said confirming Harry's suspicions.

"Thanks, Sherry. I think I can put some things together now or at least I'm pointed in that direction," Harry said.

"I'm glad I could help, Harry," she told him. "So, if we're done talking, make like a submarine skipper and dive, dive, dive."

Chapter 92

Safely out of the house and on his way well before the magical six o'clock "your-ass-is-grass" deadline, Harry was lounging in his apartment reading the Daily Racing Form, cool one at his side. Since he had taken on this assignment it had become required daily reading for him—cover to cover. If there was even the smallest fact in the daily version of the racing bible that pertained to his case, Harry would find it.

A momentary mental diversion flicked an image on his internal TV screen replaying his afternoon with Sherry. He smiled. Maybe they could coexist in the same town together and treat each other civilly—just not under the same roof.

And the sex—the chemistry between them was always power-packed with the sex exploding into 4th of July fireworks any time they went skin to skin. Man what legs, and ass, and hands, and mouth, and...

Somewhere in his mind-daze, Harry's eye caught a small snippet buried within a middle-of-the-form article that detailed the buying and selling for the last two weeks. He had seen similar articles before and read them with passing interest. It was the cumulative effect that was painting him a picture he thought he needed to look closer at. Turn over the rock; see what's underneath he reminded himself.

He gathered all of the "like and kind" articles he could find from the racing forms he had saved and started to pull out the information he needed from each edition. Individual claims—sales and purchases—meant nothing by themselves unless they formed a pattern that pointed at something else.

Facts point and clues are born. Or, clues are born from facts. Or, facts are clues waiting to be born. It's some crap like that.

Anyway, when he was done compiling the claims from all the forms he could put his hands on, walah!

What's walah? Well, it's when you find something you didn't see or have before and now you got it. It's Walah! in private detectivese.

Probably voila to mere mortals.

Harry had charted the information on paper and sat back to see if he actually had something. After looking at it for five full minutes, he was convinced. The first look-see convinced him, but no reason to be hasty. There was a perfectly clear pattern of horses being entered into claiming races that were a level below where they had been racing and had been successful in the recent past. Horses that were then claimed out of those races and lost to the stable. Yes, it was money in their pocket, but they lost quality horse flesh that had been making them money on the track.

So, you say, horses get claimed all the time, every racing day of the year you say. That's correct, but how many stables consistently drop their horses down to a lower claiming level knowing they could, and should, lose them from that race. Any trainer will take a chance on a quality horse that has been running well and is being offered for sale at a cheaper price than it should command.

They'd run out of horses to enter in races and have no stable left you say. Normally that would be the end result, unless they were claiming horses from the same races or other claiming races on the same race card to restock their stable. Horses in and horses out. Horse churn—not a completely out of the question scenario when it comes to smaller stables with lower quality animals to run.

But, and it's a major but, not when the stable is part of a major international racing corporation and almost all of the horses that are being claimed from their string are being claimed by the same trainer.

Info in hand, Harry headed for the door to shoot up to Mel's office and enter what he had found in the computer. Dump it into Excel and be able to sort and manipulate the data any which way he needed. As he got to the bottom of the stairs and opened the door, there to his surprise, and pure delight, was...

Dessert.

Chapter 93

The phone ringing at nine-thirty at night wasn't all that unusual. Harry often got calls at all hours of the day or night depending on what he happened to be working on, or with who, or whom, whichever is proper.

It was the who, or whom he happened to be desserting with at that very moment that was the reason for the problem.

"Yeah," Harry said into the receiver when he finally got to the phone.

"Sounds like the whippin' post done pained your ass, my man," was the response that greeted Harry.

"Jaxy, my main man. How you be, kiddo?" Harry said as he tried to extricate himself from the entanglement he had been enjoying before the phone rang. His fellow entanglee was resisting.

"Harry, if I be any better, I'd be scurrying down that yellow brick road to the land we all know," Jaxy replied.

Harry often had no idea what in the holy hell Jaxy was talking about.

"Cool, Jaxy. You got some goodies for me?"

"Goody two shoes, socks and all; the moniker's cool, but the dude's a fool," Jaxy replied. "The fellows you be tracking are righteously good, Harry. But even if they be better than most, I'm Jaxy, and we be the Web Dudes. No match, you dig?" he said.

Jaxy would swing from music man to cool dude with the drop of a hat. You just never knew who you were going to get when Jaxy came on the line. One thing was for sure though, it would be entertaining.

To play along, Harry said, "I dig, Jaxy. You and the boys be square down. Spill."

"Spillin' and chillin', dog."

May the god of the English language have pity on my soul.

Jaxy spent the next five minutes detailing the intricate path our bad guys followed to protect the undetected and set up their new operation. Jaxy was good, I'll give him that. How he came up with the information was a good question, but not one to be asked.

"Thanks, man. You done me solid as usual," Harry told Jaxy.

"Got me smiling all the way to the bank, Harry. I'll be 'spectin a deposit soon, the usual fur sur. Give sweet-cheeks a squeeze for me, my man, and follow the wind," Jaxy said and he was in it.

"Hot damn," Harry said to nobody in particular.

"I will be if you'd forget the freakin' phone and pay a little attention my way," Bunny said in response.

Actually having forgotten she was there, he did, and the rest of dessert was too sweet for words.

~ * ~

There was a special peace Harry felt when he sat in Mel's office late at night all by himself. The monitor provided the only light and it seemed blinding in the midst of the surrounding darkness.

Harry now had a picture that pointed him toward the puss-heads that perpetrated this scheme. Didn't prove they did anything and didn't prove a crime was committed against Board Room Farms, or anyone else, but it proved they were in it up to their eyeballs. What the "it" was still needed to be doped out fully.

Start with the who, add the where, you find the what. The when be yesterday, the day before, and now. It was all beginning to fall into place and Harry finally had a good feeling about this case. Frustration can breed more frustration and lead you down paths you shouldn't waste time and energy on. It happens and sometimes you get lucky and find a nugget off the beaten path. Sometimes you just waste more time and effort.

Sometimes, as is the case here, you call Jaxy and the Web Dudes do you a fourteen carat gold solid and point the way.

Mind-taxing as conversing with Jaxy can be at times, thank god for the Web Dudes.

Chapter 94

"The Manhasset Diner at nine," the voice said when Harry answered the phone the following morning. The bedside clock read eight-ten, so he had time to perform the morning rituals and prepare himself for...he didn't know what for.

Just when you think you're on the straight and narrow, the path bends.

~ * ~

Harry was sitting in the back booth of the Manhasset Diner at five minutes to nine, his back to the door. He had added a half-teaspoon of sugar and was stirring his coffee when the waitress brought the food. She placed a plate in front of him with two eggs over easy, bacon and white toast. Across from him she placed a similar order with the only difference being rye toast instead of white.

Harry started to eat.

Mueller slid into the booth two minutes later, picked up a fork and started to break the yokes of his eggs. The Racing Form was neatly folded in half and he read as he sliced his eggs. No good morning, no thanks for the food, no words period.

"Morning," Harry tried as he continued to enjoy his eggs and bacon together.

"Since midnight," Mueller responded.

No further discussion ensued. Food and the Racing Form for Mueller, just food for Harry, with a fine version of 'Blowin' In The Wind' resounding in his head.

Sopping up the last bit of egg yoke with his toast, Mueller finished his coffee and got up. He dropped a ten on the table and said, "Let's go."

Figuring he wasn't talking to the waitress, Harry took a final sip of his coffee and followed.

The car was waiting at the curb—Harry and Mueller got in. Without discussion the driver pulled away from the curb and started on their way. Where to Harry didn't know, but they were headed there.

"Where we headed?" Harry asked to clear up the mystery.

Mueller looked at Harry, down at the Racing Form by his side, and then back at Harry.

"Track?" Harry guessed.

"Track," Mueller confirmed.

Having traveled for awhile, Harry noticed the direction they were heading was wrong. They may be headed to the track, but not to a New York track, at least not directly. There were still plenty of tracks in the United States Harry hadn't been to, he just hadn't expected today would be the day he added a new one.

"If I might be so nosy, what track will we be frequenting today?" Harry asked.

"Philadelphia Park," came the reply from Mueller. "Been there?"

"No I haven't," Harry answered. "Some reason we are headed out of New York for a lengthy car ride to go to a small track like Philadelphia Park when we have a perfectly good track back in New York?"

"Yes," Mueller answered.

Silence.

After waiting an appropriate amount of time to see if Mueller was going to elucidate, Harry jumped back into the one sided conversation.

"Okay, I'll ask. Why?"

Harumph. That's what the sound that came from Mueller sounded like.

Harumph a second time.

"One, I like the track. I used to go there a fair share and enjoy the intimacy of it. Two, cheaper horses, but quality cheaper horses. Keeps you sharp and you have to work at handicapping local horses combined with shippers from up and down the east coast."

Silence as he picked up his Racing Form again.

"No other reason?" Harry asked.

"Three, Broderick is running two horses today," Mueller said without looking up.

Which Broderick? I don't know. Look in the form or ask. A Shorts QAS with a simple solution.

"Which one?" Harry asked him.

"Ones I believe you meant to say. Pretty Lady in Pink in the third and Publishers Dream in the seventh," he responded.

Dickhead Harry thought to himself.

"No, which Broderick?" Harry had to ask.

"Why, Matt Broderick, of course."

Chapter 95

Philadelphia Park was originally called Keystone Racetrack and his dad had told Harry of trips he had made there when he was in his betting days. The apple fell out of the tree and clonked Harry on the head, which is probably why Harry went through his own period of gambling bliss.

The ex-major league baseball player Richie Allen once ran his string of horses through Keystone.

"Great place to watch the ponies scamper," his dad would say.

For no reason at all, Harry's mom made his dad give up the horses and every other damn thing that he enjoyed. That, my friends, is why Harry hasn't spoken to his mother for as long as he can remember.

~ * ~

Harry and Mueller were sitting in the enclosed reserve seating section of Philadelphia Park. The entire grandstand is enclosed which is one of the beauties of the place. Cold or heat outside doesn't matter; it's always the same inside.

Mueller hadn't spoken ten words to Harry since they had gotten to the park. Racing Form in one hand, cold coffee in the other, Mueller had spent the entire time handicapping the day's races. Or so it looked. Harry was sure Mueller had already done his work and knew exactly what bets he would place for the entire card.

Harry would do his race by race and had the first three done.

Spectator watching was a hobby of Harry's and the track produced a bevy of entertaining souls to keep Harry's interest peaked. The educated ones looked just like Mueller, Racing Form and all. Doping out the days races was the only thing that mattered. Their concentration level was unmatched. The world could go haywire around them; the form was all they would see.

The casual bettors might have the form, or they might have the "tout" sheets that the so-called track experts sold for a buck or two. They picked all the winners for you and assisted in the removal of your hard earned dollars from your person. If they were so good they would be betting their own winners and living in mansions instead of standing at the track hawking guesses.

And then there were the program bettors. You can see them watching the horses coming onto the track and looking at the track program that does nothing more than list the horses, and jockeys, and trainers, etc. The ladies that pick a horse just because the jockey is wearing a pink shirt have as much chance as the track program bettors. Close your eyes and pick a number.

But the most fun is watching the winners and losers after the race ends. Grown people jumping around and hugging everyone they can find because they just won three dollars and forty cents on Lucky Lady in the third. Or the losing ticket rippers who swear the jockey just stiffed them when they know they had the best horse by far. God love 'em all—they keep the track going and Harry entertained.

From what Mueller had told Harry and he had then confirmed in the Racing Form, Matt Broderick had horses running in the third and seventh races. Both were shipping in from other tracks for the race, and both were favorites. Prohibitive favorites. From the patterns Harry had seen in his digging through past performances during his research phase, Matt Broderick shippers that went off as favorites almost never lost. For the two running today, from what Harry could tell by their recent form and the competition they were running against, the pattern wouldn't be changing today.

The jockey listed on both horses was McDonough. The Bug.

So, why were they there? Again, the answer was I dunno. Ask Mueller. A QAS that was becoming standard issue lately.

"So, ah Mueller, why are we really here?" Harry asked Mueller.

"You can be an annoying little bastard, can't you Shorts."

"Yep, when it suits," Harry replied.

"All right, let's go," Mueller said as he got up and headed up the stairs.

Chapter 96

A very large Asian gentleman dressed in what was probably a thousand dollar suit that would fit two of Harry looked their way as Mueller and Harry approached a door that said No Entrance.

A look, a flash of recognition, the smallest hint of a smile.

"Been a while," he said to Mueller when they got close enough to the man for Mueller to reach out and shake his hand.

"Too long," Mueller replied.

"Who?" he asked.

"Broderick," Mueller replied.

"Expecting?" he asked.

"No."

"Wait," the large gentleman said and went through the door.

I guess there was entrance if you were allowed to enter.

"Friend of yours?" Harry asked Mueller.

"We've know each other," he replied.

"From the looks of him, good person to know," Harry said.

"Handy at the time," was all Mueller said.

It was probably two or three minutes before the door opened again and another man came out. He was a smidge smaller than the first man, but it didn't matter when you get to be that size. Not Asian, though. Must have been a mute, too, since he didn't say anything and just stood there, the door ajar.

You of course know it couldn't be a jar; it was a door, but let's move on.

"Go ahead," Mueller said.

"You coming?" Harry asked.

"Nope, got stuff to do. You wanted him, he's yours," Mueller said as he turned and walked away.

Harry would have asked how Mueller knew he wanted to talk to Matt Broderick, but he knew it would have been a waste of time and he would have gotten no response. Mueller just seemed to know shit.

Again Harry wondered for the umpteenth time—who the hell is this guy.

Harry was met by a skinny nervous tick of a man who said, "Follow me," to Harry.

He walked and Harry did as instructed—he followed. Before long the skinny dude opened a door and stepped aside for Harry to enter.

He entered.

"Okay, who the hell are you and what do you want?" greeted Harry as he stepped into the room.

Matt Broderick, if this was indeed Matt Broderick that Harry was looking at, and he had no reason to doubt it was, seemed shorter than Harry would have expected. Slightly built, too. Harry had expected someone that would have mirrored Mikey Broderick in his younger days. This guy didn't. His brothers from the pictures Harry had seen on the net did. Must be the runt of the family.

"Name's Harry Mickey Shorts. You don't know me, but I spent a little time with your dad recently and I'm interested in the horse racing business."

"I give a fuck why?" was the retort.

Broderick continued to eye the day's entry sheets and still hadn't even looked up at Harry.

"Listen, as I just said, we don't know each other from a hole in the wall. I can piss on your left shoe and you can piss on my right shoe. You know what we end up with—shoes full of piss. We didn't get anywhere," Harry responded.

Broderick finally looked Harry in the eye.

"Harry whoever the fuck you are, I'm busy. I'm a mover and a shaker heading to the big time and I don't have time for little pukes like you. So, go peddle your shit elsewhere or I'll piss all up and down both your legs."

"I…," Harry started before he was rudely cut off by Broderick raising his hand in a stopping motion.

"Don't say another word," Broderick said in Harry's direction as the walking tick entered the room from a side door.

"What do you want Hutchinson?" Broderick snarled.

"Matt, ah Mister Broderick, sir, the…the…the… the stewards are ask…asking for you," he stuttered.

"Fine. Tell them I'll be right there."

He ran for the door.

"Turning back to Harry, Broderick said, "Nothing else, good, then we're done," and he looked down at his papers again in dismissal.

Turning to leave, Harry looked back over his shoulder and said, "See you on your way back down when the Mick's done with you, too."

Broderick's head snapped up instantly and Harry knew he had hit a nerve. He also knew he had just confirmed another important piece of the puzzle.

~ * ~

"Get what you needed?" Mueller asked as Harry sat in the seat next to him in the grandstand.

"We had a less than pleasant chat; but yes, I got what I needed."

No response from Mueller.

"You know him?" Harry asked.

"Of him," Mueller responded. "I'm gonna bet the first," and he got up and left.

Chapter 97

On the ride back to New York after their day at Philadelphia Park, Harry and Mueller talked about the races and who and why they bet on the horses they did. Mostly Harry talked while Mueller nodded and spoke an occasional word or three.

"You bet out on both of Broderick's horses?" Harry asked.

"Yes. Made my day," Mueller responded neglecting to say how much of a day it made for him.

"You come down here just to bet those two horses?" Harry continued.

Negative nod of the head in response.

"You come down here to bet those two horses and make sure I got to see Broderick while we were here?" Harry tried again.

A barely recognizable shrug of the shoulders seemed to point Harry in a direction to follow.

"How'd you know?"

"Just did. That's all you get on that topic, so drop it. Anything else you need at the moment?" Mueller asked.

"Shouldn't you be telling me since you seem to know what I need and want better than I do," Harry responded.

"Shorts, I'm doing my thing here and sometimes I'm gonna cross over into your thing. That happens, you get the benefit. I'm not here to hold your hand, or do your job, or tell you how to do your job. I come, I go. Simple as that. You dig, kiddo?" Mueller said with a smile.

"I dig, kiddo. And thanks for today, it helped clear up a few things and gave me an unexpected bonus on top."

"Good," Mueller said. "Now don't fuck up."

With that the car exited the turnpike and Mueller exited the car at the rest area.

"What the fuck?" Harry asked.

"Gots to see a man about a horse. Car will take you home and I'll catch up with you another time," Mueller answered, closing the door and walking away.

"The phone is for you, sir" the driver said to Harry when they had begun motoring again.

"Phone?" Harry asked.

"Lift the armrest in the middle of the seat under your arm and the phone will be inside. Just pick it up," the driver instructed.

Move arm, lift armrest, find phone—just like the man said.

"Hello," Harry said tentatively.

"Harry, its Doc. Some guy just called and said I was thinking about you and I should just talk to you instead. How'd he know I was thinking about you, Harry? And how'd he find me and hook me up with you? This is weird, Harry. Very weird," Doc said.

"Doc, you don't know the half of it. The guy majored in weird in college I think. Long as you're on the phone, how are you?" Harry asked.

"I'm missing you, Harry, that's how I am. I tried not to, I tried real hard, but I can't. You coming this way any time soon?" Doc asked.

"What, the boys need something to croon about?" Harry joked.

"Very funny, asshole. And it's not the boys that need something to croon about; it's me, Harry."

"I'm busier than a three legged dog trying to bury a bone on a frozen lake. No time to think, but I'm missing you too, Doc. I'll try and get out there as soon as I can. I'd ask you to come east, but I know you have your hands full on the ranch and at the hospital."

"I do, Harry. Doesn't mean I'm not thinking about you," she said.

"I'll do my best, Doc. Say hi to the boys for me, will ya?"

"I will, Harry. And this phone thing, it works from east to west, too."

"I hear ya, Doc. You take care, kiddo," Harry said.

"You too, Harry," Doc said and the phone went dead.

Chapter 98

When Harry got home he checked his phone for messages. Sherry had left him a message earlier that day and asked him to call when he got in, whatever time.

Interested enough, he called.

"Hey, Sherry," he said when she answered on the third ring.

"Hi, Harry. Out all day?" she asked.

One of the major things that caused Harry to head elsewhere when they were married was Sherry's constant insistence on knowing where Harry was all the time—day or night. Since Harry was away from home much of the time, it was a lot.

Old habits never die.

"Yes, Sherry, I was out since early this morning. I can run down my day for you if you need it, but I don't think you really need to know where I was all day, do you, Sherry?"

"I'm sorry, Harry, it just came out," she said.

"No problemo, kiddo. What's up?"

"I just wanted to tell you the kids are bugging the hell out of me trying to figure out what you have planned for them next Saturday. I have to admit, I'm a little curious myself. Can you give me a hint what you have planned for them?" Sherry tried.

"No dice, Sher. And by the way, you're still invited to come along if you want. I can have a car pick you up and take you to…," Harry let hang in the air.

Harry could tell Sherry was thinking about what Harry had said, pondering the offer.

"I wouldn't want to intrude on your Saturday outings with the kids, Harry. They're special to the kids and they look forward to them so much," she said.

"You wouldn't be intruding, Sher. Without spilling any of the beans, you'd have a good time hanging with some people I know, while me and the kids are doing our thing. Be fun to see them doing it, I promise," Harry urged.

"Let me think about it, okay, Harry? I just don't want to step on something that's so good for Max and Briande. And you, too, Harry. I know you really dig these Saturdays with the kids. Give me a day or two and I'll get back to you," she finished.

"Sure, Sherry. Whenever you decide is fine. I'll set it up just in case you decide to come. I can always cancel it later."

"Thanks, Harry. And just so you know, I enjoyed the time we spent together. It's good to be around you and have fun. You can be lots of fun, Harry, in all kinds of ways, if you know what I mean?"

Johnson was telling Harry he knew what she meant.

"And just so I know, Harry, anything special I would need to wear for where we'd be going? You know, outdoors or inside, extra clothes to change into later, that kind of thing?" she tried.

"Just look gorgeous like you always do, Sherry, and the rest will take care of itself."

"You're no fun, Harry," she said.

"That's not what you said last time we got together," Harry reminded her.

"That's a different kind of fun, Harry, a whole different kind of fun."

"You got that one right, kiddo. I gotta split. Call me when you decide, okay?"

"I will, Harry. And Harry, thanks for thinking of me," she said.

Chapter 99

Mel was busy doing the hard sell on the phone while Harry updated his case file in the rear of the office. Everything was pretty well tied down by now and Harry wanted to get a copy of his notes to Randle so he could digest what Harry had found out before he saw him again.

"Of course it's the right house for you," Mel was saying into the phone. "It's the right house, at the right price, and she's going to love it when you bring your bride home from the honeymoon."

Mel paused while he listened and rolled his eyes at Harry indicating bullshit was pouring forth from the other end of the connection.

"Yes, yes, and yes. All things are good about this deal and if you don't jump on it now it's gonna evaporate right out from under you. You're in first and you have until the end of business today to okay the deal. If not, the house goes back out to other bidders and you may either lose it or get hosed on the price. Either way, you lose."

More rolling of the eyes from Big Mel.

"Good, smart boy. I'll call it in and get the papers to you before the end of the day. You are going to thank me for this when that new wife of yours sees her new home and bangs your brains out in the front hallway as a thank you. Trust me on that one," Mel finished.

Phone call completed, Mel turned his attention toward Harry and laughed.

"What?" Harry asked.

"Poor schmuck's marrying a broad half the guys in town would gladly give their right nut to jump in her panties," Mel told him.

"Just half?" Harry asked.

"Yeah, just half," Mel replied. "That's because the other half have already been there. Big tits, great ass, and she just loves to hump and be humped. Any time of the day or night, makes no difference to her."

"Do you happen to come upon this knowledge from firsthand experience?" Harry asked.

"I'm part of the unfortunate half that doesn't have said firsthand knowledge," Mel told Harry. "First, she goes for the money, looking to bag somebody like the one she finally got her hooks into. And second, the wife would cut my dick off if she ever found out. I'd like to keep my dick attached for future use. They are some great looking tits and ass though," he smiled.

Finally realizing who Mel was talking about, Harry said, "She wouldn't be the one I…," before Mel cut him off.

"That's the one; Ms. Dover as she is affectionately referred to around town," Mel confirmed.

"You are right, my man. She has some great tits and an ass to die for. Plus, she's like that little battery bunny—goes all day and keeps on coming back for more."

"Spare me the details for Christ sake," Mel said.

"Did I tell you the trick she does with her…," Harry was starting to say before Mel threw his mini basketball at him to shut him up.

"They won't last a year," Mel said.

"Yeah, but for him, what a year it will be," Harry chimed in.

Mel laughed and said, "I can't believe the dude's marrying Ms. Ben Dover."

Chapter 100

The next few days were spent tying up a couple of loose ends and setting up a meet with Mikey Broderick, Sr. Word had it he was due in town for a few days and Harry was using his Trundle contact to make the meet happen.

Horse racing would be the topic of discussion once they got started, but it didn't necessarily have to be the subject used to set up the meet. The Brodericks would be front and center once Harry got down to business with one Broderick in particular. There was the potential for a messy scene, but messy scenes weren't anything new to Harry and he was sure they weren't anything new to the Broderick clan either.

~ * ~

After a quick bite and a pair of cool ones down at the pub, Harry was walking down Plandome Road heading back to his apartment. Things were quiet on the case front and he was thinking about Sherry and the kids, and Doc. Combined it was a bushel to think about for sure, but he was feeling good about his world, the case, and what was happening in general.

A sense was all it was. A sense something was there. Harry had felt it before and it had served him well in the past. No rhyme or reason for him to get "a feeling" of something being there; but he did and there was.

He came out of the shadows and stepped in front of Harry, blocking his way. As big as he was, blocking Harry's way wasn't hard.

"How are ya on this fine evening, laddie?" he said with a brogue Harry had heard for a fleeting second once before.

"Well, I'm just fine," Harry replied. "Thanks for asking."

Harry attempted to move around him but he was blocked again as the big fella moved in unison with Harry.

Three feet separated them. Tension filled the gap.

"You should be minding yer own business, laddie. Buttin' into other blokes business can get ya hurt if yer not careful, ya know," he brogued on.

"Excuse me," Harry said trying to move around him again to no avail.

"Is there a problem here, Shawn?" came a voice from the same shadows big boy had emerged from.

Without turning, he replied knowingly, "That you Mueller? Been a wee while since you and I tangled, hasn't it now?"

Mueller stepped out of the shadows and gestured with his eyes to Harry that this was his to deal with. As big as this guy was, and remembering what happened the last time they collided, Harry gladly obliged.

"Let the gentleman pass, will ya now, Shawn. He hasn't done anything to rile you now has he?" Mueller said.

"He's been stickin' his nose in other people's business for no reason when he shouldn't have. The boss wanted it stopped. And if ya wants me to let the laddie pass, yer gonna have ta make me now, Mueller. Ya know ya will," Shawn replied.

"No reason to waste any time, Shawn. Let's have a go at it then," Mueller answered.

"Don't worry, you'll be next, laddie," Shawn told Harry with a smile.

Shawn turned and took two steps toward Mueller as he prepared to get into a fighting stance. He never made it. In what Harry could only describe as a flying helicopter side kick, Mueller lifted himself off the ground, spun in the air, and knocked Shawn into left field. If you blinked, you would have missed it.

"What in the holy name of fuck was that, Mueller?" Harry asked in awe.

"Shawn's too dumb and doesn't know when to quit. I felt it would be better to end it quickly before he got a chance to get going. Our last set-to took almost ten minutes before I finally got him to cry uncle," Mueller explained.

"You are one surprising dude, Mueller," Harry said.

"That's the way I like it," Mueller replied. "He's yours to clean up if you choose to," Mueller said as he turned and walked back into the shadows.

Harry took one look at the mass of humanity spread out on the ground and promptly exited—stage right.

Chapter 101

Harry woke early on Saturday morning feeling like a million bucks. He had been looking forward to today since he had put the plans in place. Max and Briande were great kids and deserved everything he tried to do for them. He did enough "to" them early on in their lives; he might as well try and make it up to them by doing things "for" them now.

Mel's buddy Shack pulled into the driveway right on time at 8:45 driving the biggest Hummer limo Harry had ever seen. Shack had told Harry he would surprise him and surprise him he did.

"Shack, dude, that mother's nearly a block long," Harry told him as Shack climbed out to greet Harry.

"Hot off the assembly line, Harry," Shack responded. "Got it delivered yesterday and you and your brood will be the first to christen it."

"The kids are gonna flip," Harry told Shack.

"Plus, the trip's on me, Harry," Shack said. "The whole shebang. While I'm enjoying the day, this baby is going to be sitting in the parking lot with a big sign advertising 'Shack's Limo Service' and its fleet of exotic stretch limos."

"Never miss a beat, do you Shack?" Harry replied.

"Not a one, Harry, not a single one. Let's motor."

Shack pulled up in front of the kid's house precisely at 9:00 am and hit the horn. The "horn" sounded like a carnival of beeps, screeches, blips and who knows what else that definitely announced their arrival.

Bouncing out of the house and down the steps, the kids stopped in mid-step as they spied their "ride" for the day.

Opening the door, Shack proclaimed, "Master Max and Ms. Briande, your transportation has arrived."

"You da man," Max declared as he high-fived Shack and jumped into the ride.

"Very nice," Briande deadpanned as she proceeded to jump high in the air while laying a solid high-five upon Shack as well.

Squeals of joy and delight abounded.

While the kids jubilated with Shack, Harry had walked halfway up the front walk to meet Sherry. Dressed in a pink tank top, tan shorts and light pink sandals, Sherry was an early morning vision to behold.

With a quick peck on the cheek, Harry whispered in her ear, "Looking good enough to eat, Sher."

"That comes later, Harry" she responded.

"Your lips to God's ears," Harry whispered back.

"Cut the shit and get in the car—IHOP awaits," Shack yelled.

As they got in the back of the Hummer, Harry said to Shack, "IHOP it is then James."

"I'll James you, you prick," Shack said as he slammed the door to the sound of laughter everywhere, himself included.

IHOP was a full-blown fiasco with enough food ordered and consumed to feed two armies. Sherry put down a stack of pancakes and a double order of bacon herself and she was the lightweight at the table. Even Briande outdid herself in Mom's presence.

Wiping his mouth with his napkin, Max proclaimed, "Let's blow this popsicle stand and get the party going, kiddos."

Harry paid and they prepared to get it on.

Chapter 102

The ride out East on the Long Island Expressway was less crowded than usual. The atmosphere inside the Hummer could almost be explained as "family" like—mom and dad spending the day out with the kids. Harry being a current outsider—normally looking in from the outside—was forgotten for a while.

The sound system in the mondo-limo was dynamite and Shack piped in a steady stream of tunes. Madonna for Briande got things started followed by an Irish singer by the name of Maire Brennan for Sherry. The Beatles serenaded for a time and then Jethro Tull rocked the Hummer into their destination for Max and Harry.

Almost exactly an hour into the ride, the Hummer came to a stop. With the heavily tinted windows preventing them from seeing much of the ride while they were traveling, the kids weren't sure exactly where they were. Sherry—she didn't have a clue, and Harry had refused to give them any hints while en route.

Shack announced, "We're here," and got out to come around and open the doors for them. Before he could, Harry said, "This day is for you two, Max and Briande. I hope you enjoy it."

The door opened and the kids stepped out to see the Bayport Schooners Stadium before them.

"Huh," Max said.

"Ah, huh," Briande mimed.

"Harry?" their mom and Harry's ex-wife asked in question form.

Getting fully out of the Hummer, Harry turned to Shack and said, "What are we doing here, Shack? What did you do?"

Shack looked at Harry and the kids, then Sherry, and shrugged his shoulders.

"Harry, I thought you said...I could have sworn you wanted to...oh, I must have thought I heard you say...oh, man, I'm in trouble."

Raising his voice, Harry yelled something at Shack and Shack yelled back equally as loud. The small crowd that had gathered in the parking lot looked on. Looking like they were about to duke it out, they starting laughing and did their own high-five routine.

Harry turned to the kids and they jumped him ready to pummel him to death. Sherry said, "From my lips to God's ears, Harry," and she laughed as well.

"Come on guys, let's go inside and you'll understand what's up," Harry said to the kids. "You too, Sher. The fun's about to get started. Later Shack."

"I'll be around, Harry. When it's time to head back, the monster will be ready," Shack replied.

"Enjoy the day and we'll see ya later," Harry told Shack.

Walking them up to the player's gate, Harry ushered the kids and Sherry inside.

"Yo, dad, you're not a player. How come we got in through the player's gate?" Max asked.

"All in due time, my man, all in due time" Harry answered.

"What's going on, Harry?" Sherry asked as she gave him one of her looks.

"You'll see," Harry said as he walked them down the corridor and turned left toward the field instead of a right into the locker rooms.

As they entered the field and looked up at the scoreboard in centerfield, in big, bold letters they saw—

WELCOME MAX & BRIANDE

The look on the kid's faces said it all. Smiles as wide as the outfield on both of them; even Sherry showed an appreciative smile.

"What the...?" was all that came out of Max's mouth.

"Hey, Harry, glad you could finally make it," the field and General Manager of the Schooners said as he approached them.

"Guys, you know Mister Curran," Harry said in introduction.

"Hey, guys," Curran said. "On behalf of the entire Schooner organization—let me say welcome."

"Ah, thanks," Max replied tentatively.

"Now, as I'm sure your dad has kept you in the dark, why don't I explain what we have planned for today. That okay with you, Harry?" he asked.

"It's your show now, Mister Curran. I have some things to get to," Harry said as he turned and proceeded to walk over to a group of players near the batting cage.

"Typical Harry," the GM said to Harry's back.

Sherry burned a hole in Harry's back with one of her "laser" looks.

Chapter 103

Curran was about to begin telling Sherry and the kids what plans had been put in place for the day when two men came walking toward them. The GM turned toward them and gestured them over.

"Good timing, guys," he said. "Come on over here."

Turning back toward Sherry and the kids while pointing toward the shorter of the two men, Curran said, "I believe you all know our Assistant GM, Richie."

"Hey guys, Sherry," Richie greeted them. "It's a pleasure to see you again."

"Max," Curran started, "Richie is going to walk you around and introduce you to the players as they come out onto the field for their pre-game warm-ups. Then, he's going to take you for a tour of the stadium, a behind the scenes tour nobody else gets to see. Press boxes, underground batting area, training facility just to name a few places. Finally, he'll show you around the locker room again as the players get ready for the game. Maybe get a few autographs. Sound okay?"

"Way cool," Max replied with a wide grin on his face. "I can't wait."

"Great," Curran replied. "Now, for your day, Briande. This gentleman's name is Bob Alexander, and as soon as he opens his mouth, you will immediately recognize him as the voice of the Bayport Schooners. The young lady heading our way from behind me is Autumn Lilly who works in our PR department with Richie. Everyone involved with the Schooners pulls double or triple duty around here. Autumn will show you around some and get you ready for the pre-game ceremonies."

"Pre-game ceremonies?" Briande repeated.

"Well, Briande, your dad has told me quite a bit about you and what you want to do with your life. Before today's game starts, just as you have done before several of the high school football games, you will be singing the National Anthem. Autumn will get you looking your best and we have a voice coach here to help you practice if you want. Would you like that?" he asked.

"Well, sure, it was always a dream of mine to sing the anthem before one of dad's games," Briande said.

"I know," Curran said, "and today you will be fulfilling that dream. Once the anthem is done, Bob will escort you up to the announcer's booth where you will assist him with the audio play-by-play for today's game. Give you a little jump-start towards your desire to get into communications later on."

Turning toward Sherry, with a tear in her eye, Briande said, "I can't believe all of this, mom. Singing the anthem and getting to announce a game, and on the same day, it's awesome."

"Don't look at me. I didn't have anything to do with any of this. I believe it's the Schooners you have to thank and maybe that guy over by the batting cage as well."

"Thank you so much," Briande said to the GM.

"It's a pleasure, Briande. Enjoy your day and let me know if there is anything we can do for you."

"Sherry, why don't you go along with Autumn and Briande. Once Briande starts her day's activities, Autumn will take you up to Mister Trundle's private box for the game. There was a rumor going around a few of the New York Giants might be here for the game today. And, I thought I heard Richie saying something about some Irish singer being here today—a Maire something who is scheduled to be in the box as well."

Hard to tell who's smile was bigger—Briande's or Sherry's.

Lunch will be at noon in Mr. Trundle's private dining room just outside his box. You will all meet there and after lunch someone will take you wherever you need to be next. "Everyone good with our plans?" the GM asked.

"Oh, yeahs," all around.

"Good, then let's get going. I have a ball club to run."

When Sherry and the kids looked over to where Harry had been standing, he was gone.

"Where's dad?" Briande asked.

"I've been asking the same question for as long as I've known him, honey. Why should today be any different," her mom replied.

Chapter 104

The next few hours flew by. Autumn showed Briande the dress Mr. Trundle had commissioned a top fashion biggie to design for her. When she tried it on, it brought a tear to her mom's eye. She looked that beautiful.

The personal voice coach to several of today's top stars worked with Briande and complemented her natural god given talent. "You keep working on that voice of yours and you'll be a star yourself one day," the coach told her.

Next it was off to make-up and a session with a famous hair consultant; Briande was having the time of her life. It was hard for her to believe the fun part of the day hadn't even begun.

~ * ~

Max was eating it all up. The players were giving him high-fives, low-fives, every "five" there was. The current hitting star on the Schooners was in the batting cage and he was smacking balls high and far. When Richie and Max passed behind the cage, he put up his hand and told the batting practice pitcher to hold up for a minute.

"Yo, kid, you got any game?" he said to Max

"Got some," Max answered confidently.

"Well, let's see it," the slugger replied as he moved out of the cage. He reached into a bat bag next to the cage and pulled out a bat that was a perfect length and weight for Max.

"Here you go, Max. Let's see what ya got."

Since his dad was nowhere to be found, Max looked at Richie and shrugged an, "It all right?"

"Go ahead and take that dead arm out there on the mound deep," Richie told him.

Max entered the batting cage, took a few practice swings, and then signaled for the pitcher to let it fly. The first pitch was high and tight and knocked Max right on his ass. All the players had gathered behind the cage and proceeded to laugh their collective asses off.

"Stick the next one in his ear," slugger yelled.

Max got up, dusted off his shorts, and signaled for the batting practice pitcher to bring it on. He smacked the next pitch on a line right back at the pitcher knocking down the protective net in front of him. The players cheered and Max took a bow. He took a dozen more swings spraying the ball all over the park—one to left, one to center, the next to right. Just like he was taught by his old man who was watching all of it, totally out of sight, from a corner of the dugout. Watching proudly he would have added.

"Way to go kid," the team's slugger said to Max as he came out of the cage. "And here, this is from the guys," he continued as he handed Max a bat signed by the entire team.

"Cool. Thanks, man," Max said in the direction of the entire team.

"Let's go into the clubhouse and get you cleaned up before lunch," Richie told Max. "If we can't get that dirt off, I'll find something else for you to wear."

Entering the clubhouse, Richie started leading Max toward the bathrooms at the other end of the room. A few players were lingering before heading back out onto the field. Half way down the row of player lockers, Richie stopped and two players moved away from the locker they had been standing in front of. There, on a hanger in the open locker, was a Bayport Schooner uniform with the name on the back—Max Shorts.

"What's that?" Max asked Richie.

"Why, it's the uniform the batboy for today's game is going to wear," Richie responded.

"For real?" Max asked in anticipation.

"You bet, Max. Put it on and let's get you up to lunch before you have to go out on the field for the game."

"This day can't get any better," Max beamed.

Richie smiled behind Max's back.

~ * ~

Sherry and Briande were chatting with the New York Giants players who had also been invited to lunch. When Max came into the room they had all they could do to take their ogling eyes off the hunks they were talking to.

Mom noticed him first.

"Max, you're in a uniform," Sherry declared.

"Well, what would you expect the batboy for today's game to be wearing," he replied as he turned and showed off the name on the back of his uniform shirt.

"Oh, Max, you look great," she said. "You always wanted to do this and now you are."

"I know, mom. Despite some of the stuff he does, he's something, isn't he," Max declared proudly. "He never ceases to amaze me."

"Yeah, Max. Sometimes he really is amazing."

Noticing his sister for the first time, Max said, "Not bad, Bri. You don't look half bad when you gussy it up."

"Thank you, Max. You don't look half-bad yourself," Briande replied.

"Hey, let's eat. We're starved," Eli Manning said to the Shorts crew. "And here, catch this, Max," he said as he tossed him a football. Max caught it and saw it had been signed by the entire Giants team.

"It really can't get any better," Max said.

Richie just smiled a knowing smile from the doorway.

Chapter 105

The players had finished their pre-game warm-ups and were in their dugouts ready for the game to begin. Max had spent time on the field with the players and was now getting the equipment in order before the game started.

Funny, but Max still hadn't seen his dad since they had been talking with Mr. Curran earlier in the day.

Bob Alexander walked out onto the field and approached the microphone that had been set up by home plate.

"Ladies and gentlemen—welcome to all of you. To sing the National Anthem before today's game, the Bayport Schooners are proud to have with us today, for your enjoyment, a very special guest. With great pleasure I ask you to stand and give a rousing Schooner welcome to one of our own—Miss Briande Shorts."

Briande made her way to the microphone escorted on both sides by one of the New York Giants. Thanking each of them with a kiss on the cheek, she turned to the mike and said to the crowd, "It is a tremendous honor to be here today on a field where such great players have played the game of baseball, including the greatest of them all, at least in my heart, Harry Mickey Shorts."

The crowd let out a loud roar and as they quieted, Briande began to sing the National Anthem. And sing she did, hitting all the high notes to perfection while belting out a rendition that would not soon be forgotten. When she was done, smiling broadly, knowing she had nailed it, she bowed to the crowd and walked back toward the dugout to the sounds of a standing ovation.

Max met her at the steps, gave her a high-five, and said, "Not bad for a Shorts. But don't forget, they were already standing."

They both smiled.

The Schooners raced out onto the field as Bob Alexander, just off to the side of home plate, again took the mike to address the crowd.

"Ladies and gentlemen. If I could have your attention once more. Throwing out the first pitch for today's game, we are proud to have another of our own. Please give another rousing Schooner cheer for—Max Shorts.

Practically breaking his neck as he snapped around at the sound of his name, the players pushed Max up the steps and out onto the field. The fans stood and cheered as Max made his way to the mound. Once there, he took the ball that was waiting on the pitching rubber and was ready to deliver the first pitch.

"Hold on there, Max," Bob Alexander announced over the loud system. "I have one more change to today's game program to make before we get started."

A dull roar started down the right field stands as Bob spoke. At the same time, the catcher behind home plate began walking back to the dugout as Bob Alexander addressed the crowd.

"With the recent injury to our backup catcher, the Schooners have signed a player to a one day contract for today's game. There is also a change at starting catcher for today's game. That player is coming to home plate from the bullpen in right field. Ladies and gentlemen, the starting catcher for the Bayport Schooners for today's game, who will now receive the first pitch from Max Shorts, I give you Harry Mickey Shorts."

With that announcement, the crowd went wild.

Max, who couldn't believe what he was hearing and seeing, broke into a huge smile as the Schooner reserve catcher approached home plate.

When Harry got to home plate, he immediately went down into his crouch behind the plate. Max, who was already on the pitching rubber, bent down to look in for the sign from the catcher.

Harry flashed the sign…and Max shook his head "no" to wave off the sign.

The crowd loved it and immediately started a chant—MAX…MAX… MAX…

Harry flashed another sign and Max nodded his approval. He wound up and fired a perfect strike that Harry caught. He immediately fell backward from the force of the throw landing flat on his ass.

To the continued chants of—MAX…MAX…MAX… from the crowd, Max ran in and jumped on his dad.

The crowd, the players, Sherry and Briande all ate it up.

Watching from the dugout, Mr. Curran turned to his Assistant GM, Richie, and said, "I'll give him credit; our Harry really knows how to play a crowd."

"Yeah," Richie agreed, "and the apple doesn't fall far from the tree, does it."

~ * ~

As the Schooners came to bat in the bottom of the second inning, the guest announcer for today's game could be heard saying: "And now leading off the second inning for the Bayport Schooners, batting sixth and catching, Harry Mickey Shorts."

The crowd got on their feet and gave Harry a standing ovation that lasted over thirty seconds. When they had quieted down and Harry was about to get in the box, he heard over the loud speaker:

"Go get 'em, daddy."

Chapter 106

"Yes, Mister Trundle," Harry was saying into his cell as he jumped into the waiting limo. "Yes, sir, I talked to Mister Broderick yesterday and he's on board," he continued before listening for further instructions.

"No, Mister Trundle, ah Randle, I don't know that yet. As soon as I get there I'll call you back with that piece of information," Harry told Trundle. "Everything is set for tomorrow evening and all the players will be there."

Call completed, Harry sat back to try and relax for the remainder of the ride to Board Room Farms. J'Orr and Stu had things ready for him and it was time to put the last pieces of his plan in place. If Harry was right, and he was fairly sure he was, he had figured out what the bad guys had been up to and how they had planned to accomplish their ingenious scheme.

Harry must have dozed off and he woke with a start when his cell phone went off.

"Shorts," he answered.

"I've seen them, but I much prefer you without them," the voice said.

"Do I know you?" Harry kidded.

"In the biblical sense and much more," she responded.

"It's the 'much more' that usually does it," Harry continued.

"Much, much more with whipped cream on top," was the reply.

"How are you, Sherry?" Harry asked.

"Great, Harry. I just wanted to call and tell you again how great Saturday was. The kids haven't stopped talking about it and they called everyone they know as soon as we got home. My cell phone bill is going to go through the roof."

"Saturday night as well?" Harry asked.

"Especially Saturday night," Sherry answered.

"Saturday was a blast," Harry told Sherry. "It took some doing to pull it off, but give Mister Trundle a challenge and you had better jump back. The man amazes me."

"You amaze me, Harry. If you're not careful, I might actually get to like you," Sherry purred.

"I love it when you purr, Sher," Harry whispered.

"Keep doing stuff like you did for the kids on Saturday and you will find this little kitty rubbing up against you a lot more often. Bye, Harry," Sherry said as she disconnected.

The phone rang again almost as soon as Sherry had hung up.

Thinking twice before he answered, Harry said, "Yeah."

"Harry, its J'Orr. Just checking to see where you are and when you're gonna be getting here."

"I'm in the car and should be at Board Room Farms in half an hour. Doc around by any chance?" Harry asked.

"She's over at the hospital 'til later this afternoon, Harry. She asked me to tell you she would be back around five," J'Orr told Harry.

"Thanks, J'Orr. Maybe I'll try and catch her before we go in for dinner."

"That'd be good, Harry. I'm sure the boys would like that," J'Orr said with a laugh.

"Fuck you, J'Orr," Harry said as he hung up.

Harry was hoping the boys would like it a lot.

Chapter 107

"I don't know, dammit. Didn't I just get finished telling you for the third time I DON'T KNOW," he practically screamed into the phone. "If I did know I'd tell you, but I don't. Now, are you going to be there or not?" he asked.

Listening for only ten seconds, he interrupted the other person on the phone and said, "When he tells me he wants something, I do it. We don't ask questions when he tells us to do something in his 'Do it or I'll kick your ass' voice. You understand what I'm saying; I have no choice. I'll be there and you better be there too," he concluded.

Another ten seconds and he finished the call with a, "Good, dammit."

~ * ~

The limo pulled into Board Room Farms and Harry was glad to see J'Orr waiting for him when he got out of the car.

"Good to see you again, J'Orr," Harry said.

"It's good to see you again too, Harry," J'Orr replied as they shook hands.

"Any new developments?" Harry asked.

"No, nothing new to speak of," J'Orr replied. "We got everything set for tomorrow night and we can finish what we need to get done with this here fella right away if you want."

"Let me store my stuff and I'll meet you in the conference room if that's all right with you?" Harry asked.

"Take your time, Harry. We'll keep our little friend occupied 'til you get there," J'Orr told Harry.

"Same room as last time?"

"Yeah, if it suits you, you're set up in the same room, Harry."

"Good. See you in a few."

~ * ~

Stepping into the conference room, Harry found J'Orr and Stu on opposite sides of the conference table. Seated at the head of the table was the guest of honor and main player in the following evening's set-up.

"How are you, Hutch? Are these gentlemen treating you well?" Harry asked him.

"Awrights, I reckon," Hutch replied. "Don'ts know why I'm here though."

"We just wanted to have a little chat with you and see if you could help us out with something. You wouldn't mind helping us out if we made it worth your while, now would you?" Harry asked.

"Don't mind helping folk out," Hutch replied, "Especially if it be worth my while as you said."

"That's good, Hutch. That's real good. Now, here's what we need you to do. It's pretty simple in fact. We have made some arrangements and we need you to put a call in to someone you already know and say the words 'It's all set' to him on the phone. That okay with you Hutch?" Harry asked him.

"Don't sound so hard," Hutch answered. "Who's this fella I already knows I need to call?"

"When is the last time you spoke to your brother, Hutch?" J'Orr asked on cue.

"My brother?" Hutch repeated. "What's Denny got to do with anything?"

"Denny Hutchinson his name?" Stu asked.

Hutch turned toward Stu, then J'Orr, then Harry.

"Who's askin me stuff?" Hutch blurted out.

"Why, I guess we all are, Hutch. That a problem, Hutch? Calling your brother, Dennis, is it a problem, Hutch? You're not having a problem with helping us out now, Hutch?" Harry rapid fired at Hitch.

"There a problem, Hutch?" Stu followed up.

"Calling Denny a problem, Hutch?" J'Orr chimed in.

Hutch put his hands on his ears and said, "Stop. I can't be listenin to all this here from all yous all at the same time."

Nobody said a word in response. They waited.

"Denny's my brother and I can call him if you needs me to. Don't have no problem with that. I just don't know what Denny's got to do with anything," Hutch said.

As Hutch finished, Harry slammed the palm of his hand down on the table. Hutch jumped out of his chair and ran into the corner of the room like a cornered rat.

"Hutch, the worst thing you can do from this point forward is to say one more word that isn't true. Say one word that I don't believe and you will regret it for a long time. Do you understand?"

Hutch looked only at Harry.

Pointing his finger at Hutch, Harry said, "This hillbilly cowpoke bullshit routine you're pulling stops now. You hear me, Hutch. It stops right this very second."

The door to the conference room opened and two guys walked into the room.

"Recognize these two guys, Hutch?" Harry said pointing to the guys that had entered the room. "I believe they had dinner at the same restaurant as you two nights ago. Sat at the table right next to you in fact. They also were having drinks at the Round Table Bar earlier this week. Sat at the bar not two seats away from you."

Hutch started looking very uncomfortable.

Harry continued. "They will testify in court that you carried on a conversation with two other guys on both occasions. They will testify also that a hillbilly you ain't; and in fact, you are quite educated aren't you, Hutch?"

"What is it you want?" Hutch asked in a totally different voice.

"James, you will call your brother and tell him exactly what we tell you to. You will convince him to do what we say and you will assist us with the last bit of information we need. Okay, James?" Harry said.

"And if I don't?" Hutch asked.

"What do you think would happen to a man who ends up in a southern prison with word out he impersonates hillbillies and mocks them and their heritage, James."

Hutch thought for a second, rolled his neck, and then said. "Sorry, Denny. What do you want me to say, Harry?"

Chapter 108

Promptly at six-thirty, the dinner bell rang. Harry had made it back to his room after making a social call and had just enough time to complete the three S's before dinner time. The room was fairly full by the time Harry made it downstairs.

As Harry made his way into the dining room, he saw Doc walking in just ahead of him. As she got to her seat next to J'Orr, three of the boys rushed over to pull out her seat for her. At the same time, three more of the boys rushed over to pull out the chair for Harry as he got to the last empty place at the table directly across from Doc.

"Right nice of you boys to help out," J'Orr said loudly enough for everyone at the table to hear. "As tuckered out as they must be after saying howdy to each other a little while ago, I'm sure they appreciate you helping them with their chairs."

A few of the boys laughed so hard they actually fell out of their chairs. Doc and Harry joined in the fun at their expense knowing just how well they had said howdy, and how many times.

~ * ~

After dinner, Doc and Harry found themselves sitting on the small porch behind Doc's house. Sipping Absolute Gimlets, they were both quiet with their individual thoughts.

Doc finally broke the silence.

"So, Harry, you'll be heading back East after this business is done?"

"I would expect so," Harry replied. "I don't have to go back immediately, but sometime soon."

They sat quietly again sipping their Gimlets.

This time Harry broke the silence.

"You know I've been a wanderer, Doc. I seem to have settled back in New York for right now, but who knows if that will last. Even I don't know," Harry confessed.

"I know that," Doc answered. "I'm not asking for anything, Harry. I was just asking."

"I know you weren't, Doc. And if I could give you a better answer, I would. I'm still trying to figure things out for myself right now and I haven't come up with too many answers for myself, never mind you. You deserve more than that, I know, but it's all I got for now."

Harry leaned over and gave Doc a serious kiss, then leaned back in his chair.

"When you get it figured out, you'll let me know?" Doc asked.

"The day I get my sorry act figured out, you'll be the first to know, Doc," Harry told her.

They sat quietly for a while.

"My day's pretty full tomorrow and I know you have this thing later on tomorrow, Harry. Since I need a refill, why don't we head inside, get us some refills, and then give the boys something to remember our last night by?"

"Doc, for that, I do have a definite answer."

~ * ~

As Doc and Harry headed back inside for refills and other activities, a plane touched down at the nearby private executive airstrip. Mr. M. Randle Trundle deplaned along with his brother and the rest of his entourage. Within the hour, the Trundles and Ms. Timmons would arrive at the house Randle owned for the few days a year he spent in Lee's Summit. The rest of the entourage would spread out at several low profile motels to avoid detection.

"Everything has been attended to?" Trundle asked Ms. Timmons.

"Yes, sir," she responded. "All invitations were issued and accepted. I've confirmed the parties in question have made reservations as we would have expected, where we would have expected."

"Precautions have been taken?" Trundle continued.

"Exactly as you directed, Mister Trundle," Ms. Timmons confirmed.

Danny was about to say something before Randle cut him off with a look.

"Danny, if I wanted you to know what was going on, I would have told you. I obviously didn't."

"But, I…" Danny tried to interrupt before another of Randle's looks shut him up.

"Get in the car, Danny. You'll know soon enough."

Randle looked over at a member of his entourage and nodded, received a nod in return, then he got into the car.

Chapter 109

It was pouring like a mother. That was the first thought that popped into Harry's head when he woke up the following morning. Pouring cats & dogs, and a few larger animals as well. He had asked his mother when he was small why she would say it was raining cats and dogs when there obviously weren't any cats or dogs falling from the sky. She never answered him. She just said it was.

The second thought that popped into Harry's head, well maybe the third after Doc, and he, and what they did...never mind that, his thought was what went on at a horse farm when it was raining cats and dogs.

Looking at the clock on the night stand next to his bed, the bed Doc was not in, Harry saw it was twenty minutes after six. Realizing he didn't give a rat's ass what went on at a horse farm when it was raining cats and dogs, he rolled over and went back to sleep.

~ * ~

"Get your ass out of bed, Harry," was the next thing he heard.

Looking at the clock on the night stand next to his bed, the bed Doc still wasn't in, Harry saw it was eight oh five in the am.

"That's right, Harry. It's now five minutes after eight and you are late for your breakfast meeting with Mister Trundle, the one that was scheduled for eight am. That was eight am *sharp*," Ms. Timmons emphasized.

"How about I pick up my cell, call Mister Trundle and tell him I'll be a bit late. Then, you jump in the sack, and we can both work up an appetite?" Harry suggested.

"I'll tell Mister Trundle you will be down in ten minutes," Timmons replied. Before Harry could get out a single syllable, she was gone.

One of these days Harry mumbled to himself as he got out of bed, one of these days.

~ * ~

"Good morning, Harry, glad you could make it," Trundle greeted him. "You slept well, I presume?"

"As always, you presume correctly, Randle," Harry replied.

"Would you care for some Eggs Benedict this morning, Harry? The Canadian bacon is especially tender," Trundle inquired.

"Might as well be sociable," Harry replied.

"Anything else with your Eggs Benedict, Harry?" Trundle continued.

"Well, since you've inquired, some extra bacon, orange juice and coffee would be great."

"Your wish is my command," Trundle said.

"Oh yeah, when pigs fly," Harry threw at Trundle.

"The pigs are dead, Harry. Where do you think the bacon came from?" Trundle retorted.

They looked at each other, they laughed, they ate. With the tension of what lay ahead of them now dissipated for the moment, the group relaxed and began to enjoy their meal.

"Where's Doc?" Harry asked.

"She ain't here," Danny responded.

Randle frowned in Danny's direction.

"Thank you, Danny," Harry said. "Since I don't see her, I surmised as much. Will she be joining us?" Harry asked in Randle's direction.

Danny began to answer, saw his brother's continued frown, then didn't.

"Kate was off to the hospital at the crack of dawn this morning and will be accompanying one of our young horses up to Arlington Park this afternoon. He races there tomorrow," Randle informed Harry without looking up from his breakfast.

"How long will she be gone?" Harry asked.

"A few days," Randle replied.

"Humm," was all Harry said in reply.

~ * ~

The rest of the day was all about preparations. Harry and Randle met privately for over an hour right after breakfast. They were joined later in the conference room by J'Orr, Stu and Ms. Timmons for a scheduled 10:30 am meeting.

"Have we confirmed everyone's arrival?" Randle asked Ms. Timmons before she even had a chance to get settled in her chair.

"The planes arrived and the passengers in question were all present and accounted for. The last person is in route as we speak and confirmed as having boarded the plane," Timmons told the group.

"Good," Randle answered. "Let's make sure they check in as expected, where expected, and confirm their departures later today."

"Our people are already on all of the above," Timmons assured the group, Randle in particular.

"Excellent. Most excellent," Randle responded.

"Any change to the plans we discussed last week?" J'Orr asked.

"None," Randle answered, "none at all. We go exactly as we discussed and finish this business tonight. And I do mean finish," Randle emphasized.

In unison, the group nodded in agreement.

Chapter 110

At four thirty that afternoon, the same group reconvened in the same conference room. Randle always used that room since he had personally commissioned the double sound-proofing when it was converted into a conference room.

Never too careful.

"Thanks for coming, everyone," Randle started.

He got acknowledging nods from everyone at the table.

"I assume everything is in place by now. Does anyone have any questions, comments, thoughts?" Randle asked.

Slightly smaller nods from everyone at the table indicated there were none, or that nobody wanted to admit to one.

"Good. Harry, is there anything you can think of that we should be concerned about?" Randle directed at Harry.

"Other than the continued well being of one very large Irish bloke, no, nothing I can think of," Harry replied.

Smiles all around after Harry's comment.

"Okay then, everyone knows what they have to do. Be careful and be safe," Randle told them. "While I don't believe we have anything to be concerned about, it is much better to be safe than sorry. We will meet back here after this business has been taken care of. Agreed?" Randle concluded.

"Agreed," everyone responded in unison.

One thing was for sure—the "business" may not go down exactly as planned, but the group had the "in unison" thing down pat.

~ * ~

The daily activities on a horse farm were proceeding as normal just as on any other day. The horses were safely tucked away in their respective stalls and the hands were winding down the day's chores.

"Ready, Harry?" Stu asked.

"Let's get 'er done," Harry responded.

They jumped in Stu's truck and headed down the road that led out of Board Room Farms. They were the last piece to the puzzle to fall into place. It was a few minutes before six, a few minutes before show time.

A few minutes before payback was to be issued for causing pain and suffering that wasn't really necessary.

The caravan of vehicles was clearly visible behind the truck Harry and Stu were riding in. As they turned into the Rogers place, the parade had caught up to them. Stu pulled the truck up to the barn and he and Harry jumped out to meet their guests.

"Be cool, Stu," Harry said

"Cool's my middle name, Harry," Stu replied with a confident smile.

Harry returned the smile with the same amount of confident.

The first car pulled to a stop and the driver came around to open the door for his passengers.

"Howdy there, pardner," Stu drawled to the first passenger as he got out of the car. "My name's Stu from over at Board Room Farms. You must be Matthew Broderick," Stu dragged the name out.

"Yeah," Matt replied not even bothering to look in Stu's direction.

With his eyes on Harry, he said, "You're that guy from New York. Harry somebody, isn't it?" Matt asked.

Harlan Weatherbay had now emerged from the car.

"Harlan, what the fuck is he doing here? Come to think of it, what the fuck are we doing here, Harlan?" Matt asked.

"Good to see you again as well, Matt. And you too, Harlan. Glad you could join us," Harry offered.

"Join you. How about fuck you," Matt spat in Harry's direction.

"No thank you, Matt. I'm well taken care of in that particular category. But thank you for the gracious offer," Harry responded with a smile.

Stu must have liked Harry's response from the small laugh that escaped his mouth.

"You think this is funny, dude ranch cowboy?" Matt threw at Stu. "You want a piece of me?"

"Oh, I'd love a piece of you, Mister Broderick, sir. I'd just love to take you apart piece by piece. But, the boss said don't hurt anybody unless we have to, so I better not," Stu responded with a wide grin on his face.

Matt took a step toward Stu, but Harlan grabbed his arm before he could get too far.

"My guess is that would be a huge mistake on your part, Matt," Harlan told him. "But should you insist, I will swear I tried to stop you from getting your ass handed to you, in spades, as you Americans say."

"Good guess, Weatherby," Harry told him. "That would be a very good guess."

"If Shawn was here…" Matt started.

With that, the occupant from the second vehicle joined them.

"Ah, the mysterious Davey Boy McGarry I presume," Harry said.

"How the hell do you know me?" Davey Boy asked.

"Your reputation precedes you, Davey Boy, if I may," Harry continued.

"If you may what?" Davey Boy asked in confusion.

Not a wizard Harry thought to himself.

"Let me thank you as well for joining us, Mister McGarry," Harry interjected.

With that, the barn doors opened.

Chapter 111

"What the…" came out of Matt's mouth.

Matt's failure to complete his thought mirrored the open mouth wonderment of Weatherbay and Davey Boy. The barn doors opened wide, but there was nobody on the other side of the doors. They seemed to have opened by themselves. Magic. A gust of wind on a calm day. Shit happens—you decide.

"Gotcha, didn't we guys?" Harry laughed.

Stu joined him.

Matt, McGarry and Weatherbay weren't laughing.

"Come on, laugh you guys. It's the last chance you will have to laugh before the world descends on your sorry asses and you won't be able to laugh anymore."

"What the fuck are you talking about?" Matt sputtered.

"Please, allow me, Matthew. Please explain this charade, Mister Shorts," Weatherbay said.

"Charade. I like that one," Stu said.

Davey Boy turned and was about to head back to his waiting car. Unfortunately, the car pulled away at that very moment. The car that Matt and Weatherbay had arrived in followed suit.

"Stick around, Davey Boy. The fun's just getting started," Harry told him.

Harry turned and, as any good magician would do, raised his arm in the direction of the inside of the barn.

Presto. Well, maybe not presto, but J'Orr and another man walked into view from the right side of the barn. The man with J'Orr clearly wasn't happy to be there and his presence didn't make Harry's guests all too comfortable either.

"That is J'Orr, if I may, and I may. And the person with him calls himself Hutch. But, you gentleman already know the guy with J'Orr, don't you. At least you do, don't you Davey Boy. And I believe you do as well, don't you Weatherby?" Harry said.

"Weatherbay?" Matt asked.

"Shut up, Matt,' Weatherbay told him.

"We met him as a numnuts cowpoke named Hutch, but we soon came to know him as James Hutchinson. Turned out to be a very sociable and well educated man. A wee bit more intelligent than his brother—Denny Hutchinson," Harry told the group.

"Denny's his brother? What's going on, Harlan?" Matt asked Weatherbay.

"I told you to shut up, Matt. Now shut the fuck up. Don't say another word," he responded obviously perturbed.

Again raising his arm toward the barn, this time with exaggerated flair, Harry produced out of thin air the aforementioned Denny Hutchinson, brother of James Hutchinson and assistant trainer to Matt Broderick.

"What the hell are you doing here, Denny? What's he doing here, Harlan?" Matt asked.

"Perhaps you should clue in the poor unfortunate boy, Harlan," Davey Boy piped up.

Harlan turned and gave Davey Boy a glare that spoke daggers worth.

"Clue me in on...?" Matt began to ask before Harlan whirled and backhanded him across the face knocking him flat on his ass.

"Tsk, Tsk, Tsk," Harry said. "Stu, I believe the kiddies are beginning to play rough."

Stu, showing a little magical flair of his own, snapped his fingers producing four Board Room Farm hands from behind the barn doors. Each hand had a long gun that they pointed at Harlan and Davey Boy to discourage any further roughhousing.

"Nicely done, Stu," Harry complimented.

"Thanks, Harry," Stu said taking a bow.

Matt had gotten back to his feet and was slowly inching his way away from the group.

"Oh please, don't leave us yet," Harry directed at Matt. "I assure you the best is yet to come. And for your information, Matt, your sidekick Shawn is currently answering to the Dublin constables for several acts committed in their fair city. He may be detained for a long, long time. You may thank me for the delivery of his sorry ass to them."

Silly enough to take a swing at Harry, Harry duplicated Harlan's backhand and promptly knocked Matt back on his ass.

Chapter 112

When Matt was back on his feet again, Harry directed him to close ranks with his fellow confederates in crime.

"Before we present the grand finale to the Harry & Stu Magic Show, let me set the stage by telling you what I know to be fact. You may correct me at any time but, since I know the facts I am about to relate to you to be rock solid true, I doubt any of you will waste our time with frivolous denials."

Harry waited for any comments or reactions from Davey Boy, Harlan or Matt. Receiving none, he continued.

"So as not to bore you with all of the details, I will be as brief as possible. First and foremost was the burning desire to make Dave Boy McGarry and his horse racing stable a force in the United States thoroughbred world. Being a force in the UK and Europe wasn't enough. Greedy, Davey Boy, very greedy. To do so you needed a stable of top quality horses in the US without diluting your stable across the sea."

Harry looked at the three individuals before him for recognition and saw the beginnings of doubt on Davey Boy's face. Matt's expression indicated he was still clueless.

"Let me continue. With a plan firmly established, Davey Boy McGarry sends one of his trusted minions to the United States to set things in motion. With some needed and already entrenched assistance, which I will get to shortly, one James Hutchinson gets his little brother Denny a job as assistant trainer with Matt Broderick. The infiltration of the Broderick racing empire was a critical piece of the plan to supplant the Brodericks as number two and take aim at the number one stable in the United States.

"With visions of a promised big time position in the McGarry stable dancing in his head, as his beloved brother Hutch had guaranteed, Denny methodically stalled the training of a half dozen talented and promising fillies and mares from Matt's string of horses so Davey Boy could claim them at prices much cheaper than they were actually worth. That accomplished, quite nicely and efficiently, Denny would soon have moved on to Mikey Broderick Jr.'s camp to perpetrate the same evil doings."

Harry turned toward the group inside the barn, shook his head at Denny and said "You were a very bad boy, Denny. Shame on you."

The look on Matt Broderick's face was one of utter shock and disbelief.

"I claimed some horses, big fucking deal," McGarry stated matter-of-factly. "Happens every day. Don't know what this Denny did or didn't do—I don't care either," he concluded.

"Denny, you prick," Matt spit out and started toward him. Stu convinced him otherwise and Matt retreated to Harlan's side.

"The important piece to that puzzle was that it enabled Davey Boy to keep several of his best mares in their stalls and not run them here in the US. Why ship them overseas from Ireland in the first place you ask? I'll get to that in due time," Harry told everyone listening.

And to be sure, everyone was listening!

"Meanwhile, halfway across the country, the second phase of the master plan was in play. Hutch was personally handling the details and some of the actual hands-on work as well. Weren't you, Hutch?" Harry asked as he turned to Hutch.

"Eat me, Shorts," was Hutch's reply.

J'Orr, who considered Harry a friend and was clearly agitated with Hutch, punched Hutch in his right kidney doubling Hutch over in severe pain.

"Thank you, J'Orr," Harry said.

"If I might, I now will run through some of James Hutchinson's indiscretions. As I already mentioned, he put his brother Denny in Matt's camp with directions to sabotage Matt's horses. We have found a reliable witness who can put Hutch in the truck that hit Jackson and put him in the hospital. That allowed his guy Buddy to take control of Brian Boru's care on a daily basis. J'Orr's boys caught him red-handed up on the hill to the Rogers' spread spying on Board Room Farms. And, two good-for-nothings got drunk in town and blabbed they were the ones knocking down the fences on BRF's land—yep, at Hutch's direction."

"All your blabbering don't mean shit," Hutch said, still in some obvious pain. "That guy stepped out in front of my truck and the rest of it's nothing but bullshit."

Before J'Orr could massage Hutch's other kidney, Harry held up his hand to indicate he'd be happy to respond.

"When we're done with you, you'll admit to running Jackson down with your truck with malice of forethought. Trust me on this, kiddo, you'll be glad to admit it."

Harry looked at Denny and the expression on his face made Harry sure he could hear him saying to himself, "He hit him with *a malice four times he thought.*"

Harry shook his head in disgust.

Chapter 113

Turning back to face Davey Boy, Harlan and Matt, Harry continued.

"As I have previously stated, Hutch over there was working at the direction of one Davey Boy McGarry. A rather ingenious and daring plan I might add. The fact you actually thought you could get away with it was plain stupid, but it was ingenious, I'll give you that."

"You ain't giving me Jack Shit," Davey Boy spat at Harry.

"Yours will come, Davey Boy. Yours will come," Harry replied.

"You had Hutch get the two local yokels to take down a portion of Board Room Farms fences to see how tough it would be and how long it would take the Board Room Farms guys to find it and fix it. Why? Okay, I'll tell you why. You planned to have the same two yokels take down a portion of the fence that bordered the Rogers' place and kidnap Brian Boru. Once you had him, you'd breed him to the mares you already had here in the states to build your stable in this country. After a month or two, when the heat died down, you planned to ship him over to Ireland and keep his breeding services all to yourself."

Stone cold silence from Davey Boy in response to Harry's accusations.

"Preposterous!" Harlan exclaimed. "That rubbish is utterly preposterous I repeat," Harlan repeated.

"Hang tight there, Harlan," Harry told him. "I'll get to you when I'm finished with this turd and I'm good and ready to deal with you."

Matt pointed to himself and said, "What about me?"

Harry laughed and said, "Matt, if I were you, I'd listen to what Harlan told you. I'd shut the fuck up and hope I got out of this with my ass in one piece."

Matt did the smart thing and remained still.

Turning his attention back to Davey Boy, Harry continued, "Yeah, an ingenious plan if you had pulled it off and the rewards would have been immeasurable. But, since you didn't actually get to the kidnap part of the plan, you're probably thinking you're off the hook because you didn't commit any crime. You directed Hutch to get the two local dumb-asses to take down the fences on BRF's land—that makes you an accessory to destruction of property. You directed Hutch to take out Jackson—makes you an accessory to attempted vehicular homicide. You orchestrated Denny's interference with the proper training of Matt's horses—if that ain't a crime, we'll make one up."

"Bullshit. Prove I done any of it," Davey Boy challenged.

Harry and Stu smiled at each other.

"You obviously weren't listening to me before," Harry responded. "When we're done chatting with Hutch, he'll be swearing on a stack of bibles you are responsible for everything I just stated."

Just as Harry finished speaking, J'Orr produced a frightening scream from Hutch's mouth that confirmed Harry's contention.

"Thank you, J'Orr," Harry said.

"My pleasure," J'Orr said in reply.

"Little by little your plan came apart," Harry directed at Davey Boy. "What started as a brownish drizzle will eventually turn into a full stream shit geyser. There were two things you couldn't plan on. Number one, Brian Boru decided to visit the Big Corral in the sky. He just plain died of natural causes before his time should have been up. Second, and your worst nightmare, Harry Mickey Shorts…"

Chapter 114

Taking his eyes off Davey Boy, Harry turned his attention to Weatherbay.

"And now you, Weatherby."

"I'm sorry, but I'm not party to this…ah, this mess as you Americans call these things," Weatherbay stated.

"Ah, but you are a party to this mess as we Americans call it. You're a party to the whole plan in fact. In fact, it was your plan from the beginning, Weatherby. You concocted it, you picked the players, you orchestrated it step by step, and you stood to gain the most should it succeed," Harry said loud and clear for all to hear.

"Utter poppycock," Harlan responded.

Unfortunately, another vision of what was now running though Denny's mind appeared before the now famous Harry Mickey Short's minds-eye. It went something like, "What's a cow's udder got to do with this shit. And flowers, and who's dick is he talking about…"

Clearing his thoughts, Harry continued.

"It's not poppycock by a long shot, Harlan. Let me elucidate how this…"

Harry looked at Stu.

"Charade," Stu offered.

"Quite appropriate. Thank you Stu," Harry replied.

"Yes, how this charade was perpetrated for everyone. The master plan, Weatherby, your plan, the grand master plan went something like this:

1.   The initial step in the plan was to fund a young up-and-coming horse trainer in Ireland who needed the where-with-all to expand his stable and compete on a much grander scale.

2.   Patiently biding your time, you slowly incorporated a US component into this now established trainer's stable.

3.   You infiltrated the inner workings of the racing empire for which you continued to toil with an "outsider" who was there to sabotage a piece of that empire.

4.   You personally funded the purchase of a horse farm in Lee's Summit—the Rogers' place—and retrofitted the outer buildings as needed.

5.   You put in place the pieces of the puzzle that would have ensured the success of the plan's final steps—a breeding operation in Virginia for temporary use and a private plane to fly Boru out of the country to a private landing strip in Ireland.

With that, Harry stepped back to let what he had just said sink in.

"Rubbish. Hearsay, it's all hearsay," Weatherbay said immediately.

"Afraid not, Harlan," Harry replied.

Turning toward Stu, Harry said, "I believe it is now time for the grand finale. Do you agree, Stu?" Harry asked.

"I do, Harry," Stu concurred.

With as much flourish as Harry could muster, he turned toward the inside of the barn, raised both hands in the air, and said, "Hocus-pocus, Fats Dominocus, Abba sing me a cadabra…"

Like Noah before the Red Sea, the floor within the main part of the barn parted. As the two pieces of floor separated and lifted to the left and right, a solid platform rose from below and came into view. Standing on the platform were M. Randle Trundle and Mikey Broderick, Sr.

Like a Ring Master of Ceremonies inside the Big Top, Harry boomed, "Ladies and Gentlemen, I give you the stars of our show, Randle and Mikey!"

Chapter 115

Eyes wide in bewilderment, Harlan shit himself. Well, not literally, but you get the picture.

"Hello, Harlan, you look concerned," Broderick directed toward Weatherbay.

Regaining his composure, Weatherbay replied, "Concerned, no I'm not concerned, Michael. The rubbish this man Shorts spews forth will prove to be nothing but that, rubbish. The sun will shine another day."

"Yes, Harlan, the sun will surely shine another day, and many more after that. Mister Trundle and I will get to enjoy those fine sunny days, Harlan. You, as we say here in our country, Harlan, I wouldn't bet the rent on you seeing too many sunny days where you are going to find yourself," Broderick replied.

Weatherbay started to speak, but Broderick gestured for him to stop.

"Don't waste your breath," Broderick told him. "I'm going to tell you what I know, and what we can prove. My good friend Randle and I have resources far beyond your knowledge, or imagination, Harlan. We have copies of your banking records proving you bankrolled McGarry's operation in Ireland from the very beginning. I have a copy of the deed to the small horse farm McGarry uses as his base in the United States. The owner of that farm is Carolyn Weatherbay who just so happens to be married to Harlan Weatherbay. Coincidence, I think not, Harlan.

"Let me go on," Broderick said. "We have copies of phone records proving you spoke on numerous occasions with Hutch and his brother Denny before, and well after Denny was hired as Matt's assistant trainer. Pauly confirmed you personally vouched for Denny and recommended we hire him. Pauly okay'd his hire without checking his references based on your recommendation. I'll deal with Pauly on that separately."

Harlan's mouth was now hanging wide open, but not a sound came out.

"If I may," Trundle spoke up. "No reason for you to have all the fun, Michael. Your attempts to conceal the rest of your plan's needs were good, but not that good. The Rogers' place was purchased by a corporation that eventually traced back through three sub-corporations to a company owned by a woman named Madeline Devine as CEO and sole owner of the company. Shame on you for using your stepmother's name as a means for ill gotten gains, Weatherbay. Plus, you shabbily used another corporation that traced back to your daughter-in-law to do all the retrofitting on the property. Phone records show eighty-three calls from you to Mister Hutchinson, or he to you, over the period this work was being done. Very sloppy, Weatherbay, very sloppy indeed. In case you doubt my word, we have copies of documents proving everything I have just detailed."

"Nicely said, Randle," Broderick complimented.

"A few more nails in your coffin if you can stand it, Harlan. The audio surveillance equipment we uncovered planted throughout Board Room Farms was purchased by Mister Hutchinson and installed by Buddy. Twenty-five bugs in all were scattered around the stables and barns, plus two in the main house. We have the tapes by the way. Between Hutch watching BRF and the audio recordings, you were able to know everything that went on at the ranch. Plus, you had Brian Boru's daily and evening schedule down to the second. Mister Hutchinson and Buddy have already confirmed these 'accusations' as fact, Harlan."

"Is that what Doc said she heard inside Boru's stall when she went in to examine him the morning after he died?" Harry asked.

"Yes, Harry," Randle confirmed. "The bug in Boru's stall had malfunctioned and it was what led us to find it and the rest of the bugs as well," Randle confirmed.

"I'll be damned," Harry said.

"No, that would be the two gentlemen standing beside you, Harry," Broderick corrected.

"Two final points," Broderick said. "Randle and I both have extensive contacts in the private airplane and airfield circles. The firm you contracted with that specializes in private planes to transport thoroughbred horses has as its number one customer a personal friend of Randle Trundle. A contacted B, who talked to R, who spoke with me, that made a dead man of you."

"Very clever, Michael," Trundle said.

"Thank you, Randle, I rather liked it myself."

"The last point was perhaps the one that gave us the most trouble pinning down, Harlan. How do you get Brian Boru from Board Room Farms to the Rogers' place? Once he was here, the set-up you had constructed under this barn and accessed via the lift Randle and I used to make our entrance would have been good for months, if necessary. But, how do you get Boru here. The answer eluded us until Harry figured it out."

At that moment a car came to a halt behind McGarry and Weatherbay. The driver, Tom Broderick, walked around and opened the rear passenger door. Out stepped McDonough, the "bug" jockey that worked for Board Room Farms and now rode almost exclusively for McGarry.

"I believe everyone is familiar with the jockey that exercised Boru to keep him in shape," Trundle spoke up. "The jockey that would have ridden Boru from the field bordering the Rogers' property right off the BRF grounds and over to the Rogers' place. That is correct, Mister McDonough, isn't it?" Randle asked.

"Yes, sir, Mister Trundle," came the reply.

"And, at whose direction would you have done this?" Trundle continued.

"Mister McGarry said Mister Weatherbay wanted me to do it," McDonough confirmed.

"Thank you, Tom, that will be sufficient. He is all yours," Broderick told Tom Broderick. McDonough got back in the car to be driven to you don't want to know where.

Chapter 116

A hush had fallen over the crowd. As the car that was carrying McDonough off to his appointed fate faded down the road, all eyes fell back on Michael Broderick, Sr.

"Now that I believe we have proven our case to everyone's satisfaction, let's get down to what we are going to do about it. Randle," Broderick said deferring to Trundle.

"Everyone listen closely. I don't want to have to say this more than once. The Hutchinson boys will be left for J'Orr to deal with. There was interest in bringing Denny back East by some East Coast law enforcement entities, but we have convinced them the local constabulary will deal with the Hutchinsons appropriately. I don't believe anyone in the racing industry will have to worry about them any time soon," Trundle told them.

It was now Mickey's turn.

"Matt, the car approaching will take you directly to the airport. The driver will provide you with a ticket for your nine o'clock plane to the West Coast. Pauly's man will meet you at the airport and take you to the San Diego compound. Perhaps Pauly will be able to make you a Broderick; I've surely tried and I am sick to have to say that I have failed miserably," Mikey Broderick said in disgust.

"So, that leaves Davey Boy McGarry and Harlan Weatherbay," Trundle said. "Stu, if I could ask you to escort these two to the conference room in the main house over at Board Room Farms, would you do that for me?" Trundle asked Stu.

"I would be pleased to 'escort' these two to the ranch. If I'm lucky, one of them may force me to escort them with 'malice of forethought' which would be my utmost pleasure," Stu said with a wide smile.

Harry joined Stu in a smile.

"Harry, you'll join Michael and I as we head back to BRF?" Trundle asked.

"That would be my pleasure," Harry replied.

"Then let's get everyone where they belong and 'get er done'," Trundle deadpanned.

~ * ~

A short time later, Harry found himself in the BRF conference room with Davey Boy McGarry and Harlan Weatherbay. Neither was saying a single word, so Harry joined them.

Harry could out-silence the best of them.

Five minutes became ten. Harry was about to get up for a soda when the door opened. In walked Michael Broderick, Sr. and M. Randle Trundle sharing a good laugh, best of buddies, or so it seemed.

"Good one, Mike," Trundle said.

"You should have been there," Broderick said.

They sat in chairs at the right and left side of the head of the table, neither wanting to assume the primary position. Best of buds deferring to the other.

Trundle spoke first.

"So, guys, what do you suggest we do with you?" he asked.

McGarry looked at Weatherbay. Weatherbay looked back. Neither said a word. They didn't know what the hell to say in response.

"Come now, neither of you has a suggestion on how we may resolve this mess we find ourselves with?" Broderick chimed in.

A minute of silence passed; still not a word from either Davey Boy or Harlan.

"That's too bad. Michael and I were willing to allow you to decide your own fate. Since you didn't, you're shit out of luck," Trundle said. "Shit out of luck express it appropriately, Harry?" he asked.

"Quite appropriately," Harry agreed.

"Let's start with you, Mister McGarry," Trundle said.

"My people are still investigating your misdeeds and what crimes may be attached to those misdeeds. I do know the shit you pulled with Matt Broderick's horses was not the first time you stocked your stable at the expense of others. The Irish racing authorities would like to speak with you concerning how you got to prominence in your career, especially early on. It seems several of your previous trainers are lined up to offer testimony on the who's, what's and where's connected to your prior activities."

Concern crept into McGarry's eyes.

"As I said, my people are investigating you, Mister McGarry. You would be surprised at how far my reach extends and my people are very good at what they do. Several agencies here in the states also have interest in you, Mister McGarry. I have every confidence they will deal with your indiscretions and neither I nor Michael will ever have to set eyes on you again. When they are done with you, the Irish can have what's left of you.

"Lastly, on behalf of Board Room Farms and the Broderick racing stable, we accept your generous offer. The horses you "stole" from Matt Broderick will be purchased back for one dollar each. Since you and your silent partner, Mister Weatherbay, will no longer be involved in the racing business, Michael and I will jointly purchase the remainder of your stable and manage it as a new international venture under the name Boru Stables. Feeney has agreed to stay on as its trainer."

McGarry opened his mouth, thought twice, and shut his mouth.

Trundle looked disgusted as he said, "My man will escort you to meet with certain people. Now, get his sorry cheating ass out of my sight before I puke."

The door opened at the sound of Trundle's command. Two men entered, lifted McGarry out of his chair, and carried him out the door.

Harry looked out into the hallway through the open door and said, "What the…" catching himself before he continued on. There, waiting to take charge of McGarry was Trundle's man—Mueller. Davey Boy stepped through the door and he, and Mueller, were gone.

"Something wrong, Harry?" Trundle asked him.

"No, everything is fine," Harry replied. "I thought I saw someone I knew, but I must have been mistaken."

"Good, then let's carry on," Trundle said.

Michael Broderick rose from his seat and went over to sit in the seat next to Harlan Weatherbay.

"Your fate, my most unfortunate man, is my responsibility. You will come to wish it weren't so, but it is."

Chapter 117

Order was now restored in the conference room. Michael Broderick's words must have scared Weatherbay terribly. Upon hearing them, he bolted from his chair and attempted to flee from the room. It gave Harry great pleasure to knock him on his ass and drag him back to his chair.

The continuance of order was never in doubt.

Broderick and Trundle never moved.

"Please remain seated, Harlan," Michael Broderick said. "I may be much older than Mister Shorts, but I will surely hurt you if you give me cause. And Harlan, rest assured, I would enjoy every second of it for what you have done to me, my family, my friend, and the racing industry I so love."

Harlan turned to stone as if he was afraid to even breathe.

"Good then. Mister Trundle and I differ on how we should deal with you, Harlan. Randle has utmost faith and believes in the system we have in this country to deal with people like you. I do as well, but not to the degree that Randle does. I also believe that what you have done, and the crimes that may be attached to your acts, would not come even close to fully account for the pain and suffering you have caused.

"Harlan, you have hurt me deeply. After all the years you have been with me, and there have been too many to count, you stab me in the back and twist the knife. Through the good times and the bad, we fought through it and came out winners. I considered you my friend, Harlan, and you have betrayed that friendship. You know as well as I that Brodericks don't accept betrayal, Harlan. As you have witnessed, we firmly believe in an eye for an eye."

Broderick sat back realizing his face was now mere inches from Weatherbay's.

Weatherbay showed the look of a man now scared out of his wits.

"So, Harlan, with Randle's semi-blessing, you will be sent back to the old country and work on the Broderick family horse ranch. John will assign you the most back-breaking work and you will be happy to do that work from sun up until sun down. One of Tom's men will watch you like a hawk, and should you decide you don't want to continue, you will be turned over to the Irish Racing authorities. Along with the US racing authorities, they have been informed of your past activities. All of them. Both groups are most anxious to deal with you as well. They will have to wait though until we are done with you. And Harlan, as God is my witness, give me cause and you will never see the light of day again."

Broderick took a sip of water and looked around the room.

Looking back at Harlan, Broderick said, "A fine animal has left us before his time. That would have been bad enough. But, Harlan, you have intensified the pain with your unthinkable acts of selfishness and greed. For that you will pay dearly."

"Harry, would you escort Mister Weatherbay from the room, please. There are several men outside waiting to take him via private plane to his new station in life," Trundle said. "And Harry, give Michael and I a minute if you would."

"Of course, Randle," Harry replied.

Harry grabbed Weatherbay by the arm and hauled him out of the room.

~ * ~

"Randle," Broderick started, "you and I have had our battles over the years, both in racing and our outside business ventures as well. Some of them memorable. But there was always a mutual respect for the ability and hard-earned success of the other. I am truly sorry for your loss of Brian Boru and any suffering you may have endured due to the indiscretions of anyone connected to my organization. May this new venture of ours bind our friendship, and in some ways, work to heal the wounds caused by its creation."

"Michael," Trundle said in reply, "friendship can get dented and chipped at times. It can experience near complete fracture even. But true friendship endures all, and the Brodericks have been friends with the Trundles for a long time. As long as I am alive, that will continue to be so."

Broderick and Trundle stood and shook hands. Then they hugged as true friends do.

Picking up his water glass, Broderick raised it up and said, "To Brian Boru, the Greatest Champion of all time."

~ * ~

Harry was sitting on the back porch with J'Orr and Stu, all of them working on polishing off a few long necks.

Trundle came walking up the steps and sat down next to Harry.

"Any of those long necks left?" Trundle asked.

"I think we can rustle up one for the boss, don't you Stu?" Harry replied.

"Sure enough, Harry," Stu said as he handed Trundle a beer.

"Thanks for your help today, boys. We got us some bad guys and now we should be able to put the death of Brian Boru behind us. I will, and I hope you boys can as well," Trundle said.

Lifting his bottle, J'Orr said, "To Brian Boru."

"To Brian Boru," came the refrain from all four of them.

Chapter 118

Harry and Trundle were sitting in the owner's box along the first base line watching the Bayport Schooners wax a hapless opponent. They were both enjoying a hot dog and a beer at the time.

"Your boys look good today," Harry commented.

"They have been on a hot streak and haven't lost this month," Trundle replied.

Harry looked at him and said, "It's only the fifth of the month."

"So," Trundle said, "they still haven't lost this month."

They laughed the laugh of friends.

Swallowing a sip of beer, Harry asked, "You send Doc up to Chicago with that horse?"

"Yes," Trundle replied.

"So she wouldn't be there while it went down?" Harry continued.

"Yes," Trundle replied again.

"And wouldn't be around when it was done?" Harry went on.

"Yes," was Trundle's reply.

"Knowing I'd probably have to leave before she got back?" Harry continued.

The crowd got to its feet and roared as a Schooner homered to deep left.

Harry waited.

"Yes," Trundle finally said.

Harry drank his beer and waited.

After a while, he said, "Okay, why?"

Trundle drank his beer and waited.

"So I'd have time away from her and think about her. So I'd get to the point of need vs. want if it was there. So I'd know?" Harry asked.

Trundle finished his beer and got up to get two more beers. He had stopped having his "people" do shit for him and did for himself whenever possible.

Trundle returned, handed Harry a beer, drank his beer and waited.

"So I'd know?" Harry repeated.

"So you'd know," Trundle responded.

They drank their beers and waited.

"You know?" Trundle asked.

"Not yet," Harry conceded.

Trundled nodded and said, "You'll know."

"I know," Harry agreed.

After a while, Harry said, "Sorry about Boru."

"Thanks," Trundle replied.

They sat there the rest of the afternoon, drank their beer, ate their hot dogs, and enjoyed the game of baseball, the most glorious game on earth.

www.ingramcontent.com/pod-product-compliance
Lightning Source LLC
Chambersburg PA
CBHW051541260626
47170CB00003B/1047